本书为国家社科基金一般项目
"李渔在英语世界的历时接受与当代传播研究"
（立项号：13BWW012）结项成果

# 李渔在英语世界的历时接受与当代传播研究

唐艳芳　杨　凯————著

ZHEJIANG UNIVERSITY PRESS
浙江大学出版社

**图书在版编目（CIP）数据**

李渔在英语世界的历时接受与当代传播研究 / 唐艳
芳，杨凯著. —杭州：浙江大学出版社，2021.9
ISBN 978-7-308-21751-4

Ⅰ.①李… Ⅱ.①唐… ②杨… Ⅲ.①中国文学—古
典文学—清代—英语—文学翻译—研究 Ⅳ.①I206.2
②H315.9

中国版本图书馆 CIP 数据核字(2021)第 186622 号

**李渔在英语世界的历时接受与当代传播研究**

唐艳芳　杨　凯　著

| | | |
|---|---|---|
| 责任编辑 | 郑成业 | |
| 责任校对 | 董齐琪 | |
| 封面设计 | 春天书装 | |
| 出版发行 | 浙江大学出版社 | |
| | （杭州市天目山路 148 号　邮政编码 310007） | |
| | （网址：http://www.zjupress.com） | |
| 排　　版 | 杭州青翊图文设计有限公司 | |
| 印　　刷 | 杭州良诸印刷有限公司 | |
| 开　　本 | 710mm×1000mm　1/16 | |
| 印　　张 | 10.75 | |
| 字　　数 | 221 千 | |
| 版 印 次 | 2021 年 9 月第 1 版　2021 年 9 月第 1 次印刷 | |
| 书　　号 | ISBN 978-7-308-21751-4 | |
| 定　　价 | 39.00 元 | |

# 前　言

　　李渔(1611—1680)是清初著名戏曲家、小说家、文论家,其作品早在 18
世纪初就开始向域外传播,19 世纪初译入英语,在西方世界有相当的影响。
本书运用翻译史研究方法和文化翻译理论,对李渔在英语世界两个世纪以
来的传播与接受进行了系统深入的调查和分析,梳理了李渔作品英译的概
况,对各个阶段的翻译策略有了比较全面、准确的了解。在掌握大量真实史
料的基础上,本书试图分析不同时期李渔作品英译策略背后的时代背景和
文化交流状况,探索翻译与社会历史文化之间的交互影响,并从翻译策略的
历时演变中寻找对当代典籍翻译事业有借鉴意义的认识论和方法论启示。

　　研究表明,李渔在英语世界的形象是后者按照自身不同时期的规范和
需要建构起来的,建构的手段主要包括选材偏颇、翻译改写、评论引导等,而
经过英语世界建构之后的李渔形象已不再是中国文学文化语境中那个真实
的李渔了,译介过程中的各种操控行为,对李渔的文学声誉和中国文学的整
体形象都造成了一些负面的影响。进一步的翻译史和文本调查显示,从 19
世纪初到 21 世纪初,李渔作品英译的策略发生了比较大的变化,表现为语言
方面由粗而精、文学方面由俗而雅、文化方面由“入”而“出”、副文本方面由
泛而专等趋势。这些变化反映了中西方文化力量对比和交流状况的历时变
化,也为当代翻译的策略选择提供了历史借鉴和方法参考。

　　本书对翻译研究的启示有二:一是翻译的传播与接受必须通过翻译史
的历时研究才能获得比较客观真实的结论;二是成功的文学翻译绝非孤立、
偶然的行为,一定是两种文化之间的一场系统而深入的对话,除了译者,还
有双方众多读者、评论者和研究者、出版商等力量的积极参与,因而是一种
集体的行为,不能把翻译的成败只归功(咎)于译者个体。对于我国当代典
籍翻译实践的启示,一是典籍翻译的原作选材应力求全面、准确,坚持“存疑
不译”“译无不尽”的原则;二是翻译策略和方法应忠实、完整,贴近译出语语
言文学文化特点,重视并大胆运用副文本策略,坚定不移地走深度翻译的道

路,为我国当代的典籍翻译事业探索行之有效的方法,更好地助推中国文化走向世界。

本书为国家社科基金一般项目"李渔在英语世界的历时接受与当代传播研究"(立项号:13BWW012)的结项成果。书稿得以付梓,要感谢嘉兴学院人文社科处、外国语学院的鼎力支持,他们在项目推进、出版资助等方面提供了不遗余力的帮助和保障;同时也要感谢浙江大学出版社相关编校人员的辛勤付出,他们对图书的出版规范提出了许多专业的建议;更要感谢所有引用及参考文献的原作者,他们的研究成果和思想结晶闪耀着人类文明的熠熠光辉,为本书的撰写奠定了坚实的基础。

由于时间有限,书中疏漏之处在所难免,恳请广大读者不吝指正。

唐艳芳

2021 年 9 月

# 目　录

# 第一章  绪  论

## 第一节  研究背景和意义

李渔(1611—1680)是中国古代为数不多的一位集小说、戏剧、诗词曲赋、杂论等成就于一身的伟大作家,而且研究兴趣相当广泛,在文艺理论乃至园林建筑、休闲养生等非文学领域也有独到的见地和不菲的建树。但这样一位多才多艺的作家和百科全书式的人物在走向世界的过程中,却遭到了不同程度的遮蔽、篡改和误读。在中国文化大踏步走向世界的背景下,对李渔及其作品在海外的历时传播和接受情况作一梳理,为当代中国典籍外译实践探索更有成效的策略,是对这位中国古代文坛巨匠的最好纪念。

本书聚焦李渔在英语国家的传播和接受,基本研究思路是:将李渔在英语世界的传播与接受置于近现代以来东西方文化交流的大背景下进行全面观照,尝试揭示文化力量和权力关系对翻译的操控,在此基础上探索李渔作品的当下传播策略,为全球化时代的典籍外译和中国文化"走出去"战略提供理论和实践支持。本书的理论意义有三:(1)文化翻译学意义。后现代文化翻译理论认为,译者对原文本的选择、翻译过程中对文本内容的增删、调整或改写,背后都有着权力或意识形态的影响。李渔在英语世界的传播和接受,较为典型地反映了作家形象在跨文化传播过程中是如何被操控和误读的,对此进行探索和研究,可以揭示文本旅行过程中的各种权力关系,从而有助于深刻理解文化翻译的本质和内涵。(2)翻译史价值。李渔作品英译的历史跨度较大,从可以查考的德庇时《三与楼》(1815年)到晚近的《李渔小说选》和《李渔诗赋楹联赏析》(2011年),历时近两个世纪,其中既有重译又有新增译作、既有外国人和中国人各自主译的也有中外译者合作翻译的,可谓一部所谓的汉籍外译史,将其完整整理出来,可以为我国的翻译史研究提供重要的史料补充。(3)接受美学和跨文化传播学意义。文学文本从一种语言/文化进入另一种语言/文化的传播过程中,既会在某些方面(如题材内容、语言技巧、文学手法等)迎合译入语受众的期待视野,同时也必然会影响甚至塑造后者的阅读体验。李渔作品的英译及其传播与接受,涉及一系列接受美学与跨文化传播学的理论和实践命题,包括译者对受众期待视野和认知能力的评估与判断、译作对于建构李渔在英语世界的形象所起的作用或产生的影响等,具有重要的研究价值。除此以外,本书的实际应用价值还包括为海内外李渔研究搭建桥梁、推动国内外李渔研究学者的沟通和交流、为典籍外译工作提供方法论参考,等等。

## 第二节　研究内容与方法

本书主要围绕以下几方面的内容开展研究:

(一)翻译选材

翻译选材可以直观地反映翻译过程中权力对译者和翻译作品的干涉与操控,也必然影响作家在译入语文化中的形象建构。英语世界对李渔作品的选择,从现有的文献调查结果来看,无疑是很不全面的,其直接后果就是在西方读者心目中塑造了一个与中国文学史上真实的李渔相去甚远的作家形象。本书试图在梳理李渔作品英译史的过程中,对影响翻译选材的各种主客观因素开展深入调查,并探讨翻译选材的后续效应,为打破权力对翻译的限制与操控、重塑李渔在英语世界的形象作学理铺垫。

(二)翻译策略

翻译策略上的操控主要体现于译者对文本内容的增删、对原作语言是否尊重等。本书将依据国内已经出版的《李渔全集》及其他相关文献,对英译本作详细的文本比对调查,了解译者是否在翻译策略上有操控之举、在多大程度上实施了操控、原因何在、影响如何等,并从中归纳和提炼对当前李渔作品英译有启发或帮助价值的规律或经验教训。

(三)译市接受

了解以往译本的接受情况,目的是为重塑李渔在英语世界的形象提供读者接受方面的信息,其中涉及单一译本的受欢迎程度、多译本的接受度差异等。此类信息与译本的翻译策略调查结合起来将有重要的方法论价值,可为当前及今后一段时期的李渔作品英译以及其他典籍作品的外译实践提供决策参考。

(四)当下传播

当前李渔作品的英译,是在全球化时代和后殖民语境下传播中国文化、争取中国文化身份与地位的努力之重要组成部分,其翻译主体应以中国译者为中心、英语国家的汉学家或译者为重要支持力量,翻译策略应坚持以原作为中心、兼顾译文语言的通顺与可接受性等。本书将结合已经取得的翻译实践成果,积极探索更有成效的传播策略,为李渔作品在英语国家的当下传播以及当代其他典籍的外译提供借鉴。

研究方法上,本书主要采用历史学和传播学研究方法,梳理李渔作品在英语世界的传播史,探索传播的规律和效果,为李渔乃至更多中国作家"走出去"提供历史学和传播学理据。此外,本书还将采用译本调查和文化批评的方法,对英语世界已有的李渔作品译本开展深入的文本调查和研读,了解译者翻译策略的全貌,分析和批评其文化动因,为李渔作品的当代传播提供翻译学和文化学的理论视域和实证支持。

## 第三节　本书框架

本书共五章,主要内容如下:

第一章为绪论,介绍研究背景、意义、内容、方法等。

第二章对李渔及其作品在英语国家的传播情况进行总体梳理,重点关注作品译介概况,拟按传播的主要特点分成若干个历史阶段展开讨论。

第三章围绕英语世界对李渔作品的取舍及其对李渔形象建构的影响展开。首先介绍李渔作品译入英语的文类和篇目,并分析译者"操控"原作取舍的原因,在此基础上提出,选材偏颇是导致英语读者片面认识甚至曲解李渔作家形象的主要原因,而这种基于片面和偏颇的翻译选材所造成的对作家形象的歪曲式建构,有可能造成严重的后果和负面影响。

第四章对李渔作品英译策略的历时演变开展研究,选取 19 世纪初、20世纪中叶、20 世纪末至 21 世纪初这三个时期的译本,开展深入的、全方位的文本调查与分析,了解不同时期译本的语言、文学、文化、副文本等翻译策略并归纳其演变规律,探索翻译策略变化背后的社会历史和译者主体原因。

第五章为结语,概括本书主要发现和观点,总结本研究对翻译研究和当代典籍翻译的启示,指出不足之处并提出后续研究展望。

# 第二章　李渔在英语世界的传播：
## 历史的回顾

　　李渔作品的英译和英语世界对李渔的研究，前后长达近两个世纪，其间经历了滥觞、冷寂、复苏、繁荣等多个阶段。从各个历史时期的译介和研究情况来看，李渔在英语国家的传播主要可分为三个阶段。① (1)19 世纪滥觞期：以零散译介和传播为主，译者多为来华商人、传教士和外交官，按照各自需要或偏好选择原作，翻译策略以改编为主，译者的语言观和翻译观有比较浓厚的"东方主义"色彩，相关研究不多。(2)1960—1980 年代"复兴"期：以《肉蒲团》和《十二楼》的英译为代表，西方译者不加考证的猎奇式翻译和华人译者为促进文学交流而采取的删削取径式翻译策略交织在一起，选材和翻译策略的操控迹象明显，此间李渔研究掀起热潮。(3)1990 年代以降的繁荣与成熟期：译介方面继续拓展，更多作品译入英语，研究方面日趋深入、多元、稳定。本章拟对各个时期的译介和传播情况作一爬梳，为开展本研究奠定学术史基础。

## 第一节　19 世纪：李渔英译之滥觞

　　根据现有的资料，李渔作品中最早进入英语世界的是短篇小说集《十二楼》。《十二楼》成书于清顺治末年，是李渔继《无声戏》之后创作的一部拟话本小说集。全书收录小说 12 篇，每篇以一座楼的名字作为题名，故事有长有短，回目数也各不相同，最长的有六回(《拂云楼》)，最短的只有一回(《夺锦楼》)。与成书稍早的《无声戏》相比较，《十二楼》在语言艺术、人物塑造、创作手法等方面更加成熟、新颖，非常生动地反映了我国明末清初时期的社会生活，这是它被 19 世纪英国来华人员首选译入英文的重要原因。

　　最早翻译《十二楼》的是德庇时爵士(Sir John F. Davis,1795—1890)，他

---

　　①　何敏将李渔小说在英语世界的研究归纳为三个阶段：滥觞期的先河、发展期的拓展和繁荣期的多样化。参见何敏.李渔小说在英语世界的研究述论.中华文化论坛,2013(11):94-101.笔者认为这样的三分法也适用于李渔在英语世界的整体传播与接受。

多次来华参与商贸和外交活动，是个中国通，曾任英国驻华公使和第二任香港总督（1844—1848），卸任外交官之后潜心向学，成为 19 世纪英国三大汉学家之一。① 《十二楼》的翻译是他早年在东印度公司广东商馆任职期间完成的。德庇时总共翻译了《十二楼》中的三篇小说，即《三与楼》《合影楼》《夺锦楼》，其中《三与楼》最初于 1815 年在广州出版过单行本，题为 *San-Yu-Lou*：*Or the Three Dedicated Rooms*，次年被《亚洲杂志》（*Asiatic Journal*）转载。德庇时后来又完成了《合影楼》和《夺锦楼》的翻译，将三篇小说译文连同他自己收集、翻译的 126 条中国谚语格言一同结集，于 1822 年交由 John Murray 出版社出版，完整书名为 *Chinese Novels, translated from the originals；to which are added Proverbs and Moral Maxims, collected from their classical books and other sources*。所收录的三篇小说分别为 *The Shadow in the Water：A Tale. Translated from the Chinese*（《合影楼》）、*The Twin Sisters：A Tale. Translated from the Chinese*（《夺锦楼》）和 *The Three Dedicated Chambers：A Tale. Translated from the Chinese*（《三与楼》），其中《三与楼》译文在 1815 年初译的基础上作了较大修改。② 德庇时为这本 250 页的书写了一篇长达 50 页的导论，题为《中国语言文学观察》（"Observations on the Language and Literature of China"）（Davis，1822：1-50）。他开门见山地指出：

> 在我们英国人所取得的知识方面的总体成就中，与中华帝国及其文学相关的主题一直都是无足轻重的。在马戛尔尼使团首次访华（1793 年）之前，全英上下对于一个与我们贸易量如此巨大的民族居然近乎一无所知，这一点令人大惑不解，而法国人是将近一个世纪前就已经在孜孜矻矻地开展研究且卓有建树了。（*op. cit.*：1-2）

德庇时认为，即便不考虑其他任何因素，单凭中英之间贸易历史之久、贸易量之大，就足应引起人们对中国文学的关注和研究（*op. cit.*：2-3）。他进而指出，英国人对于中国的了解深受欧洲天主教来华传教士的影响，而这

---

① 另外两位分别是理雅各（James Legge，1815—1897）和翟理斯（Herbert A. Giles，1845—1935）。

② 宋丽娟指出，德庇时《中国小说》1822 年译本主要在三个方面修改了原文：(1) 书名翻译，除《三与楼》译名较好地遵循了原作的题意，其余两篇的译名对原作书名的象征含义和主题都有所消弭和转移；(2) 译文体制改编，包括删去入话、回目、诗词歌赋、文末点评等；(3) 文辞情节改动，《三与楼》1815/1816 年译文与 1822 年译文相比，在体制和文辞句法的语法两方面更贴近原作。参见宋丽娟. "中学西传"与中国古典小说的早期翻译(1735—1911)——以英语世界为中心. 上海：上海古籍出版社，2017：108-122.

些传教士出于某些冠冕堂皇的理由,大多会对其真实的中国报道加以修改,篡改后的记录与其说是在传播信息,不如说是在误导读者,因此当务之急就是要把英国普通民众认知世界里被传教士错误渲染的中国色彩抹去,用正确的记录还中华民族一个本来的面貌,惟其如此,英国人才会发现,中国人既非聪明绝顶亦非道德高尚,他们偶尔也会沦落到需要靠清官和猛将来挽救整个民族的地步(*op. cit.*:5-6)。

德庇时导论的主要内容是宏观介绍中国语言文学,涉及三篇小说及其翻译的内容并不多,诸如《合影楼》中男女之情所反映的人性、《夺锦楼》中清官巧断家务事所昭示的权力问题等,也只是一笔带过(*op. cit.*:10-12)。其中关于《三与楼》部分,德庇时在简单介绍了一下早期英译和出版、发表的情况之后说:"译者一直觉得这篇初试牛刀的译作在翻译时过于严格贴近汉语的表达习惯了,译文如果能少一些字斟句酌,则不仅会让英语读者赏心悦目,也能更好地传达原作的精髓。因而译者对译文全文作了修订。"(*op. cit.*:12)

1841 年,大英博物馆古代部汉学家、埃及古物学者、考古学家伯奇(Samuel Birch,1813—1885)摘译《生我楼》,发表于《亚洲杂志》,同年出版单行本,题为 *Yin Seaon Low, or the Lost Child. A Chinese Tale*。① 但单行本仅 6 页,只相当于原作的一个梗概,文学影响和研究价值均十分有限。伯奇于 1836 年获聘大英博物馆古代部研究职位时,所凭借的主要就是他的中文造诣(当时英国懂中文的学者不多),但其兴趣很快转向埃及和亚述研究,因此在中国文学的翻译和研究方面再无建树。

1887 年,大英博物馆汉学家道格斯爵士(Sir Robert K. Douglas,1838—1913)重译《夺锦楼》,发表于《布莱克伍德杂志》(*Blackwood's Magazine*),题为"The Twins: From the Chinese of Wu Ming",后与他选译的其他 9 篇故事和 2 首诗歌一同收入 William Blackwood & Sons 出版社 1893 年出版的 *Chinese Stories* 一书(Douglas,1893:82-124)。值得一提的是,道格斯的译文对原作内容的改编幅度相当大,仅保留了一小部分主要情节(即一对双胞胎女儿、父母因分头择婿引发争议而告到衙门、睿智的官员以才选贤替两个女儿择得金龟婿等),其他如人物姓名与身份、细节描写、人物对话乃至故事结局等完全不同,译文与原作可说已无可比性。由表 2-1 可以看出译文和

---

① Birch, Samuel, and LI, Yü, pseud. *Yin Seaon Low, or the Lost Child. A Chinese Tale.* [*An Abstract of a Tale from the* Shih êrh Lou *of Li Yü. Signed B., i. e. Samuel Birch.*] *Extracted from the* Asiatic Journal, *etc.* London, 1841. Web.

原文差距之大。[①]

表 2-1　《夺锦楼》原文与道格斯英译文要素对比

| 主要<br>指标 | 原文 | 译文 |
|---|---|---|
| 标题 | 夺锦楼 | The Twins：From the Chinese of Wu Ming |
| 主要<br>人物 | 钱小江(鱼行经纪)、边氏夫妻 | Mr. Ma，ex-chemist，and Mrs. Ma |
| | 双胞胎女儿(佚名) | The twin daughters：Daffodil and Convolvulus |
| | 断案及主持夺锦择婿的官员：武昌府刑尊(佚名) | The prefect of King-chow town：his Excellency Lo |
| | 求亲四家姓氏：赵钱孙李 | Surnames of the four suitors：Tsai，Fung，Yang and Le |
| | 二女夫婿：袁士骏 | Husbands of the two sisters：Tsin and Te |
| | 无 | Mr. Ma's friend：Ting |
| | 袁士骏好友、夺锦特等第四名：郎志远 | 无 |
| 内容<br>细节 | 无母女之间关于择婿的直接交流，亦无钱小江与朋友商议择婿办法的情节 | 母女之间直接对话，详细交流择婿(偶)态度；Mr. Ma 和 Ting 之间多次沟通择婿办法 |
| | 袁士骏直至夺锦胜出取为特等第一名方见到二女 | 二女与 Tsin、Te 早已相识并两情相悦 |
| | 夺锦择婿的设计与实施等均由刑尊一人操办 | 二女与 Lo 频频互动(书信、面谈等)，甚至暗示后者选题，得到命题信息之后透露给恋人助其获胜 |
| 文学<br>手法 | 第三人称叙事：全知视角 | 出现第一人称叙事，以邻居身份出现，两边劝和：全知＋半知视角 |
| | 直接引语对话数量适中，对话多与叙述夹杂在一起，较少单列成段；全文无二女直接引语 | 直接引语对话数量多，对话按英文习惯，多单列成段；二女大量直接对话 |
| 结局 | 二女嫁一夫(袁士骏) | Daffodil 嫁 Tsin，Convolvulus 嫁 Te |

---

① 另见本书第四章例(22)《夺锦楼》开头及道格斯译本(22b)，两相对比会发现道格斯译文几乎是另起炉灶重写的文本。

正如道格斯在 *Chinese Stories* 导论《中国小说》("Chinese Fiction")一文中所言,"由于已经充分说明的原因,这些故事并非逐字译自原文,而是在忠实保留情节和事件的同时(对原文)作了删减和改编,以符合西方读者的要求。它们是中国通俗文学的范例,而非一时之引人入胜。它们可以说是树立了一面中国人生活的镜子,使我们明白了这样一个事实:长江两岸和泰晤士河畔虽地隔万里,却人同此心。"(Douglas,1893:xxxvii)

纵观 19 世纪李渔作品在英语世界的译介,可以明显看出西方学界风行的"东方主义"倾向。萨义德在《东方学》一书中开门见山地指出:"东方几乎是被欧洲人凭空创造出来的地方。"(1999:1)他认为,在东方学的形成过程中,作为对象的东方自始至终都未真正在场,一直以来都是欧洲的东方主义者们在以东方"代言人"之名行本质主义界定之实,即按照欧洲自身不同时期的需要而对东方作各种想象和建构,致使后者的形象千变万化。在萨义德看来,这种漠视对象的存在及其权力的做法,使得东方学"带有 19 世纪和 20 世纪早期欧洲殖民主义强烈而专横的政治色彩"(*op. cit.*:3),"与其说它与东方有关,还不如说与'我们'的世界有关"(*op. cit.*:16-17)。从 19 世纪为数不多的李渔作品英译情况来看,东方主义主要体现在以下三个方面:

一是翻译目的。德庇时在感叹英国人对中国这样一个与之有多年贸易关系且贸易量巨大的国家居然几近一无所知的同时,明确提出翻译的主要目的是出于英国自身利益的需要而增进对中国的了解,其中最重要的一点是要改变被欧洲传教士高估了的中国及其人民的形象,使英国人意识到中国人只不过是和他们差不多的一个民族,高明不到哪里去(Davis,1822:6)。道格斯在这一点上与德庇时如出一辙,也是期望通过翻译使读者明白长江两岸的中国和泰晤士河畔的英国是"人同此心",而译文删减和改编也是为了"符合西方读者的要求"(Douglas,1893:xxxvii)。从两位译者这些服务英国自身利益需要、提升本国国民文化自信等利己主义的翻译目的,不难看出其东方主义立场。

二是译者对原作和译出语语言文化的态度。19 世纪的英国汉学家和译者们在面对来自东方的文本时,已经不再像他们的前辈那样心存敬意了。德庇时长篇大论地介绍中国语言和文学,主要是为了帮助英国人通过语言文学来认识和了解中国,从而达到与中国人打交道时"一方至少能充分理解另一方的语言"和"促进双方相互交流"(Davis,1822:3)的功利目的,而不是从心底里对中国语言文学充满敬仰之情。他在提及广东话给中英双方商务交流带来的困难时,甚至用了"卑贱而令人厌恶的黑话"(base and disgusting jargon）这样的表述（*ibid.*），显示了他对汉语语言（包括方言）的极度蔑视。① 如果说 19 世纪初处在中英第一次鸦片战争前的德庇时对中国语言文学的态度还算克制，用语也还算比较客气的话，那么在英国实力已完全占了上风的 19 世纪末，道格斯译本导论的字里行间已经充满了不屑的口吻，开篇就把中国人在文学文化方面的"自大"和对孔孟之道的"迷信"淋漓尽致地数落了一通（Douglas,1893：xi-xii），然后不无优越感地说："怜悯和轻视是这种逆水而游之举给人的唯一感觉。"（*op. cit.*：xii）他批评中国小说风格拖沓、叙事冗长、情节琐碎，"在欧洲要是出版这样的作品就全完了"，并宣称这种缺陷"是自《天方夜谭》以降所有东方作品的一个原罪，东方人要想在这方面进行改革，只能先去东方化"（*op. cit.*：xviii-xix）。这已经是对包括中国在内的所有东方文明轻蔑之情溢于言表了！更有甚者，道格斯在导论中至少有三处提及中国人时用的是"Chinaman/Chinamen"这样的蔑称（*op. cit.*：xvii, xviii, xxi），一副满不在乎和不屑一顾的口吻，与萨义德笔下那些"以东方为业却难掩对东方之极度鄙视"（Their professional involvement with the East did not prevent them from despising it thoroughly.）的"白种东方人"（White Orientals）（Said,1978：238）何其相似！

三是翻译策略和方法。对原作和译出语的态度直接影响着译者的翻译策略和方法，尊重者往往选择贴近原文，轻视者则一般不太在乎原作的内容和形式，而是会按译入语的需要或译者个人的偏好对译文进行增删或改编，调整的程度与译者对原作和译出语的轻视程度有直接关联。从 19 世纪李渔作品的三种英译来看，或多或少都存在着删削或改编的情况。相比较而言，德庇时译本应该是三者之中最贴近原作的，但即便如此，其中还是有不少删省，最明显处就是原作每篇小说开头的导入性铺垫，即"入话"（约 800～1000字不等）被悉数删去，译文直接从故事本身发生的时间，即"元朝至正年间""明朝正德年间"和"明朝嘉靖年间"开始。德庇时在《三与楼》题注中解释删省的原因是原作的入话失之"冗长"（tedious）（Davis,1822：154）。但这种入话是中国传统话本小说常用的写作手法，往往发挥着铺陈背景、导入情节、表达观点乃至教化读者的作用。翻译过程中若是只考虑英语文学规范的要求和读者的阅读习惯，简单地以"冗长"为由对这些内容随意删削，难免给人

---

① 当然，德庇时后来做外交官，乃至最终成为一名汉学家之后对中国语言文学的态度发生了较大转变，那是后话，但至少在翻译《三与楼》的青年时期，他对当时广州地区通行的贸易用语粤语是很不喜欢的。

自我中心主义和不尊重原作的霸道之感,同时这样的删削还有可能让读者误以为原作的叙事方式与英语文学作品并无二致。不过德庇时的译文除了上述这些删削,总体上还是比较贴近原文的,"比较朴素,没有冗词,也不夸张"(赵长江,2017:144)。而其他两位译者对原作的改动幅度则要大得多。伯奇的译文只是原文的一个梗概,除了一点可以满足一下猎奇心理的情节,几乎一无所有;道格斯更是只从原作借了个母题,其他全部自创,差不多可以算是一篇原创的英文短篇小说了!其中最有可能误导英语读者的并非人物信息和故事结局的差异,而是细节描写方面——译文为了符合英语小说的需要而杜撰了许多原作没有的交流细节,包括两个孪生女儿之间以及她们与母亲、意中人及 prefect 之间的多轮对话,但这样一来,原作里的两个待字闺中足不出户、自始至终"欲语还羞"、没说过一句话的未婚女子,到译文里就成了两个抛头露面、为追求个人幸福而殚精竭虑(甚至不惜从prefect 处套取考题来帮助自己的恋人)、敢做敢当的"小辣妹"了!原文与其社会文化背景之间的联系纽带被粗暴地切断,读者所面对的,早已不是真正的东方女子形象。这样的翻译,又何以帮助读者认识和了解真实的东方呢?

综上,19 世纪李渔在英语世界的译介主要集中于短篇小说集《十二楼》的翻译,翻译主体是英国汉学家、来华商人和外交官等,主要目的是藉翻译了解中国,译者大都有东方主义倾向,轻视原作和中国语言文化,译文有程度不一的删削改编现象。从传播媒介看,三篇小说都既在英文期刊上发表过也出版过单行本,多数是先在期刊上连载,然后出版单行本。其中《三与楼》稍有不同,最先于 1815 年由 E. I. 公司出版过单行本,但"在中国印数很少"(Davis,1822:12),之后于 1816 年被《亚洲杂志》转载,最后才与其他两篇小说结集出版。此外,在译介时间的分布上,从德庇时到道格斯中间间隔时间比较长,译介缺乏延续性,疑因中英之间鸦片战争影响所致。总体而言,这一阶段的译介规模不大,相关研究也不多,但为 20 世纪中叶之后英语世界李渔译介和研究的复兴打下了基础。

## 第二节　1960—1980 年代:李渔译介和研究的"复兴"

道格斯之后,英语世界的李渔译介和研究进入了"休眠"期,在长达半个多世纪的时间里，几乎成了一片无人问津的空白领域。① 造成这一局面的主要原因是两次世界大战使西欧各国满目疮痍、无暇他顾，而我国这段时期也是内忧外患、国运多舛，完全无力襄助文化外传事业。进入 1960 年代，随着欧美各国先后摆脱二战影响、经济社会发展蒸蒸日上，李渔在英语世界的传播也进入了"复兴"期。

这一阶段在翻译上的重要成果，一是理查德·马丁（Richard Martin，生卒年不详）从德文转译的《肉蒲团》；二是茅国权（Nathan K. Mao，1942—2015）翻译的《十二楼》。

1959 年，德国翻译家弗兰茨·库恩（Franz Kuhn，1884—1961）将《肉蒲团》首次译入德语，在西方国家也掀起了轩然大波。1961 年美国汉学家海陶玮（James R. Hightower，1915—2006）在德国《远东学报》（Oriens Extremus）第 8 卷第 2 期发表"Franz Kuhn and His Translation of *Jou P'u-t'uan*"一文，专门评论译作（Hightower，1961：252-257）。1963 年马丁将《肉蒲团》从德语版译入英语，书名为 *The Prayer Mat of Flesh*，由纽约格洛夫出版社（Grove Press）出版。翌年美籍华人学者夏志清（C. T. Hsia，1921—2013）在《亚洲研究杂志》（*The Journal of Asian Studies*）第 23 卷第 2 期发表"Review of *Jou Pu Tuan*（*The Prayer Mat of Flesh*）. By Li Yü. Translated by Richard Martin from the German version by Franz Kuhn"一文予以绍介和评论

---

① 根据羽离子的说法，第一次世界大战前有一位国籍不明的译者乔·格雷戈里（J. Gregory）曾将李渔十种曲之一的《玉搔头》译入英文，题名 *The Dreamy Life*。参见羽离子. 李渔作品在海外的传播及海外的有关研究. 四川大学学报（哲学社会科学版），2001(3)：71. 但大英图书馆未能查到相关信息，国内其他学者亦未提及，故无可考。除此以外，这一时期译介李渔最多的当属林语堂，他 1930—1940 年代出版的一些著述，包括《吾国吾民》（*My Country and My People*，1935）、《生活的艺术》（*The Importance of Living*，1937）等，就有多处引用或摘译《闲情偶寄》的相关内容，涉及声容部、居室部、饮馔部、种植部、颐养部等。参见 Lin Yutang, *My Country and My People*（New York：Reynal & Hitchcock, Inc.，1935），p. 99，169，pp. 317-318，325-328，332-333，338-340. 及 Lin Yutang, *The Importance of Living*（New York：The John Day Company，1937），pp. 42-43，p. 205，211，240，255，pp. 268-273，p. 298，pp. 304-305. 林语堂后来在《古文小品译英》一书中更是直接摘译了《闲情偶寄》声容部"选姿第一"之"态度"、颐养部"行乐第一"之"富人行乐之法""贫贱行乐之法""随时即景就事行乐之法"（睡、行、坐、立）等篇目的内容。参见 Lin Yutang, *The Importance of Understanding*：*Translations from the Chinese*（Cleveland & New York：The World Publishing Company，1960），pp. 214-215，216-217，232-235，258-263. 以上引用和摘译详见本书附录1：林语堂英文著述引用/摘译《闲情偶寄》情况一览。松田静江认为在李渔进入美国的过程中，林语堂的《生活的艺术》和《古文小品译英》居功至伟。参见 Shizue Matsuda, "Li Yu：His Life and Moral Philosophy as Reflected in His Fiction"（Columbia University diss.，1978），p. ii. 另外，美国汉学家恒慕义（Arthur W. Hummel，1884—1975）所编《清代名人传略》（*Eminent Chinese of the Ch'ing Period*［1644—1912］，1943）一书也收有李曼瑰对李渔生平的介绍（Hummel，1943/2010：495-497），库恩译本译者序作了节略引述（参见 Martin，1965：284-286）。但总体上，1960 年代之前李渔在英语世界的译介非常少。

(Hsia,1964:298-301)。1965 年马丁转译本由英国 Andre Deutsch Ltd. 出版社再版,书名改为 *The before midnight scholar* [*Jou Pu Tuan*]。英译本的内容简介这样评价原作:"这部小说的引人注目之处在于它所营造的宁静而幽默的氛围,时不时地会令人捧腹大笑。小说情节安排缜密,像戏剧一样包含多幕内容完整、结构紧凑的场景,既是博人一笑的行为喜剧,又是对性和心理的观感。"(Martin,1965:v)然而,由于《肉蒲团》的情色题材和内容,它在译入西方世界后产生了广泛的影响,包括影响西方读者对中国传统小说的印象、对原作者文学形象的认知和接受等,尤其是在李渔的作者身份尚未完全证实的情况下,作品的外译和传播对李渔在西方的文学声誉产生了较大的负面影响。本书第三章将对此另述。

　　1973 年,美籍华人学者茅国权将《鹤归楼》(《十二楼》之九)译成英文,发表于香港中文大学翻译研究中心主办的《译丛》(*Renditions*)杂志秋季号第 1 期,题为"Tower of the Returning Crane"(Mao,1973:25-35)。茅国权在译文插注里简要介绍了原作者李渔的生平,解释了《十二楼》书名的意思和《鹤归楼》题名中的"鹤归"典故,同时还发布了《十二楼》全译本即出的信息(*op. cit.*:26),并在译文末尾附了其他 11 篇小说题目的原名与译名对照表(*op. cit.*:35)。1975 年,茅国权的《十二楼》英译本由香港中文大学出版社出版,书名为《李渔十二楼》(*Li Yü's TWELVE TOWERS*)。这是《十二楼》英译历史上的第一部,同时也是唯一一部全译本。但所谓的"全译"只不过是就篇目数而言的"完整"翻译,实际上茅国权采用的是一种"译述"(retelling)式的翻译方法,对每篇故事的内容和情节都有较大幅度的删削改编。此前发表的《鹤归楼》译文在《李渔十二楼》译本中的题名改为 *The Stoic Lover* (*Ho-kuei lou*)(Mao,1975:88),"鹤归"的字面意思则用尾注形式加以解释(*op. cit.*:134)。① 1979 年译本再版时,茅国权将书名改为《十二楼:李渔短篇小说集》(*Twelve Towers:Short Stories by Li Yü*),并根据他和柳存仁(Liu Ts'un-yan,1917—2009)合著的《李渔》一书第一、四章(Mao & Liu,1977:11-30;78-89)的内容对初版引言作了较大修改和替换(Mao,1979:xvii-xxxvi),另外还就"译述"法专门写了一篇再版序(*op. cit.*:xiii-xv),解释"译述"同逐字对译和过度意译的区别:

---

① 原作所有篇目的字面意思在茅译本中均用尾注作了解释。

我决定不采用逐字对译的方法，因为我首先考虑的是译文读者：我是在为学术圈的同事翻译，还是在为范围更广的普通读者而译？如果是为前者，则译文读者只会圈于为数不多的几个教授和研究生，那就没有理由花好几年的时间来翻译了。显然我是意在普通读者的，因为我相信李渔是一个善于讲故事的人，他的有些故事对于一些西方读者来说可能颇有娱乐性乃至启发性，如果翻译不为这些读者考虑，他们就会错失阅读李渔作品的机会。

但竭力赢得广大读者的青睐并不意味着我就得采取林语堂"复述"中文故事的那种彻底重写的自由译法，或者是像伊万·金翻译老舍《骆驼祥子》那样改变小说的结尾，又或者是像斯奈德翻译寒山诗那样展开诗一般的想象，而是意味着在保留原作精髓的同时，只需改一改故事的题目、删除重复多余的细节、重新安排句子结构、省略回目名称及模糊指代等，即可达此目的。(*op. cit.*：xiii)

茅国权进一步解释了他采用"译述"法的主观动机和客观需求：

简言之，逐字对译固然有其优势，但采用可靠的"译述"式翻译方法，尤其是对近世以前的中国文学用此方法，并非全无优点。在中美关系不断加强、民众对中国日益好奇的时代，我们这些从事中国研究的人必须采取一切可用的办法和手段来满足这种好奇心。"译述"法作为一种翻译手段，哪怕再不完美也能吸引读者走近译作，总比他们完全不读要好，单凭这一个理由，译述法就应该受到我们所有人的积极关注。(*op. cit.*：xv)

从再版序可以看出，茅国权的翻译动机非常清楚：通过"译述"的方法提高文本的可读性，吸引普通读者走近译作。尽管当时中美建交在即，但就文化而言，中西方仍然处在隔阂甚至对立的冷战时代，或者准确点说，是处在冰雪消融的前夜，茅译选择这样的翻译方法，应该说是审时度势的明智之举。

除了以上两部小说的英译，这一时期李渔的其他一些非小说作品（主要是《闲情偶寄》）也开始译入英语。这些译文虽非全译，却有如为英语读者打开了一扇窗，使其窥斑见豹，得以看到李渔小说之外的辉煌成就，从而改变对作家李渔的原型印象。

1960 年，林语堂出版《古文小品译英》(*The Importance of Understanding：Translations from the Chinese*，1960)一书，该书以 460 页的宏篇，摘译、汇集了中国古代众多著名作家和文人的名篇片段，旨在向西方介绍中国传统文学精华、促进东西方理解。其中第 40 篇"How To Be Happy Though Rich"（Lin,1960:214-215）、第 41 篇"How To Be Happy Though Poor"（*op. cit.*:216-217）、第 45 篇"On Charm in Women"（*op. cit.*:232-235）和第 52 篇"The Arts of Sleeping,Walking,Sitting and Standing"（*op. cit.*:258-263）分别摘译自李渔《闲情偶寄·颐养部》行乐第一"富人行乐之法"篇（40）、"贫贱行乐之法"篇（41）和"随时即景就事行乐之法"篇（52），以及《闲情偶寄·声容部》选姿第一"态度"篇（45）。① 林语堂在其中一篇的按语中对李渔给予了高度评价：

> 李笠翁是一位富于原创、多才多艺的作家,他与其说是一位学者不如说是一位生活艺术大师,所撰《芥子园画谱》（施蕴珍译,伯林根系列丛书之 49）的序言脍炙人口,另有多部畅销书籍传世,包括我年幼时读过的一部楹联创作方面的书。他写过 12 部短篇小说和 10 部传奇,以喜剧题材为主。《闲情偶寄》反映的是他在戏曲、表演、居室、饮馔、园艺等方面一以贯之的原创思想。（*op. cit.*:214）

1974 年,《译丛》秋季号第 3 期刊登了文世昌（Man Sai-cheong,1944—2015）节译的《李笠翁曲话》,题为《李渔论表演艺术》（"Li Yu on the Performing Arts," Man,1974:62-65）。译文前的编者按语作了如下介绍：

> 李渔（1611—1680?）的多才多艺在《译丛》第 1 期刊载的一部短篇小说中已可见一斑,此处所刊曲话则显示了他在戏剧方面的才能。李渔本人就是剧作家和戏班班主,办了一个四处巡演的戏班,上演自创的戏曲,其中他本人至少写了 10 部。因此他对戏曲的见解超越了纯文学方法的局限,是从表演艺术的角度来看戏剧,四邻八舍皆为观众。……（*op. cit.*:62）

这篇译文是文世昌从其硕士论文（Man,1970）征引的李渔关于戏曲表演的言论中遴选出来的,全文共 14 个部分,涵盖李渔在词采、选剧、授曲、教白、习技

---

① 原文和译文详见本书附录 1。

等方面的见解,①是李渔戏曲理论英译的有益尝试。但因系节译,全文仅 4 页,内容失之简略,未能展现笠翁曲话原作的全貌和丰采,茅国权和柳存仁评价译文"作为一般参考还可以"(Mao & Liu,1977:167)。

在作品英译的影响和推动下,这一时期英语世界的李渔研究进入了复兴期,主要表现在以下几个方面:

一是研究数量明显增加。这一阶段在英语世界发表于各类报刊杂志的李渔研究或与李渔相关的评论文章、正式出版的学术专著以及各类学位论文数量,用"雨后春笋"来形容亦不为过,与之前数十年的冷清局面形成了鲜明对照。但稍加梳理即不难发现,大部分研究成果都与《肉蒲团》脱不了干系,正如宋柏年(1994:580)所言,"在李渔所有的作品中,只有《肉蒲团》在西方闻名。"杨力宇等人《中国古典小说》(Yang *et al.*,1978:70)亦持此见。按照日裔美国学者松田静江的说法,1971 年春她首次涉足李渔短篇小说这一研究领域时,她实际上是全美唯一把李渔作为一位重要的白话短篇小说家来研究的人(Matsuda,1978:ii)。这意味着英语世界 1960—1970 年代的李渔研究是"言必称'蒲团'",人们的注意力基本都集中在《肉蒲团》上,《无声戏》和《十二楼》这两部确系李渔创作的经典短篇小说集反而无人问津了。从笔者掌握的资料来看,1960 年代以降的汉学家和李渔研究者中有不少人都认为李渔就是《肉蒲团》的作者,或者是把李渔同《肉蒲团》及中国古代色情文学放在一起相提并论,如高罗佩(van Gulik,1961)、茅国权(Mao,1967)、茅国权与柳存仁(Mao & Liu,1977)、松田静江(Matsuda,1978)、杨力宇等(Yang *et al.*,1978)、何谷理(Hegel,1981)、雷威安(Lévy,1986:460-461)、马汉茂(Martin,1986:557-559),以及韩南(Hanan,1981;1988)等。当然,也有部分学者对李渔的作者身份提出过质疑,例如海陶玮(Hightower,

---

① 一般认为,笠翁曲话就是指李渔《闲情偶寄》中"词曲部"和"演习部"的内容,其中"词曲部"分为"结构第一"(计 7 款:立主脑、脱窠臼、密针线、减头绪、戒荒唐、审虚实)、"词采第二"(计 4 款:贵浅显、重机趣、戒浮泛、忌填塞)、"音律第三"(计 9 款:恪守词韵、凛遵曲谱、鱼模当分、廉监宜避、拗句难好、合韵易重、慎用上声、少填入韵、别解务头)、"宾白第四"(计 8 款:声务铿锵、语求肖似、词别繁减、字分南北、文贵洁净、意取尖新、少用方言、时防漏孔)、"科诨第五"(计 4 款:戒淫亵、忌俗恶、重关系、贵自然)和"格局第六"(计 5 款:家门、冲场、出脚色、小收煞、大收煞);"演习部"分为"选剧第一"(计 2 款:别古今、剂冷热)、"变调第二"(计 2 款:缩长为短、变旧成新)、"授曲第三"(计 6 款:解明曲意、调熟字音、字忌模糊、曲严分合、锣鼓忌杂、吹合宜低)、"教白第四"(计 2 款:高低抑扬、缓急顿挫)和"脱套第五"(计 4 款:衣冠恶习、声音恶习、语言恶习、科诨恶习)。但文世昌的译文中还有《闲情偶寄》"声容部"名下"习技第四"之"歌舞"款的内容。参见 Sai-cheong Man,"A Study of Li Yü on Drama"(The University of Hong Kong diss.,1970),pp. 142-143,162-163. 亦见 Sai-cheong Man trans.,"Li Yu on the Performing Arts,"*Renditions* 3(Autumn,1974):63,65. 本书第四章关于翻译策略的探讨将涉及文世昌译文。

1961:256)就指出,"就现有证据而言,我认为李渔作为《肉蒲团》作者的可能性不大",并建议"最好把他的姓名从(德译本)封面上删去"。夏志清(Hsia,1964:299)认为海陶玮的论证"令人信服"。[①] Ingalls(1964:60)甚至还提出《肉蒲团》原作封面所署的"情隐先生""有可能是一名女性"。此外也有持中立立场的,例如从事李渔戏曲研究的 Henry(1980:261)就表示,尽管《肉蒲团》和李渔的短篇小说乃至戏剧作品有诸多相似,但他不愿在此问题上纠缠,因为一是与李渔戏曲赏析无关,二是有相似之处也并不代表就能最终确定作者身份。不过,与主流学术界的意见相比,质疑者和持异议者的声音十分微弱且应者寥寥。不仅如此,茅国权和柳存仁(Mao & Liu,1977:91-95)还对海陶玮和 Ingalls 的观点提出了批评;他们引用刘廷玑(李渔同时代学者)、鲁迅、孙楷第、德国汉学家马汉茂(Helmut Martin,1940—1999)等人的意见,辅以《肉蒲团》与李渔《无声戏》《十二楼》中的短篇小说在人物塑造、情节结构、语言特点等方面的相似之处作为证据,强调《肉蒲团》确系李渔所作。

欧美读者和学人对《肉蒲团》的喜爱和热捧,部分原因是当时适逢西方的性解放运动如火如荼之际,性题材的作品大行其道、风靡一时,《肉蒲团》的西译"一定程度上迎合了当时西方盛行的色情狂热"(宋柏年,1994:580);而且,这样一部来自遥远东方的"深藏不露的文学宝藏"(a hidden literary treasure,库恩语,转引自 Martin,1965:287),在作品寓意、情节编排、语言技巧等方面处处体现了原作者的匠心和中国语言文学的奇趣,给读者带来了新奇的异域文化体验和文学想象,因而自然会受到读者的普遍青睐。但另一方面,在整个西方世界对《肉蒲团》毫不了解的情形下,初译者库恩把原作者这顶帽子扣在了李渔的头上,[②]致使包括转译者和相当一部分学者在内的

---

① 事实上夏志清在 1964 年发表的这篇评论中除了指出库恩译本的错误及其对马丁转译本的影响之外,自始至终没有涉及作者问题。参见 C. T. Hsia,"Review of *Jou Pu Tuan* (*The Prayer Mat of Flesh*),by Li Yü,translated by Richard Martin from the German version by Franz Kuhn," *The Journal of Asian Studies* 23,2 (1964):298-301. 他在后来的著作中提及《肉蒲团》时,也只说"这是一部比《金瓶梅》更明晰紧凑、更有艺术性、也远为生动的作品",避而不谈其作者问题,这也说明他并不认同李渔的作者身份。参见 C. T. Hsia,*The Classic Chinese Novel:A Critical Introduction* (Hong Kong:The Chinese University of Hong Kong Press,1968/2015),p. 187. 中译文参见夏志清. 中国古典小说导论. 合肥:安徽文艺出版社,1988:227.

② 库恩是根据鲁迅、蔡元培、孙楷第等中国学者的观点作此判断的,参见 Richard Martin trans. ,*The before midnight scholar* [*Jou Pu Tuan*]. By Li Yu. Translated from the German version by Franz Kuhn (London:Andre Deutsch Ltd. ,1965),p. 284. 但事实上这些学者的观点只有片言只语,并无实质佐证。

受众先入为主地接受了"李渔就是《肉蒲团》作者"这一原本存疑的观点，①也使得西方 1960—1970 年代以来涉及《肉蒲团》和中国古代色情文学的研究，无论肯定与否，②都打上了李渔的烙印，对李渔在英语世界的作家形象和文学声誉产生了难以估量的影响。后文另有专述，此处不赘。

二是研究范围扩大。尽管《肉蒲团》在相当长的时间里一直都是西方读者和学界关注的热点，但这一阶段还是有些研究者把目光投向了李渔的生平以及文学（小说、戏曲等）和艺术（绘画、园艺、建筑等）等领域的思想；文学作品方面的研究也由《肉蒲团》拓展至他的短篇小说和戏曲等作品。

文世昌是最早系统研究李渔戏曲理论的学者，其硕士论文《李渔戏剧理论的研究》（"A Study of Li Yü on Drama"，Man，1970）全文共 7 章，详细介绍和分析了李渔在戏曲观众、戏曲功能、情节与结构、唱腔与对白、演员调教与表演等方面的见解，并对李渔在中国乃至世界戏曲批评史上的地位和价值作了较高的评价。Eric P. Henry 的《中国娱乐：轻松活泼的李渔戏剧》（*Chinese Amusement：The Lively Plays of Li Yü*，Henry，1980）是第一部李渔戏剧研究专著，③全书共 6 章，④探讨了李渔 4 部戏曲（即《比目鱼》《巧团圆》《风筝误》和《奈何天》）的主题内容、构思技巧、文学地位等，尤其是对李渔戏曲和小说之间的渊源作了有益的探索，对英语读者了解李渔戏曲作品和戏剧理论颇有帮助。此外，威斯康辛大学麦迪逊分校东亚语言文学系教授、汉学家倪豪士（William H. Nienhauser，Jr.）主编的《印第安纳中国古典文学指南》（*The Indiana Companion to Traditional Chinese Literature*，1986）一书收录了亚利桑那大学奚如谷（Stephen H. West）和芝加哥大学费维廉（Craig Fisk）的文章，二者均肯定了李渔在戏曲上的成就和地位，认为中国文学史上"系统的戏曲研究始于李渔"，因为李渔"把戏曲看作是一门既重剧本创作又重舞台表演的整体艺术""不仅关注剧本台词和唱词的创作，而且关注台上唱念做打的方式"（West，1986：27），"戏剧概论，尤其是戏剧结构

---

① 杨力宇等人认为李渔 1960 年代在西方名声大噪的主要原因就是库恩的《肉蒲团》翻译。参见 Winston L. Y. Yang，Peter Li and Nathan K. Mao，*Classical Chinese Fiction：A Guide to Its Study and Appreciation-essays and Bibliographies*（Boston：G. K. Hall & Co.，1978），p. 70.

② 事实上前文所引大部分学者都是从正面角度来研究《肉蒲团》及相关问题的，笔者只是试图提醒读者：《肉蒲团》的作者问题从来没有真正解决过，任何想当然的以讹传讹都是不负责任的行为。

③ 据作者在前言中说，该书是在其耶鲁大学博士论文基础上完成的，参见 Eric P. Henry，*Chinese Amusement：The Lively Plays of Li Yü*（Hamden，CT.：Archon Books，1980），p. ix. 但博士论文具体信息无可考，疑应晚于松田静江（Matsuda，1978）。

④ 其中最后一章"Li Yü and His Critics"已译成中文发表。参见埃里克·亨利. 李渔：站在中西喜剧的交叉点上. 徐惠风，译. 戏剧艺术. 1989（3）：115-122.

和创作方面的最佳见解,就是李渔的《闲情偶寄·词曲部》"(Fisk,1986:56)。

茅国权和柳存仁的《李渔》(Mao & Liu,1977)是第一部专门研究李渔的著作,全书共7章,其中探讨《无声戏》《十二楼》和《肉蒲团》等小说的内容各一章,其余各章介绍李渔的生平及生活艺术、小说创作思想及成就、戏曲理论等,内容比较全面,有助于读者全方位了解李渔其人其作其论。

松田静江的《李渔小说中的生活与道德哲学》("Li Yü:His Life and Moral Philosophy as Reflected in His Fiction",Matsuda,1978)是英语世界第一部专门研究李渔小说的博士论文,全文共3章,分别探讨了李渔的生平、其短篇小说以及《肉蒲团》的作者问题,有一定的参考价值。此外,如前所述,松田静江是美国较早关注李渔白话短篇小说的研究者,她在1970年代初就研究过李渔短篇小说中的"才子佳人"式爱情主题(Matsuda,1973:271-280),对后来者颇有启发。

韩南是1980年代之后英语世界最重要的李渔研究专家,他于1960年代开始投身中国古典文学研究,在金学、红学、中国古代白话小说、李渔研究、晚清言情小说以及中国现代文学等领域均有不凡的建树。这一时期他有2部重要著作与李渔有关:《中国话本小说》(The Chinese Vernacular Story,Hanan,1981)①和《李渔的创作》(The Invention of Li Yu,Hanan,1988)②,其中前者专辟一章介绍李渔(Hanan,1981:165-190),对他的戏曲理论(op. cit.:168-171)和小说创作(op. cit.:171-187)作了较为深入的分析,并把李渔的小说与稍晚成书、同样充满喜剧想象的酌园亭主人的《照世杯》作了对照,从历史的角度指出中国传统小说中的正统道德框架的变化和瓦解(op. cit.:187-190);后者则为李渔专论,全书共8章,系统介绍和分析了李渔的创作动因、作品主旨、写作技巧、文学成就以及在休闲享乐等方面的造诣。

除此以外,李渔在其他领域的造诣和见解也引起了一些学者的注意,例如香港著名书画家和收藏家、文化学家、香港中文大学教授赖恬昌(T. C. Lai)发表于《译丛》1978年春季号第9期的文章"精选美食——袁枚与李渔美食思想辑录"("Choice Morsels-Some Food for Thought from Yuan Mei and Li Yü",Lai,1978:47-80),就从文化角度对袁枚《随园食单》和李渔《闲情偶寄·饮馔部》中关于食材和烹饪的部分内容作了译介,涉及李渔部分包

---

① 又译"中国白话小说史"。参见韩南.中国白话小说史.尹慧珉,译.杭州:浙江古籍出版社,1989.

② 亦译"创造李渔"。参见韩南.创造李渔.杨光辉,译.上海:上海教育出版社,2010.但笔者认为该译名存在歧义。另外也有译为"李渔的发明"的,参见张春树,骆雪伦.明清时代之社会经济巨变与新文化——李渔时代的社会与文化及其"现代性".王湘云,译.上海:上海古籍出版社,2008:182.

括他对蔬菜（笋、蕈、菜、葱蒜韭等）、肉食（蟹等）、汤、果食茶酒等食材的辨识、烹饪、食用等心得。Edwin T. Morris 的《中华园林》（*The Gardens of China：History，Art，and Meanings*，1983）一书中多次提及李渔在南京的芥子园（Morris，1983：23，76，117）以及与之相关的《芥子园画谱》（*op. cit.*：92，147，164，170）。①

　　三是研究水平大幅提升。如前所述，这一时期英语世界发表了大量李渔研究方面的期刊论文和评论文章，但该领域研究水平显著提升的重要标志，乃是专题硕博士学位论文的提交和学术专著的出版。文世昌的硕士论文（Man，1970）、松田静江的博士论文（Matsuda，1978）以及茅国权和柳存仁（Mao & Liu，1977）、Henry（1980）、韩南（Hanan，1988）等人的专著，在很多方面都是前无古人的首创研究，成为李渔英译与传播史上的里程碑，同时也把这一时期的李渔研究提升到了一个很高的层次，为1990年代之后李渔译介和研究的繁荣打下了坚实的基础。

　　综上，1960—1980年代的李渔英译主要围绕小说《肉蒲团》和《十二楼》展开，另外还有《李笠翁曲话》的部分内容节译发表，但影响不大。其中《肉蒲团》因题材迎合了西方的性解放运动而受到广泛关注，但同时原本存在争议的作者身份也被初译者先入为主地安在了李渔身上。李渔研究方面进入复兴期，在研究数量、范围和水平上都大大超越了前人，成为一个承前启后的重要历史阶段。

## 第三节　1990年代以降：全球化时代的繁荣与成熟

　　继1960—1980年代"复兴"期在翻译实践和相关研究等方面取得大量突破性进展之后，从1990年开始，英语世界的李渔译介和研究进入了一个相对平稳的繁荣和成熟期，翻译实践方面继续开拓，将李渔更多的作品译入了英语，研究方面也不断挖掘，在深度、新意、方法等方面均取得了一些

---

① 羽离子称 Morris 在书中"引介了李渔的园林建筑的思想以帮助美国人理解中国园林"，另外还提及 Alison Hardic（应为 Hardie。——笔者注）1988年从中文翻译的 *Craft of Gardens*（《园林匠艺》）一书（中英文书名均有错误：英文书名应为 *The Craft of Gardens*，中文原作应为《园冶》，系明代造园家计成［1582—？］的传世之作。——笔者注）中"论及李渔的园林理论"。参见羽离子. 李渔作品在海外的传播及海外的有关研究：77-78. 但这两点据考证皆不实：（1）Morris 虽数次提及芥子园，但大多只是一笔带过，关于李渔讲得最多的也只是他的生平和主要作品，并未涉及他的园艺思想；（2）计成《园冶》一书成书于崇祯四年（1631），崇祯七年（1634）刊行，而据李渔年谱记载，芥子园落成于康熙八年（1669），收录李渔园艺思想的《闲情偶寄》则刊行于康熙十年（1671），前者比后者早了40年，不可能论及后者的理论。参见李渔. 李渔全集第十九卷. 杭州：浙江古籍出版社，1991：67，76.

进步。

这一时期的翻译活动主要是《肉蒲团》的重译和《十二楼》《无声戏》的英译。

1990 年,韩南重译的《肉蒲团》由纽约 Ballantine Books 出版社出版,这是继 1960 年代马丁转译本之后《肉蒲团》在英语世界的再度亮相,也是这部小说第一次直接由中文译入英文。韩南译本的封面上印有美国当代著名旅行作家保罗·泰鲁(Paul E. Theroux,1941—)的评语:"这本陌生而令人喜爱的书是中国色情文学中最生动的一部作品,展示了中国社会裸体的一面。韩南的译文富于启发、流畅而详尽——不但有学术性,还很性感。"韩南在译本引言中介绍了李渔的创作特色、中西色情文学传统的差异、《肉蒲团》与其他色情小说的不同、原作成书年代及版本演变情况、小说各章主要内容等(Hanan,1990a:5-18)。他宣称:"如果说中国色情小说有经典范本的话,则非李渔《肉蒲团》莫属。"(*op. cit.*:8)。译本封底的书评称《肉蒲团》是一部有重大影响的小说、"一部被重新发现的经典",是克莱兰(John Cleland,1709—1789)《芬妮·希尔》(*Fanny Hill*,1784)和劳伦斯(David H. Lawrence,1885—1930)《查泰莱夫人的情人》(*Lady Chatterley's Lover*,1928)这两部英语世界公认的色情小说的"真正鼻祖"。

韩南重译本出版之后在英语世界再次引发了轰动效应,很快售罄,于1992 年、1995 年、1999 年多次再版和重印,甚至还推出了录音磁带版,1990年被《纽约时报》书评栏目评为"1990 年度著名小说",1995 年被美国《出版者周刊》(*Publisher's Weekly*)杂志评为年度最佳图书(参见羽离子,2001:71-72;2002:26),[1]在世界各大图书馆也受到读者热情追捧,借阅人数屡破纪录。[2] 评论界的反响也很大,且褒贬不一。例如 Hauf 认为,与马丁节译本比起来,[3]韩南的重译本"棒极了"(excellent),而且还提供了富有启发的引言和注释,"从此英语里就能找到这部小说的完整版了"(Hauf,1990:7)。

---

① 据何敏(2013:94)的说法是 1996 年。

② 笔者曾调阅伦敦大学亚非学院(SOAS)图书馆所藏的一部《肉蒲团》韩南译本的非电子借阅记录,据不完全统计,该书在 1990—2005 年总共被借阅了 40 次,其中 1991 年 4 次,1992 年高达 10次,1993 年也达 8 次。这已是相当高的借阅纪录。

③ Hauf 认为马丁转译本的原文——即库恩译本——依据的是中文的一个删节版。参见 Kandice Hauf, "Review of *The Carnal Prayer Mat*, by Li Yu, translated with an introduction and notes by P. Hanan," *Harvard Book Review*,17/18 (Summer-Fall,1990):7. 但韩南译本和马丁转译本的回目总数应该是一样的(韩南译本是二十回,马丁转译本则把第一回改成了引言,因此看起来少了一回),可能只是所依中文原本不同。由于笔者不认同李渔是《肉蒲团》的作者,不拟作进一步考证。

1992 年 7 月美国的《科库斯评论》(*Kirkus Reviews*)上有人撰文评论说:"中国的社会和喜剧般情爱的精妙把魅力赋予了一位真正大师的作品。而这一作品轻易地跨过了三百多年而在今天依然鲜亮和震响。"(转引自羽离子,2001:72)与此同时,批评该书充斥着"性小丑"和"胡言乱语"的也大有人在,甚至连 *Playgirl* 这样的杂志都不得不承认该书的巨大的负面影响(同前引,其他一些批评意见另参见羽离子,2002:27)。

韩南没有解释过自己重译《肉蒲团》的原因,笔者认为最大的可能性是马丁译本的出版年代去今已远,而且是从一个满篇错误的德语译本转译的,[①]问题多多,已经不能适应英语世界当代李渔研究对作品的要求了。当然,也不完全排除他有吸引大众读者的商业动机,毕竟 1950—1960 年代《肉蒲团》译入西方时的火爆和畅销令人记忆犹新,也是每位译者都希望出现的场面。然而,尽管译文十分流畅,引言和注释也都颇有启发,但读者的阅读动机恐以猎奇居多,不一定能达到译者所希望的那样领会原作寓意和教化宗旨,甚或藉此开展学术研究的目的。正如 Hauf(1990:8)所言,"最后我们看到,主人公在肉蒲团上花费了大把的时间之后幡然醒悟,而我这位'看官'得到的却不是什么顿悟,而是娱乐。"

《肉蒲团》重译本出版当年,香港中文大学出版社推出了韩南主译的另一部李渔作品《无声戏》(*Silent Operas*,Hanan,1990b)。这是这部小说集第一次译入英语,使英语世界的读者得以首次领略到李渔《十二楼》以外的短篇小说的风采。《无声戏》是李渔的第一部白话小说集,原作成书于清顺治十三至十四年(即 1656—1657 年),最早分初集和二集刊行,其中初集收录小说 12 篇,成为后世流传之《无声戏》的主要篇目(第一至十二回),二集完整版失传,其中 5 篇与初集的 7 篇小说(即第一至四回、十至十二回)后收入李渔在南京梓行的《无声戏合集》。这就是说,《无声戏》现今存世的篇目数为 17 篇。若干年后,李渔改《无声戏合集》为《连城璧全集》,并将合集中未收录的初集 5 篇(即第五至九回)以及新写的 1 篇(《说鬼话计赚生人显神通智恢旧业》)附于其后,是为《连城璧外编》,篇目总数为 18 篇。可

---

① 夏志清指出,库恩译本不仅译者序错误百出、极易误导读者,而且译文充斥着无法原谅的低级错误,包括错认原文字词、随意篡改固定表述、曲解和生造句意等,"库恩博士是西方世界备受尊重,同时也无疑是最刻苦的中国小说译家,但从他在成熟老练的年纪里完成的一部作品中居然看到他中文功底这么不扎实,想到这一点就让人觉得悲哀。可惜他在开始译者生涯之前没能做到精通这门语言(指汉语)。——笔者注)否则凭着他翻译上的高产以及那么多以他作品为基础的重译(包括《肉蒲团》英译本),他本来是能永葆一代名家之誉的。"参见 Hsia,"Review of *Rou Pu Tuan*",pp.299-301.

见,连城璧及外编与无声戏之间的关系比较复杂,既有直接渊源,同时在回目数、内容、文字、评注等方面又存在一些差别,"说二书实为一书、《连城璧》是《无声戏》的别名亦可,说二书并非一书、《连城璧》应为《无声戏》之增订别刻亦无不可"(萧欣桥,1991:2)。韩南译本总共选取了 6 篇小说,即《无声戏》的第一回《丑郎君怕娇偏得艳》、第二回《美男子避惑反生疑》、第五回《女陈平计生七出》、第六回《男孟母教合三迁》、第九回《变女为儿菩萨巧》和《连城璧全集》的第一回《谭楚玉戏里传情 刘藐姑曲终死节》。其中第五回和第九回是韩南单独翻译的,其余各篇由韩南与朱志瑜(Chu Chiyu)、孔慧怡(Eva Hung)、夏克胡(Gopal Sukhu)、魏贞恺(Janice Wickeri)等中外学者合作完成。①

韩南在《无声戏》译本引言中开门见山地指出,17 世纪是中国小说史上话本小说的重要时代,最优秀的小说家们都在写话本小说,而"其中最成功的一位便是李渔",因为他的小说总是特立独行于同时代的作家,"绝不取现成逸闻",主题也比时人更敢于针对社会,"有时胆大得令人吃惊"(Hanan,1990b:vii)。韩南认为,李渔小说的基本构成要素是社会和文学主题的倒置,而所有倒置都是为喜剧效果服务的,因此可以顺理成章地称李渔为中国文学(包括小说、戏曲和随笔)的喜剧专家(op. cit.:viii)。韩南随后介绍了《无声戏》和李渔其他小说的创作、发行及版本等情况,并分析了部分小说与李渔戏曲之间的渊源,包括《丑郎君》与《奈何天》、《谭楚玉》与《比目鱼》、《女陈平》与《巧团圆》等(op. cit.:x)。最后对原作回目标题的排列规律、开篇诗词与入话的特点、回末批评、原作注解等作了分析和举例说明。译本引言内容未直接解释原作回目的遴选标准和原因,亦未交代翻译策略与方法及其理由。

1992 年,韩南选译了李渔《十二楼》中的《夏宜楼》《归正楼》《萃雅楼》《拂云楼》《鹤归楼》《生我楼》等 6 篇故事,结集交由 Ballantine Books 公司出版,取名《夏宜楼》(A Tower for the Summer Heat)。1998 年译本由哥伦比亚大学出版社再版。再版序言中,韩南介绍了李渔对文学创作和日常生活"出新"的重视、《十二楼》原作话本小说的语体特征、"楼"的意思及篇目名称的翻译、作品的内容和结构、译本篇目取舍的原因以及原作创作年代和版本信息等(Hanan,1992/1998:vii-xi)。他称赞《十二楼》是"李渔最著名的小说类作品"(op. cit.:xi)。在介绍译本篇目取舍及其原因时,他说:"我翻译了《十二楼》的第四到七、第九和第十一篇小说。有人可能会提出

---

① 详见本书附录 2:《无声戏》韩南译本篇目一览。

疑问，觉得只译出一半篇目会损害原作。那么整部作品的形制是否因翻译而丢失了呢？事实上，每篇小说以一幢楼作为题名，这只是一条表面的纽带，把若干故事松散地串在一起，就像中国古代用绳子把铜钱串在一起一样。"(op. cit.：x)他还特别解释了未选译最后一篇《闻过楼》的原因，认为《闻过楼》描写了明末清初文人的颠沛与窘迫，一定程度上反映了李渔的个人境遇，而且也影射了当时经济和文化支配权集中于官员手中的现实，虽然题材和立意都不错，但"以李渔的标准来评判的话，它是一篇缺乏文采的小说"(ibid.)。① 与 1970 年代的茅国权译述版《十二楼》相比，韩南译本虽非全译，但就所选篇目的内容来看，删削之处不多，还是比较忠实于原作的。

进入 21 世纪之后，由国/境外汉学家和学者以及国/境外出版社主导的李渔作品英译活动告一段落，国内翻译家、学者和出版社开始登上译介舞台。2011 年，外语教学与研究出版社推出了由卓振英编著的《李渔诗赋楹联赏析》，这是李渔诗赋楹联英译的首次尝试。卓振英是"大中华文库"《楚辞》英译者、国内著名的典籍翻译家，其《天问》译文曾被 2012 年在北京召开的第 28 届国际天文学联合大会采纳为官方译文，公布在大会网站上，昭示中国人对天文学的亘古追问与梦想。《李渔诗赋楹联赏析》总共选译了 4 篇赋、14 首古风、26 首格律诗和 19 副楹联，根据上述体裁样式分为 4 章，各章按"绪论—原作—英译—评注"的顺序编排，其中绪论简介各体裁样式的特点、技巧等，评注说明或分析诗作的内容、形式、手法等，是典型的"译""研"结合的深度翻译。图 2-1 为该书选译的古风之一《行路难》(卓振英，2011:26-30)，从中可以看出每首诗从介绍、原文、译文到评注的全貌。

---

① 韩南的解释有一定道理，但像《合影楼》《夺锦楼》《三与楼》这样质量较高的小说也没有选译，大概是因为这几篇早在 19 世纪就有英译了，译者不希望重复前人的劳动；而《生我楼》之所以入选，一方面可能是因为之前只有一个摘译，重译无妨，另一方面则是该篇质量明显高于《十卺楼》《奉先楼》和《闻过楼》。

### Chapter Two: Poems in the Classical Style（古风）

#### Introductory Remarks to Poems in the Classical Style

In ancient China, there had been tetra-syllabic, penta-syllabic, and hepta-syllabic poems, without strict metrical rules governing the form, the tonal pattern and the rhyme scheme of poetic composition. When poetical meter was shaped in the Tang Dynasty, those poems were referred to as "ancient poetry" or "poetry in the classical style".

Included in *The Complete Works of Li Yu* are one hundred and six poems in the classical style, of which fifty-seven are penta-syllabic and forty-nine hepta-syllabic. The present book only contains a selection of fourteen.

#### 5. Perilous Is the Way（行路难）

行路难
请君驻马离雕鞍，
听我一歌行路难。
人生得意须行乐，
顺风舟去如飞鹃。
君不见千里江陵一日还，
又不见轻舟已过万重山。
前人赋此鸣得意，
我读此诗生长叹。
人逢佳景愁易过，
路好恨不终漫漫。
胡为自甘胸过隙，

(a)

---

图画留与后人看，
行到山穷水尽处，
曲终兴亦随之阑。
旁有达者闻我语，
莎诩连声莫之许，
我拥达者讯以故，
达者曰吾语汝，
富贵颛光异贫贱，
一来即去如飞电，
素封乞丐须臾间，
画颥颥坦倏倾变，
官好易裁潘岳燕，
势去难留王谢燕，
长夜为欢只怪迟，
万钱一食非无见，
汝功贵人缓行床，
先为显者题左券，
功名富贵可常保，
寄语桃李之花勿成片。

（唐艳芳、卓振英译）

**Perilous Is the Way[1]**

Would you, sir, halt your horse and leave your carv'd saddle?
I would like to sing to you *Perilous Is th' Way*.
Good luck, like the boats, will soon go with th' wind, thus one
Is to think before going on sprees in his day!
Have you witness'd a day's thousand-*li* voyage to Jiangling,
Or e'er seen a swift boat that flashes past many a mount.
When writing th' poem[2], the poet was light-hearted;
But I sigh o'er th' lines, for I'm vari'd on that count.
In one's good times 'tis easy to cast cares aside,

(b)

---

And when the road is smooth, to move on one's inclin'd.
Oh, when life is like a steed's gallop o'er a gap,
Why sit idle, leaving a laughing stock behind?
It is a long lane that has no turning: the time
Might come when zeal fades away at the cul-de-sac.
The so-called clever men around, however,
Make an objection to my point with sneer and smack.
Making a bow to them I ask for their reasons,
And request that they listen to my point of view:
Wealth and power are as transient as lightening,
While poverty lingers away and comes anew.
Marquises may soon be reduc'd to beggary,
And to ruins magnificent mansions may turn.
Uphill, th' official's as complacent as Pan Yue[3];
Downhill, he can't stay th' swallows' despite his concern.
Thousand-tael banquets are nothing unusual,
And th' rich regret they hadn't enjoy'd night-long sprees.
Would you please warn the powerful of frustrations
And setbacks, and the rich not to indulge in bliss?
Oh, power and fortune none can fore'er sustain:
In the wake of their zeniths often comes unwish'd—for pain!

(Tr. TYF & ZZY)

#### Notes and Commentary

1. In this poem, which reflects the insight of the poet into life, the poet alludes to historical events to warn people against the danger hidden behind indulgence, arrogance and complacence caused by wealth and successes.

2. This refers to a four-line poem written by Li Bai, the great poet of the Tang Dynasty, which goes as follows:

朝辞白帝彩云间，千里江陵一日还。

(c)

---

两岸猿声啼不住，轻舟已过万重山。

I left Baidi nestling in rosy clouds at break of day,
And in the eve I'll reach Jiangling a thousand li away;
The jabbering of apes along the banks still seems to last,
Oho, ten thousand sweeps of mounts my swift boat has flash'd past!

3. Pan Yue (247—300), another name Pan An, was known for his literary attainments and especially for his unusual handsomeness.

4. In his poem "The Black Coat Lane", Liu Yuxi of the Tang Dynasty writes: 'The swallows, which us'd to construct their nests at the splendid domes/ Of th' Wang's and th' Xie's, are now darting into common folk's homes.' Henceforth the swallow may sometimes symbolize power or luck.

Another translation of ours, which may help the reader view the conceptual realm and artistic features of the poem from a different perspective, goes as follows:

#### Ode to Hardships of a Journey

Alas, thou travellers! Pray dismount for a stay,
And listen to me on the hardships of thy way.
When things go smooth, in merrymaking do be slow,
As happiness vanishes in th' way torrents go.
A thousand-mile voyage is covered in a day,
With shallops sailing past mountains without delay.
An ancient poet rejoiced over this for long,
But I just sigh, as his naivety turns out wrong.
In better-off days men forget what they worry,
And on broad roads they hate to be in a hurry;
The swift lapse of time, alas, they ne'er bear in mind,

(d)

Their glories are but laughing stocks, left far behind.
Mountains and waters will but with their ends remain,
So will melodies, with listeners' zest on the wane.
Standing beside me was a wise man of open mind,
Who upon th' words refuted me as being blind;
Wondering why, to him with both hands clasped I bowed,
And to my request he had the following told:
Riches and honor are but a flash in the pan,
And obviously take them for long nobody can;
Millionaires may instantly into beggars turn,
In the way frescoes into decadent walls burn.
For upright officials peach n' plum flowers grow well,
And corrupt ones even swallows flee like from hell;
Merrymakers always hate to see 't late in nights,
And sumptuous banquets are not unusual sights.
Thou asked the rich in enjoyin' their life to be slow,
But what means holding left side of th' contract, thou know?
'Tis for their positions and fortunes they most care,
And ne'er like to see peach n' plum blossoms everywhere.

(e)

图 2-1　李渔古风《行路难》中英文对照及评注

　　如图,编者除了介绍李渔这首古风的主要特点,还同时提供了自己翻译的两种英译文,并附上评注供读者对照阅读和赏析。在译序中,卓振英回顾了对李渔从最初知之不多到最终决定研究和翻译其诗赋楹联的整个历程,继而介绍李渔作品的西译情况和英语世界的主要研究成果,并以大量例证介绍了李渔诗赋楹联的思想内容和文学价值,在此基础上提出了自己的翻译观(*op. cit.*:I-XVIII)。他指出:"李渔最受称道的是戏剧理论和剧本。不过,他的诗作同样值得研究。它们充满睿智和哲理,折射着诗人的批判精神,表现出超常的想象力,闪耀着人文主义的光辉。"(*op. cit.*:XIV)他认为诗词的翻译标准应该是最大限度地保留原作的审美价值;由于韵律是传达诗歌艺术内涵的工具,失韵则诗歌形制、意境尽失,因此诗歌翻译的原则应该是"以诗译诗",译作在形式上应与英诗近似;要做到这一点,翻译过程中需要考虑和解决诸如移情、总体审度、战略布局、炼词、风格近似、逻辑调适、文本考证等诸多方面的问题(*op. cit.*:IX-X)。

　　2011年,外文出版社推出了由夏建新等人翻译的《李渔小说选》(*Selections of Li Yu's Stories*,Xia et al.,2011)。这是继1990年代韩南英译《无声戏》和《十二楼》之后,李渔短篇小说英译的又一次突破。夏译本以《连城璧全集》

和《连城璧外编》为原本,选译了 8 篇小说:《全集》第二回《老星家戏改八字 穷皂隶陡发万金》(即无声戏第三回《改八字苦尽甘来》)、第八回《妻妾败纲 常 梅香完节操》(即无声戏第十二回《妻妾抱琵琶梅香守节》)、第九回《寡妇 设计赘新郎 众美齐心夺才子》、第十回《吃新醋正室蒙冤 续旧欢家堂和事》 (即无声戏第十回《移妻换妾鬼神奇》)、第十二回《贞女守贞来异谤 朋侪相谑 致奇冤》;《外编》卷之三《说鬼话计赚生人 显神通智恢旧业》、卷之四《待诏喜 风流趋钱赎妓 运弁持公道舍米追赃》(即无声戏第七回《人宿妓穷鬼诉嫖 冤》)和卷之五《受人欺无心落局 连鬼骗有故倾家》(即无声戏第八回《鬼输钱 活人还赌债》)。① 对照之下可见,夏译本与韩南译本的篇目是不重复的。因 而,李渔无声戏的 18 篇小说,至此已有 14 篇译入了英语。夏译本前言对李 渔在文学(尤其是戏曲)和其他多个领域的成就和地位给予了高度评价,盛 赞他的中国古典戏曲理论可与斯坦尼斯拉夫斯基(Konstantin Stanislavski, 1863—1938)和布莱希特(Bertolt Brecht,1898—1956)的西方戏剧理论相媲 美(Xia,2011:i)。译本还为读者提供了中文原作,集中附于英译文之后,扉 页上印有李渔生平简介,封底有译者评价,认为他"颠覆了 17 世纪中国文学 的一些公认的道德主题"。

除了以上这些翻译,美国一些学者出于研究的需要,开始将李渔的戏曲 和其他作品列入译介计划,例如华盛顿大学圣路易斯分校文理学院东亚语 言文化系的何谷理(Robert E. Hegel)等。②

这一时期英语世界的李渔研究日趋稳定和成熟,主要表现在以下几个 方面:

一是研究深度和范围稳步加强和扩大。张春树和骆雪伦的《明清时代 之社会经济巨变与新文化——李渔时代的社会与文化及其"现代性"》 (*Crisis and Transformation of in Seventeenth-Century China: Society, Culture,and Modernity in Li Yü's World*,Chang & Chang,1992;亦见张春 树、骆雪伦,2008)在多学科视野、研究方法、考证功力等方面均超越了前人

---

① 详见本书附录 3:《李渔小说选》篇目一览。

② 何谷理在东亚语言文化系官网的教师个人"目前研究"一栏中提及,他正在与沈静(音)博士 和李前程博士合作翻译李渔戏曲《比目鱼》和董说(1620—1686)的《西游补》。参见华盛顿大学圣路 易斯分校文理学院东亚语言文化系网站[EB/OL]. [2018-08-18]. http://ealc. wustl. edu/people/hegel _robert-e.

的同类研究，①对于后来者起到了很好的示范和引领作用，在很大程度上也成为引导这一阶段英语世界李渔研究走向深入的"定音器"。随着李渔作品的大量英译，李渔研究的主题日益细化，对象范围则日益扩大。王颖（音）对李渔作品中的"翻案文章"式倒置（即主题创新、不拘一格）和"作家兼批评家"式自我沟通这两种创作技巧的分析，就把研究对象缩小至李渔写作技法的探讨（Wang，1997）。张洁（音）更是细化至李渔短篇小说中的仿拟（parody）辞格的研究（Zhang，2005）。沈静（音）主要针对李渔戏曲开展研究，包括《比目鱼》的剧中剧（Shen，2010）及其角色类型（Shen，2003）和伦理问题（Shen，2008）、《风筝误》诗化爱情的反讽视角（Shen，2010）等。这些研究的共同之处就是视野宽、学术性强，其中张、骆和沈的专著代表了很高的学术水平，王颖和张洁的研究成果是博士论文，也体现了较深的学养。

　　二是学术观点多样化。学术研究领域的成熟，很重要的一个标志就是百家争鸣、各抒己见。1990年代以来的李渔研究与前一阶段相比，观点明显更加多样化。例如《肉蒲团》的作者到底是不是李渔，原本是一个颇有争议的问题，即使在国内也是如此，但回顾英语世界1960—1980年代的李渔研究不难发现，在正反双方都缺乏"铁证"的情况下，学界因受库恩先入之见的影响，认同或接受李渔作者身份的似乎居多，反对者看起来很少而且应者寥寥。② 随着韩南等重量级汉学家的加入（Hanan，1981；1988；1990a），这种一边倒的情形愈加明显。而张春树和骆雪伦凭着他们精通中英文和熟稔中外研究、尤其是史学研究的考证能力等优势，在仔细梳理了古今中外相关证据和研究之后，对"李渔作者说"的内外部"证据"逐一提出了质疑和批驳（Chang & Chang，1992：234-237），认为李渔的作者身份"从未得到符合逻辑的证据之证实"（op.cit.：236-237）。他们指出，韩南在《肉蒲团》译本序言中提到的一些证据，包括序言日期、眉批及批注者"社弟"身份、回目数、刊刻特点等，大都是17世纪通行的做法或特征，并不能证明专属于李渔；因此他们批评韩南《李渔的创作》一书缺乏令人信服的证据而断定李渔为《肉蒲团》

---

　　① 张、骆主治中国古代史研究，张春树长于政治、军事、社会经济、文学与思想、边疆、民族、法律、考古与人类学、科技等，骆雪伦长于中国古代宗教、明清社会、思想、妇女、民族与文学等。二位学者合著的这部李渔研究专论，以宽广的学术视野和"新史学"的研究理路，将李渔的生平事迹、文学思想、戏剧创作、小说作品、批判精神等置于明末清初政治社会变革、文化危机与思想革命等宏大的历史背景下展开深入分析和研究。该书英文原著共452页，参考文献和术语表达64页，中文译本在原作基础上略有改动，正文279页，征引书目达51页，其学术性可见一斑。

　　② 但实际上很多学者（尤其是像夏志清这样的华裔学者）由于不专事李渔及其创作研究，即便有不同意见也不太会专门花时间和精力去考证真伪，面对相关争论时便三缄其口、避而不谈，客观上也助长了一边倒的局面。

作者的看法是一种"主观印象",认为这样的主观印象"往往比通过学术分析得来、有可靠证据的结论更具误导性"（op. cit. :237）。尽管李渔的作者身份问题一直悬而未决（而且在找到新的证据之前也很难尘埃落定），但 1990 年代以来英语世界的许多研究者在提及《肉蒲团》作者问题时，哪怕是认为李渔就是作者的，也都开始小心翼翼地使用"attributed to Li Yu"之类更显客观（亦更利于免责）的表述。这一现象应该说与多样化观点的争鸣和碰撞不无关联，同时也说明李渔研究在新时期日益走向成熟、客观。

三是研究视角和方法多元化。新时期的李渔研究，不但可供研究的文本和文献材料越来越多、研究范围越来越广，而且跨学科的特征日益明显，研究视角与方法越来越多元化。张春树和骆雪伦（Chang & Chang, 1992）将李渔创作和思想置于明末清初社会政治背景下开展研究的历史学视野，沈静把李渔置于汤显祖（1550—1616）、梅鼎祚（1549—1615）、吴炳（1595—1648）、孔尚任（1648—1718）等明清戏曲家群体中开展对比研究的比较文学视角，王颖（Wang, 1997）和张洁（Zhang, 2005）对李渔创作技巧的文体学和修辞学研究方法，等等，都显示了该领域的跨学科特征和多元化视角与方法。我们有理由相信，在可以预见的未来，李渔研究的语言学、翻译学以及文化人类学等视角也将大有可为。

综上，英语世界 1990 年代以降的李渔译介和研究在前一阶段的基础上继续高歌猛进。译介方面可圈可点：韩南的《肉蒲团》《无声戏》《十二楼》（重）译本、夏建新等的《李渔小说选》，都是李渔小说英译史上的重要作品。其中《无声戏》从无到有，再到大部分篇目完成英译，填补了李渔小说英译的空白；卓振英的《李渔诗赋楹联赏析》首次将李渔的诗赋作品译入英语，也是李渔英译史上的创举。此外可以看到，进入新世纪以来，国内译者和学者在译介舞台上崭露头角。研究方面，相比较前一阶段，新时期的李渔研究更趋理性和成熟，研究的学术深度和广度不断提升，视角和方法日趋多样化，标志着李渔研究进入了一个繁荣而稳定的成熟期。

## 本章小结

本章回顾和梳理了李渔在英语世界的译介和传播史，将其分为滥觞、复兴和繁荣三个阶段，并分别介绍了每个阶段的译介和研究情况。通过梳理我们发现，李渔在英语世界的传播和接受，宏观上有两个值得注意的问题或现象：(1)翻译选材的偏颇。李渔小说的英译贯穿了传播史的所有阶段，而且一直处在压倒性的中心位置：他的大部分小说（包括作者身份存疑的《肉蒲团》、《十二楼》的全部、《无声戏》18 篇中的 14 篇）都译入了英语，与此形成鲜明对照的则是他更负盛名的戏曲作品，连一部完整的都没有译过（只有一出查无实据的《玉搔头》和一出传闻即出的《比目鱼》）；他的百科全书式代表作《闲情偶寄》，迄今没有系统译介过（只有少量关于词曲、声容、居室、饮馔、种植、颐养等方面的零散摘译）；以及他的诗赋作品，只有一部节译本。而欧洲其他主要语种，包括拉丁语、法语、德语等，在译介李渔时虽也存在一定程度的选材偏颇现象，但多少还能兼顾一下各类体裁和领域的作品，[1]其中德语里甚至还推出了李渔戏剧研究的皇皇巨著。[2] 这是一个值得我们思考的现象。（2）研究方面的不足。受译介内容以及国内学界的影响，英语世界对于李渔的认识还存在一些片面甚至偏见。例如《肉蒲团》的作者问题，西方学者大部分都认为是李渔，其中直接的原因是库恩初译本的影响，但追根究底还是因为国内学界观点不一致，其中某些不一定正确可靠的意见被西方学者所采纳。这就给我们提出了一个很有意义的问题：我们应该以怎样的学术观点和研究方法来影响和引导西方学者，是不负责任的信口开河还是用科学的证据和逻辑推理说话？又如，李渔的戏曲作品和理论思想（即笠翁曲话）从未以完整的面貌译入英语，导致英语世界的一些学者对其戏曲领域的成就和造诣一无所知，甚至拒不认可。英国爱丁堡大学专治中国戏剧史的著名汉学家杜为廉（William Dolby）的《中国戏剧史》（*A History of Chinese Drama*，1976）是英语国家出版的该领域首部权威著作，但其中关于李渔的内容只有三段，他的戏曲作品连名字都没有提过（Dolby，1976：115-116）；澳大利亚格里菲斯大学研究中国戏剧发展史的马克林（Colin Mackerras）在其代表作《中国戏剧：从起源到当代》（*Chinese Theater：From Its Origins to the Present Day*，1983）一书中甚至只字未提李渔。以上这两方面的现象和问题，对于李渔在英语世界的当代传播有很重要的现实启发意义。

---

① 例如李渔的戏曲《比目鱼》和《慎鸾交》《风筝误》《奈何天》的部分内容早在 19 世纪末就有了拉丁文译本并很快转译入法文。参见王丽娜. 中国古典小说戏曲名著在国外. 上海：学林出版社，1988：531-532. 亦见宋柏年. 中国古典文学在国外. 北京：北京语言学院出版社，1994：595. 又如《闲情偶寄》的《声容部》和《饮馔部》的部分内容在 1940 年就译入了德语。参见羽离子. 李渔作品在海外的传播及有关研究：74.

② 即马汉茂的德文版《李笠翁戏剧》。参见王丽娜. 中国古典小说戏曲名著在国外：532.

# 第三章  选择与操控:英语世界
## 对李渔形象的建构[①]

通过前一章的历史回顾可以看到,李渔在英语世界的传播过程中,仅就译介而言,不同体裁、不同作品之间存在着较大的出入。这种出入在一定程度上反映了英语世界对李渔作品的取舍标准,同时也对李渔形象在英语中的建构产生了一定的影响。本章拟结合操控学派等文化翻译流派的思想,探讨英语世界对李渔作品选择和操控的方式,以及这种选择和操控对李渔形象建构和接受所造成的影响。

## 第一节  关于翻译与操控

1970—1980 年代,随着西方翻译研究的文化转向,翻译中的操控现象及其背后隐藏的意识形态、诗学规范等问题日益引起学界的关注,以勒菲弗尔(André Lefevere,1945—1996)为代表的低地国家翻译研究学派独辟蹊径,从意识形态、赞助人、诗学规范等文化政治角度切入,探讨和阐释翻译中的"操控"和"重写"等现象,"操控学派"(The Manipulation School)应运而生,也拉开了后现代文化翻译研究的序幕。

操控学派站在译入语文化的角度,宣称"一切翻译都隐含着出于特定目的而对译出文本实施的某种程度的操控"(Hermans,1985:11),因此翻译的过程就是"使目标文本与某种特定模式及其衍生的特定正确性观念相一致,以保证译文获得社会接受乃至欢迎"的过程(Hermans,1991:166;qtd. in Shuttleworth & Cowie,1997/2004:101)。在此过程中,意识形态和诗学规范是影响和支配操控行为的主要因素,正如勒菲弗尔(Lefevere,1992:39)所言,"……在翻译过程的每个层面上,……如果语言方面的考量同意识形态/诗学性质方面的考量发生抵触,则后者往往胜出。"操控学派认为"重写"(rewriting,亦译"改写")是实现操控的主要手段,同时也是推动文学演进的

---

①  本章内容已公开发表。参见唐艳芳. 建构李渔:论英语世界对李渔形象的操控. 北方工业大学学报,2019(6):121-129.

重要力量。巴斯奈特和勒菲弗尔将重写界定为"有助于建构一位作家及/或一部文学作品'形象'的任何做法"(Bassnett & Lefevere，1990：10)，并指出重写绝非"清白无辜"的行为(*op. cit.*：11)，因为它与译入语文化中的政治和文学权力结构有着密切的联系。"不管重写者是做翻译、书写文学史或与之相关的简本读物、编纂工具书、编辑作品集、发表评论还是推出作品的不同版本，他们都会对原作做一些改编和操控，一般都是为了使作品与他们所处时代占支配地位的意识形态和诗学潮流相一致"(Lefevere，1992：8)。

尽管操控学派对重写的定义是建构作家/作品形象的"任何做法"(anything)，但从勒菲弗尔的研究来看，①操控学派关注的焦点显然是微观层面的操控，亦即翻译过程中出于意识形态、诗学规范等方面的考虑而对原作文本所作的改动(包括内容和字词的增删、体制的调整、情节乃至人物的改编等等)，却忽略了另一种可能对作家/作品形象建构影响更大的宏观层面的操控。这种宏观层面的操控由于不是直接发生在翻译的过程中，往往不太引人注目，但它对作家/作品形象的跨文化建构有可能产生更大、更持久的影响，而且影响一旦产生就很难改变，因为微观层面的操控尚可通过重译和多译本之间的互文对照而为人所知，亦可作理论解释或在实践中善加利用，而宏观层面的操控由于发生在翻译之前的选材阶段或翻译之后的传播和接受阶段，其影响往往是间接的、隐性的，对其影响的评估也必须跳出翻译行为自身，从历史和跨文化交流的角度，将作者及其全部作品置于两种文化交流碰撞的历史长河之中作整体和历时的考量，才有可能获得比较全面和客观的发现。

因选材原因而影响或改变作家/作品在译入语文化中的形象的例子，中外翻译史上俯拾皆是。例如，民国时期蟠溪子选译的半部《迦茵小传》(*Joan Haste*，1895)，就使英国文学史上名不见经传的哈葛德(Sir Henry R. Haggard，1856—1925)一时之间成为中国文学圈里备受瞩目的英国作家，尤受鸳鸯蝴

---

　　①　勒菲弗尔举过多个例子来阐述翻译重写背后的意识形态、赞助人、诗学规范等因素以及重写的影响，包括：古希腊喜剧《利西翠妲》诸译本对原作中男性生殖器直接表述的不同处理方式，以及各种与原作无关的添加；犹太少女安妮·弗兰克《安妮日记》荷兰语原作的两个不同时代版本(1947年版和1986年版)所反映的作者形象的自我建构和他者建构之间的差异，以及荷兰语原作与1955年德语译本之间的差异所反映的译者意识形态方面的考量；古波斯诗集《鲁拜集》原作"颂诗"体(qasidah)在英译过程中的失落所反映的诗学规范对翻译的影响，等等。参见 André Lefevere，*Translation，Rewriting and the Manipulation of Literary Fame* (London：Routledge，1992)，pp. 41-86.

蝶派的推崇。① 又如,寒山子在中国文学史上只不过是一名长期游离于正统文学之外的诗僧,却因 1950 年代斯奈德(Gary Snyder,1930—)选译了他的24 首诗而成为风靡欧美的中国唐代诗人,其域外声名甚至超过了李杜。这两个例子说明,选择译或不译,很多时候是对作家/作品形象建构起决定作用的操控行为。另外,选材方面的操控在中籍外译领域还有一种比较特殊的情况,即作者身份的错置——很多中国传统小说的作者身份由于一直存疑而无定论,而一些翻译者往往出于各种考虑,选择采信了部分中国学者的观点,导致作品在译入语文化里的形象(无论正反)被先入为主地同某些作家绑在了一起,从而对后者的形象建构产生较大影响。这种作者身份"张冠李戴"的情况似可归入"伪翻译"的范畴,②它既是中国典籍外译领域的一种独特现象,同时也是一个需要译者和翻译研究者高度重视的问题。

除了选材,宏观层面的操控还有一种情况,即译入语文化对译作的接受或拒斥。按照操控学派的观点,这种接受或拒斥主要是受译入语主流意识形态和诗学规范的支配,是一种系统的、"有组织"的集体行为;实施接受或拒斥行为的主体,除了普通读者之外,还有负责出版审查的政府部门、出版商、学者/评论者乃至大学教师等,这些群体面对一部译作,其反应和态度有时会表现出各自为阵、杂乱无序的一面,但在主流意识形态和诗学规范的影响下,更多时候是心照不宣、"同气连枝"地选择相同的立场,有时甚至还会相互引导或影响。学者/评论者的负面批评、教师对作品的视而不见、出版商对出版/再版的不感兴趣、政府审查机构对作品发行的种种限制,等等,都有可能影响译作的传播和接受,也是研究翻译操控现象时不可忽视的因素。

本节以上关于翻译和操控问题的讨论,主要是从理论上厘清操控、重写等文化翻译现象的概念和范畴,将操控区分为微观和宏观两个层面,认为操控学派关注的主要是微观层面的操控,但实际上译前选材、译后传播与接受等宏观层面的操控对作家/作品形象建构的影响可能更大。李渔在英语世界的形象建构正是这样,既有微观操控的影响,同时也受到宏观操控的影

---

① 但后来林纾将蟾溪子所删嘉茵未婚先孕等内容完整译入中文,反遭读者和蟾溪子埋怨,原作者哈葛德的形象亦随之一落千丈。这同样说明了选材的差异对作家和作品形象建构的影响,与翻译行为本身无关。

② 按照图里和拉多的观点,伪翻译(pseudotranslation)主要有两种情况:一是被当成翻译但却找不到原文本的作品,二是与原文本偏离太远而无法被认定为翻译的作品(Toury,1980;Radó,1979)。中国传统小说的作者问题比较独特,不了解中国文学传统的西方学者未予考虑也很正常,但笔者认为,在作者身份不明的情况下随意"拉郎配",终究难免伪托之嫌,因此这种情况也理应纳入伪翻译的范畴,作为一种宏观操控行为来看待和研究。

响,而且很大程度上后者的影响更多一些;把这些操控因素找出来,逐一进行研究和剖析,有助于我们总结作家形象异域建构过程中的成败得失,扬长避短,为当代典籍外译事业提供更好的理论和方法借鉴。

## 第二节　英语世界建构李渔形象的途径

按照操控学派的观点,"形象"(image)是作家/作品/文学/文化在译入语文化里的"投影"(projection),"建构"(construction)则是投射的过程。勒菲弗尔指出,翻译就是"为服务于某种意识形态的需要而对原作(剧)某种形象的投射"(Lefevere,1992:42)。由于投射和建构的背后有太多不确定性和文化政治等因素的影响,往往使得译入语文化里建构的作家/作品形象与原作相去甚远,但对于不懂原作而只能视翻译为原作的读者或观众来说,这样的形象就等同于原作者/作品的形象。后现代文化翻译理论对投射和建构持怀疑和批判态度,正是因为看到了建构的操控性以及经过投射处理的作家/作品形象"往往会比原作影响更多的读者"(*op. cit.*:109-110)这一不良后果。

英语世界今日之李渔形象,不是一朝一夕完成的,而是几代译家、学人和读者在长达两个世纪的时间里,历经无数的阅读、研究、选择和迻译,点点滴滴建构起来的。在此过程中,中国文化语境里那些组成真实李渔形象的要素,有些被放大,有些被遮蔽和忽略,还有些则被扭曲了,导致英语世界的李渔形象与中国文化语境中的李渔存在较大出入,也在一定程度上影响了英语读者对中国明末清初时期历史和文学的印象。因此有必要对这一过程中所添加、遗失和改变的各种要素作一探索和分析,以利修补和改变李渔在英语世界里的原型形象,并为当代典籍外译总结经验和教训。根据前文对李渔英译及接受史的梳理,笔者认为,英语世界对李渔形象的建构主要是通过文本选择、翻译改写和评论引导这三个途径来实现的。

### 一、文本选择

李渔是中国文学史上一位百科全书式的作家,其涉猎甚广,跨文学、美学、曲艺、园林、养生等多个领域,其作品体裁跨戏曲、小说、散文、文论、诗词曲赋以及名著批改等,此外还身体力行办书班、开书铺,在经商和实业方面也颇有成就。然而从本书第二章归纳的李渔作品英译情况可见,李渔在中国文学史上最负盛名的戏曲,包括他的《十种曲》和他阅定的八种传奇,迄今无一译入英语(其中《玉搔头》英译存疑待考);他的百科杂论巨著《闲情偶寄》只有少量涉及戏曲、养生、园艺等方面的内容被零散摘译以资绍介或研究之用,系统译介无从谈起;诗赋楹联迟至新世纪初才有第一部译作,而且是由中国译者完成、在中国大陆出版发行的,对英语国家的读者影响有限;文论、批改、韵书等更是鲜少译介和研究。最后,总体译介数量最多的小说中,只有一部作者身份存疑的《肉蒲团》在英语中"一枝独秀",其他小说均"黯然失色"。如此偏颇的翻译选材,其直接的后果就是把李渔的形象建构成了一位小说家,而且是一位擅写情色题材的小说家!

皮姆采用亚里士多德的"四因"说,把翻译发生的原因也归为四类:(1)质料因(material/initial cause),指翻译行为发生之前的、完成翻译所需要的一切外部因素,包括(假定的)原文本、语言、传播技术等;(2)效力因(efficient cause),指参与翻译的主体,即译者;(3)目的因(final cause),指可以证明翻译及其作用之合法性的目的,包括目标文化为其定位的功能以及翻译自身的理想操作过程;(4)形式因(formal cause),指翻译接受的历史规范,包括接受者(委托人、译文接受者、译者本人、其他译者等)的因素(Pym,1998/2007:149)。亚里士多德所说的"因",原非简单的"原因",而是哲学意义上的事物形成或存在的依据和条件,它们对事物的形成和存在是缺一不可的,分类只是描述的需要。皮姆借鉴四因说来解释翻译发生的原因,实际上也是想说明,翻译行为的发生和完成往往不是单一原因造成的,而是多种因素共同作用的结果。一部作品从一种语言文化译入另一种语言文化,质料因固然是很重要的因素,但正如皮姆(op. cit.:150-151)所言,"质料因并非一切",它只是翻译的必要条件,不是充分条件,因为它"无法反映翻译的真实细节",最多只能说明文本"运动是可能的",无法解释或证明文本翻译的可能性有多大、合理性怎样等问题。换言之,原作本身的各种条件(题材、寓意、情节、人物、文学性、语言,等等)即使达到再高水准也只能说明它具备了翻译的可能性,如果译者对其价值不认同或评价不高(缺乏效力因),翻译行为就不会发生;质料因和效力因都具备,翻译行为有可能发生,但如果译入语文化对该作品没有需求(缺乏目的因),或作品同译入语受众的一般口味和期待不符(缺乏形式因),则翻译行为即使勉力完成,译作的传播和接受效果也会大打折扣,而更大的可能则是译者根据对目的因和形式因的理性判断,主动调整或甚至放弃翻译行为。因此可以说,作家形象在异域文化语境里的建构,是质料因、效力因、目的因和形式因之间交互影响、博弈乃至"共谋"的结果,其中效力因是起决定作用的条件,因为正是译者的选择才使翻译的发生成为现实。当然，译者的选择也是基于对原作的评价和对译入语文学规范和需求的判断而做出的，虽有主观色彩，但总体上还是理性的选择，从中可以基本看出译入语文化对原作者及作品的选择面和接受度。

　　英语世界对李渔形象的建构过程，也是译入语文化在不同历史时期按照自身需求对李渔进行选择、阐释和"投射"的过程。在李渔的诸多作品中，小说是最早译入英语的，这里面除了作品本身的因素（例如故事性、文学性、趣味性等）之外，主要还是因为其中反映的中国明清社会文化生活等内容有助于中英文化交流早期的英国人便捷地了解中国这个陌生的国度[①]；而小说中的《肉蒲团》迟至1960年代才译入英语，也是因为当时恰逢西方性解放运动如火如荼，译入语的时代需求直接影响并促成了译者的选择（包括对作品本身的选择和对原作者身份的选择）；至于1990年代以后的译介仍然以小说为主，则是因为小说本身就比其他文体对读者的吸引力更大一些。戏曲方面，除了关于李渔戏曲思想和创作方面的为数不多的研究，其戏曲作品的英译长期处于无人问津的境地，这可能是因为英国文学传统中的戏剧历史悠久、成就颇丰，译入语文学对于来自异域的戏曲作品缺乏译介的兴趣和动机。至于诗词曲赋，中国文学史上远胜李渔的经典之作比比皆是，因此英语世界恐怕没有多少人认可李渔是位诗人，遑论读他的诗作了，长期无人选择翻译亦属正常；而像《闲情偶寄》这样的百科全书式皇皇巨著，只有极少数专治李渔生活艺术和思想的学者才有阅读和研究的兴趣及能力，普通读者往往却步于其长篇大论、奥理玄思，难以领会其中精妙，因而同样无人选译。就这样，在两个多世纪的时间里，英语世界通过一系列的选择，一步步地完成了对李渔形象的历史建构。

## 二、翻译改写

　　翻译过程中的改写有很多形式，包括内容增删、情节改编、人物变换、风格调整等。改写的幅度也有大有小：改动小的一般只涉及字词、句序等微观层面的调整，原作总体面貌保留，例如菲茨杰拉德《鲁拜集》译文总体保留了原诗的形式特征，并通过归化使之更贴近维多利亚时期的英诗特征，赢得如

---

　　① 德庇时在《中国小说》前言中指出，"要深刻了解中国，最有效的一个办法就是通过通俗文学（主要是戏剧和小说）的翻译来了解"。参见 Davis, p. 10.

潮好评;①改动大的则可能出现面目全非的"豪杰译",完全按己所需取舍原作内容,表达上怎样方便怎样来,让人几乎无法看出原作的影子,例如道格斯的《夺锦楼》译文只剩下一个原作的母题,②伯奇的《生我楼》译文只是原作的一个梗概,等等。19世纪的李渔作品英译,改写幅度总体上是比较大的,即便是相对比较忠实的德庇时译本,对原作的改写也随处可见。德庇时的改写主要表现在两个方面:(1)内容和文字大段删减;(2)叙事方式随意转换。此处我们以《合影楼》为例分别作一简单呈现,第四章翻译策略部分另有详述。

《合影楼》原作以一首右调《虞美人》开头,外加千余字的"入话"作铺垫,之后才切入正题"元朝至正年间,广东韶关府曲江县有两个闲住的缙绅,一姓屠,一姓管"(李渔,1991/9:15)。德庇时译本将诗词和入话悉数删去,开篇即直奔故事本身:"During the reign of a certain Emperor of the Yuen dynasty, in a district of the province of Canton, there lived two persons of rank, who had retired from the toils of office. Their names were Too and Kwan;..."(Davis,1822:53)。小说末尾的删削幅度也很大:

> (1)提举听到此处,颜色稍和,想了一会,又问他道:"敝连襟舍了小女,怕没有别处求亲?老亲翁除了此子,也另有高门纳采。为甚么把二女配了一夫,定要陷人以不义?"路公道:"其中就里,只好付之不言。若还根究起来,只怕方才那四拜,老亲翁该赔还小弟,倒要认起不是来。"提举听到此处,又从新变起色来道:"小弟有何不是?快请说来!"路公道:"只因府上的家范过于严谨,使男子妇人不得见面,所以郁出病来。别样的病,只害得自己一个;不想令爱的尊恙,与时灾疫症一般,一家过到一家,蔓延不已。起先过与他,后来又过与小女,几乎把三条性命断送在一时。小弟要救小女,只得预先救他。既要救他,又只得先救令

---

① 吴笛认为,菲茨杰拉德的《鲁拜集》英译主要采取了三种翻译策略:神形兼顾(忠实文本)、译创并重(归化异化结合)及合成翻译(串联独立诗节以求经典重生)。参见吴笛.菲茨杰拉德《鲁拜集》翻译策略探究.安徽师范大学学报(人文社会科学版),2017(6):758-763.但总体上菲译是保留了原作四行一节、每节一二四行押韵的形式特征的(尽管原作韵脚按字母顺序排列的特征无法保留,各诗节的独立性也被打破)。

② 本书第二章已详细介绍过道译《夺锦楼》的情况。事实上,道格斯的《中国故事》所辑10篇小说大都只保留了原作的母题,原作的人物名字、故事情节、叙事视角乃至结尾等都被改得面目全非,甚至看不出原作是哪篇小说、出处何在。据宋丽娟(2017:436-437)考证,这10篇小说的中文底本主要选自《今古传奇》(《怀私怨狠仆告主》《金玉奴棒打薄情郎》《庄子休鼓盆成大道》《女秀才移花接木》《夸妙术丹客提金》等5篇)、《好逑传》(《水小姐俏胆移花》)、《十二楼》(《夺锦楼》)和《续玄怪录》(《薛伟》),其余2篇出处不详。

爱。所以把三个病人合来住在一处,才好用药调理,这就是联姻缔好的原故。老亲翁不问,也不好直说出来。"

提举听了,一发惊诧不已,就把自己坐的交椅一步一步挪近前来,就着路公,好等他说明就里。路公怕他不服,索性说个尽情,就把对影钟情、不肯别就的始末,一原二故,诉说出来。气得他面如土色,不住的咒骂女儿。路公道:"姻缘所在,非人力之所能为。究竟令爱守贞,不肯失节,也还是家教使然。如今业已成亲,也算做既往不咎了,还要怪他做甚!"提举道:"这等看来,都是小弟治家不严,以致如此。空讲一生道学,不曾做得个完人,快取酒来,先罚我三杯,然后上席。"路公道:"这也怪不得亲翁。从来的家法,只能痼形,不能痼影。这是两个影子做出事来,与身体无涉,那里防得许多?从今以后,也使治家人知道这番公案,连影子也要堤防,决没有露形之事了。"又对观察道:"你两个的是非曲直,毕竟要归重一边。若还府上的家教,也与贵连襟一般,使令公郎有所畏惮,不敢胡行,这桩诡事就断然没有了。究竟是你害他,非是他累你。不可因令郎得了便宜,倒说风流的是,道学的不是,把是非曲直颠倒过来,使人喜风流而恶道学,坏先辈之典型。取酒过来,罚你三巨觥,以服贵连襟之心,然后坐席。"观察道:"讲得有理,受罚无辞。"一连饮了三杯,就作揖赔个不是,方才就席饮酒,尽欢而散。

从此以后,两家释了芥蒂,相好如初。过到后来,依旧把两院并为一宅,就将两座水阁做了金屋,以贮两位阿娇,题曰"合影楼",以成其志。不但拆去墙垣,掘开泥土,等两位佳人互相盼望,又架一座飞桥,以便珍生之来往,使牛郎织女无天河银汉之隔。

后来珍生联登二榜,入了词林,位到侍讲之职。

这段逸事出在胡氏《笔谈》,但系抄本,不曾刊板行世,所以见者甚少。如今编做小说,还不能取信于人,只说这一十二座亭台都是空中楼阁也。

(《合影楼》,李渔,1991/9:33-35)

(1a)—Kwan,when he had heard thus far, relaxed the rigidity of his visage, and after a little more explanation,* all parties having become good friends, they closed the day with feasting and merriment.

(*The conclusion, which in the original consists merely of a further conversation, repeating what the reader already knows, has been a little curtailed in the translation.)

(Davis, 1822:106)

可以看到,原文总共千余字的内容,除了下划线部分,几乎删削殆尽;两处下划线之间的大量对话,仅以"and after a little more explanation"寥寥数语一笔带过;译文至"尽欢而散"处戛然而止,后话略去,结尾难免有些突兀。不过德庇时译本总体上还算认真负责,举凡大段删削都会作注解释理由。又如:

> (2)珍生见了,就立住脚跟,不敢进去,只好对了管公,请姨娘表妹出来拜见。管公单请夫人见了一面,连"小姐"二字绝不提起。及至珍生再请,他又假示龙钟,茫然不答。珍生默喻其意,就不敢固请,坐了一会,即便告辞。
>
> 既去之后,管夫人问道:"两姨姐妹,分属表亲,原有可见之理,为甚么该拒绝他?"管公道:"夫人有所不知,'男女授受不亲'这句话头,单为至亲而设。若还是陌路之人,他何由进我的门,何由入我的室?既不进门入室,又何须分别嫌疑?单为碍了亲情,不便拒绝,所以有穿房入户之事。这分别嫌疑的礼数,就由此而起。别样的瓜葛,亲者自亲,疏者自疏,皆有一定之理。独是两姨之子,姑舅之儿,这种亲情,最难分别。说他不是兄妹,又系一人所出,似有共体之情;说他竟是兄妹,又属两姓之人,并无同胞之义。因在似亲似疏之间,古人委决不下,不曾注有定仪,所以泾渭难分,彼此互见,以致有不清不白之事做将出来。历观野史传奇,儿女私情大半出于中表。皆因做父母的没有真知灼见,竟把他当了兄妹,穿房入户,难以堤防,所以混乱至此。我乃主持风教的人,岂可不加辨别,仍蹈世俗之陋规乎?"夫人听了,点头不已,说他讲得极是。
>
> 从此以后,珍生断了痴想,玉娟绝了妄念,知道家人的言语印正不来,随他像也得,不像也得,丑似我也得,好似我也得,一总不去计论他。
>
> (《合影楼》,李渔,1991/9:17-18)

(2a)—When Chin-seng saw this, he stopped immediately, and did not venture to go farther. He saw Kwan, however, and requested him to ask his aunt and cousin to come out and see him. Kwan only called his wife, and would not say a word about his daughter. When Chin-seng again hinted her to him, he pretended to be deaf, or ignorant of his meaning, and gave no answer. Chin-seng, seeing his determination, did not venture to press him farther, but after sitting some time, took his leave. *

From this time, both Chin-seng and Yu-kiuen gave up their childish
curiosity, and knowing that they could not verify the reports which
they heard, did not care any thing more about the matter, but became
quite indifferent as to whether the resemblance existed or not.

(* Here follows a long speech from Kwan to his wife, about his
reasons for keeping his nephew at a distance, the real motive, perhaps,
being his enmity to his brother-in-law. )

(Davis，1822：60-61)

本例下划线部分一整段话在译文里均未译出。德庇时在注释中除了告知读
者删省的事实,还把原文管提举阻止珍生见表姐的原因归为他对连襟屠观
察的讨厌,但实际上原文并无此意（至少从字面上看不出来）。笔者认为,这
里译者省译的主要原因,乃是原文所呈现的中国传统家族的内部关系和文
化特征对当时的英语读者来说太过复杂了,如果原话全部译入英语,读者甚
至可能连其中的亲缘关系都弄不明白,更不用说理解这种关系的文化内
涵了。

诗词曲赋也多有删削调整。对于原作中与情节直接相关的诗词,德庇
时主要采取了意译的方式处理（另见第四章相关讨论）,而对于其中并不直
接推动情节发展、只起歌咏和赞叹作用的诗赋则作了删省处理：

(3)路公选了好日,一面抬珍生进门,一面娶玉娟入室,再把女儿请
出洞房,凑成三美,一齐拜起堂来,真个好看。只见:

男同叔宝,女类夷光。评品姿容,却似两朵琼花,倚着一根玉树;形
容态度,又像一轮皎日,分开两片轻云。那一边,年庚相合,牵来比并,
辨不清孰妹孰兄;这一对,面貌相同,卸去冠裳,认不出谁男谁女。把男
子推班出色,遇红遇绿,到处成牌;用妇人接羽移宫,鼓瑟鼓琴,皆能合
调。允矣无双乐事;诚哉对半神仙!

成亲过了三日,路公就准备筵席,请屠、管二人会亲。……

(《合影楼》,李渔,1991/9:30-31)

(3a)—Loo-kung fixed upon a fortunate day, and at once got Chin-
seng and Yu-kiuen to his house, where his daughter awaited her nuptials.
The marriage was then concluded, and all three appeared in the hall
together, and went through the regular ceremonies. *

When the marriage had been concluded three days, Loo-kung
directed a feast to be prepared, and invited Too and Kwan to a meeting

of relations. . . .

（*Here is omitted a rhapsody of the author's, in which he compares the ladies to flowers, and the hero to a tree; and the hero to the moon, and the ladies to two light clouds; gravely ending with calling them "a brace and a half of Deities."）

(Davis，1822：98-99)

本例前后下划线之间插入的赋文，主要起描写婚礼场面、烘托气氛的作用，话本和拟话本小说中经常出现，是说书人炫耀口才和文采的好机会，同时也是作品里最富文学性和艺术性的部分。但这种"徒"有形式之美的诗赋翻译起来难度很大，而且对小说情节的发展并无实质推动作用，因此往往是译者首选的删省对象。于是，经过德庇时的改写，原文"叔宝"和"夷光"的掌故、"琼花""玉树""皎月""轻云"等美喻以及诗赋的各种音韵之美，在译文中就只剩下注释里三言两语的几句大白话了。显然，这样的删省对原作文学性的损害是很大的，经过改写之后的作品形象，与原作已是大相径庭。

德庇时《合影楼》英译改写的另一种表现形式，是人物话语形式的转换频繁而复杂。叙事学领域对于人物话语表达形式的划分标准和方式比较多，例如英国批评家佩奇将其细分为直接引语、被遮覆的引语、间接引语、"平行的"间接引语、"带特色的"间接引语、自由间接引语、自由直接引语、从间接引语"滑入"直接引语等8种（转引自申丹，1998：38-41），不过这些总体上都可以归入直接引语和间接引语这两大话语表达形式。两种话语形式在文学作品中的使用各有优劣：直接引语长于音效和真实性、生动性，但意味着需要转换人称、时态等要素并使用冒号、引号等标点，因而会"打断叙述流"（*op. cit.*：329）；间接引语的优点是"具有一定的节俭性，可加快叙述速度"（*ibid.*），但代价是牺牲了现场感和生动性。传统汉语不用标点，句法上的竹式结构非常便于话题/主体的变换，时态方面也没有印欧语系语言那样的屈折变化要求，因此使用直接引语的技术难度比西方语言小，而且中国传统话本和拟话本小说直接服务于说书，出于表演生动性的需要也会选择直接模仿人物话语。由于以上这些因素，中国传统小说的间接引语使用较少，《合影楼》也是如此。德庇时译本在很多地方都是按英文叙事特征和风格的需要，把原文的直接引语变成了间接引语：

（4）观察要把大义责他，只因骄纵在前，整顿不起；又知道："儿子的风流原是看我的样子，我不能自断情欲，如何禁止得他？"所以一味优容，只劝他："暂缓愁肠，待我替你画策。"

（《合影楼》，李渔，1991/9：24）

(4a) Too would have corrected his son for this, but having formerly indulged him, he could not now exert his authority. He knew also that Chin-seng's disposition was the copy of his own; and since he could not restrain his own passions, how should he govern those of his son? He therefore let him have his own way entirely; but advised him to moderate his grief, and let *him* manage the affair.

(Davis, 1822：77)

(5) 一日，丫鬟进来传话，说："路家小姐闻得嫂嫂有病，要亲自过来问安。"玉娟闻了此言，一发焦躁不已，只说："他占了我的情人，夺了我的好事，一味心高气傲，故意把喜事骄人，等不得我到他家，预先上门来羞辱。这番歹意，如何依允得他！"就催逼母亲叫人过去回覆。

（《合影楼》，李渔，1991/9：29-30）

(5a) One morning, an attendant came in to announce that Kin-yun, hearing her friend was unwell, wished to come over in person, and ask after her health. Yu-kiuen, hearing this, was very much disturbed, thinking that the other, after having won her lover, and snatched away her hopes, was coming, the exultation of her heart, to boast her success over her; and that, unable to wait until the period when they were to meet, she had anticipated the time for insulting her. She was determined, however, that Kin-yun should not be gratified in her malice; and urged her mother to send a person immediately with an answer.

(Davis, 1822：94-95)

这两例中，原文即使不用标点也能从人称上看出是直接引语；译文将其改成间接引语后，叙述的效率明显提高，人物话语的生动性和情感色彩则大大削弱。除了直接引语转换为间接引语之外，德庇时译本对原文直接引语的改写还有一种值得注意的处理方式，即保留引号，但第一人称变成第三人称：

(6) 管提举想了一会，再辨不清，又对路公道："这些说话，小弟一字不解，缠来缠去，不得明白。难道今日之来，不是会亲，竟在这边做梦不成?"路公道:"小东上面已曾讲过'今为说梦主人',就是为此。要晓得'说梦'二字原不是小弟创起,当初替他说亲,蒙老亲翁书台回覆,那个时节早已种下梦根了。人生一梦耳,何必十分认真? 劝你将错就错,完了这场春梦罢!"提举听了这些话,方才醒悟,就问他道:"老亲翁是个正人,为何行此暧昧之事! 就要做媒,也只该明讲,怎么设定圈套,弄起我来?"路公道:"何尝不来明讲? 老亲翁并不回言,只把两句话儿示之以意,却像要我说梦的一般,所以不复明言,只得便宜行事。若还自家弄巧,单骗令爱一位,使亲翁做了愚人,这重罪案就逃不去了。如今舍得自己,赢得他人,方才拜堂的时节,还把令爱立在左首,小女甘就下风,这样公道拐子,折本媒人,世间没有第二个。求你把责人之念稍宽一分,全了忠恕之道罢。"

(《合影楼》,李渔,1991/9:32-33)

(6a)Kwan considered a little, but still could not make it out, and said to Loo-kung, "I cannot comprehend a single word of what you say: it is a mystery which I cannot unravel. Am I come to a meeting of relations, or am I in a dream?" —Loo-kung answered, "I mentioned the subject of dreaming in my note to you, and you should be aware that it is a subject which was first started, not by me, but by yourself, when I proposed the match to you, and when you wrote down your answer on the table. You then sowed the seeds of that dram which has now come to maturity. —But man's life is a dream; why, then, need you make a great stir about it? —I advise you to take the thing as it comes, and bring this dream to a happy conclusion!" —When Kwan had heard these words, he began to comprehend it, and asked Loo-kung, "how he, so correct a man, could practise such deceit: that if he wanted to act as the negotiator of the match, he should have spoken clearly, and not have laid this trap for his unwariness." —To this Loo-kung replied, "And did I not speak clearly? —but you, instead of giving me a plain answer, thought proper to deal in tropes and figures, as if you wanted to set me a dreaming. I therefore could not speak to you any longer in a straight forward manner; but was compelled to act to the best of my abilities. If indeed I had only sought my own particular good, and, deceiving you into the marriage of your daughter alone, caused you to look ridiculous, —this would have been an unpardonable offence:

but by giving *my own* daughter in marriage, I also effected the marriage of yours. On performing the ceremonies in the hall, I still gave your daughter the higher place, and my own willingly took the lower. There certainly, then, never was such another conscientious contriver as myself. I entreat you to relinquish your angry intentions, and practise the rule of forgiveness."

(Davis，1822：104-106)

可以看到，原文一整段都是直接引语形式的对话，译文整体上也是照直处理，但却独独在下划线部分采用了与前后不同的话语形式：看似直接引语，却是间接引语的人称。这种话语形式可能属于佩奇分类中的"带特色的"间接引语，也可能属于直接引语的一种，但不管哪一种，在前后都是典型直接引语的情况下，这句话单独把第一人称变成第三人称的处理方式显然值得商榷，一是因为与上下文对比显得突兀；二是整句的反诘语气被严重削弱：动词 ask 在意义和逻辑上只能统御引号内第一个以 how 引导的分句，与第二个分句无法构成有效搭配。这样的改写在德庇时译本中并非个例，《合影楼》原作中与情节发展直接相关的诗词，德庇时在翻译时也采用了这样的形式。但笔者认为，这种做法除了徒增译文话语形式的怪异、影响读者对原作话语生动性的评价之外，别无他用。

1970 年代的茅国权《十二楼》英译，对原文也多有删削改写，微观层面上的调整甚至比德庇时译本有过之而无不及，也可划入豪杰译的范畴。不过总的来说，内容删省、话语形式转换以及其他语言表述方面的改写，本质上还属于文本本身层面的操控，其对作家和作品形象建构的影响止于传统传播介质与受众，尚属可分析和可预见的范畴，终归有限。另一种形式的"改写"对作品传播和作家形象建构的影响比传统形式要大得多，那就是文本的跨媒介传播。在李渔西译史上，受库恩译本先入为主的影响，不管我们是否愿意接受，《肉蒲团》已被很多人认定就是李渔的作品，但是，若非该作品的跨媒介传播，其受众或许只限于文学圈和学术圈，李渔也就不至于像今天这样"臭名远扬"了。据羽离子（2001：72）所述，1990 年代美国激情出版社（Passion Press）出版的《肉蒲团》韩南译本磁带节录版，"录音本充满幽默，让人发噱"，多次再版，造成了广泛的影响。与此同时，中国香港地区 1990 年代发行的多部三级片中，麦当杰（Michael Mak）执导的《玉蒲团之偷情宝鉴》（*Sex and Zen I：The Carnal Prayer Mat's Stash of Illicit Love*，1991）和孙立基（Christopher Suen）执导的《3D 肉蒲团之极乐宝鉴》（*3D Sex and*

*Zen：Extreme Ecstasy*，2011)都是根据《肉蒲团》小说改编的，而且海报和宣传品醒目位置也都标明李渔为编剧(之一)，从而很快在更大范围的中文受众圈里坐实了李渔的作者身份。由于这些电影都是国内外双语(或粤语对白＋英文字幕)同步发行，也因为香港地处中英文化交流的最前沿，这些影片在英语世界造成了广泛的影响，并进一步强化了英语受众对原作和原作者形象的认知。① 马未都在一档媒体访谈节目中谈及周杰伦时，曾坦言自己"在《百家讲坛》讲了五十多课，也不顶周杰伦唱一首《青花瓷》"，虽是一番玩笑话，却道出了新媒介在传播和弘扬传统文化方面的速度和效率。在全球化的网络时代，音像媒介的传播速度日益加快，影响范围也越来越大，已成为当代典籍外译领域不可忽视的重要因素，同时也启发我们：李渔在英语世界的当代传播，应积极利用多种新媒介的优点，减少改写造成的负面效应，为英语读者重塑真实的李渔形象。

## 三、评论引导

译入语的评论者(也包括集翻译和研究于一身的学者型译者，例如韩南)对于译本的传播和接受也发挥着重要的引导作用。按照操控学派的观点，评论者的意见也反映了译入语的意识形态和诗学标准，是译文进入异域文化之后决定其接受效果的关键因素之一；评论界是重视还是轻视、肯定还是否定、客观还是偏颇，对于普通读者的影响非常大。就李渔作品的英译来说，19 世纪英语世界译介中国小说的主要目的是帮助英语读者初步了解中国社会、文化、生活等方方面面的信息，译者关注较多的是故事本身，作品文学性和作者之类的问题尚未进入其视野。德庇时的《中国小说》前言只简单介绍了所译 3 篇小说的主题和寓意，对故事情节未置一词，原作者李渔更是连名字都没有提过(Davis,1822:10-12)；这还是译文比较贴近原文的译者的做法，其余两位则一个是摘译、一个把原文改得面目全非，遑论顾及原作的文学性和其他优点了。与这种普遍漠视原作、囫囵吞枣式的豪杰译相对应的是，这一阶段基本上没有针对原作和译作的评论和研究。进入 1960 年代以后，随着李渔作品英译的数量明显增加，相关评论和研究也如雨后春笋般涌现，从而将作家李渔从幕后推上了前台，并通过评论和译介之间的交互影

---

① 维基百科英文版"The Carnal Prayer Mat"条目(参见 https://en. wikipedia. org/wiki/ The_Carnal_Prayer_Mat)下的"Later Popular Culture"部分专门提及这两部电影并有链接，详细介绍片名、故事情节、编剧、制片与发行公司、导演、演职人员、票房情况等信息(分别参见 https://en. wikipedia. org/wiki/Sex_and_Zen 和 https://en. wikipedia. org/wiki/3D_Sex_and_Zen:_Extreme_Ecstasy)，足见影视作品在英语世界的影响之大。其中尤其提到了作为编剧/作者的李渔。

响乃至"共谋"，合力投射和建构了今日李渔及其作品在英语世界的形象。这种"共谋"，首先表现为作品译介对读者和评论者的先入为主的影响，然后是评论和研究反过来固化由作品译介造成的印象，再经过多种因素和力量之间的反复博弈，最终造就了一个符合今日英语受众需要的李渔。

如前所述，受《肉蒲团》的译介和关于其作者的先入之见的影响，自1960年代以降，西方学界对李渔的作者身份几乎是一边倒的肯定，大有言(李)必称"蒲团"之势。早在《肉蒲团》转译入英文之前的1961年，荷兰汉学家高罗佩在其《中国古代房内考》(*Sexual Life in Ancient China*, van Gulik, 1961/2003:301-306)一书中就介绍了李渔，包括他的生平、他以女同性恋为题材的戏曲《怜香伴》以及他在《闲情偶寄·声容部》中对理想女性形象的概括，尤其是比较详细地介绍了《肉蒲团》的主要内容。高罗佩研究成果的付梓时间疑应早于海陶玮质疑李渔《肉蒲团》作者身份的文章①，因而似乎从未考虑过《肉蒲团》作者身份存疑的问题，开门见山就说"(《肉蒲团》)作者李渔(号笠翁，1611—1680?)，是明末最著名的作家之一，同时也是一位才华横溢的戏曲家、诗人、散文家以及品鉴女性和雅致生活的行家里手"(*op. cit.*:301)，并指出李渔是"一个公开承认好色的人，事业生涯中曾与女戏子、女乐师、高级妓女以及陪他到处打抽丰的女子多风流艳情"(*op. cit.*:301-302)。由于高罗佩研究主题的特殊性，他对李渔以上几部作品的选择性介绍以及对李渔身份的这番界定，至少给不了解李渔的读者造成了两个印象：(1)李渔好色；(2)《肉蒲团》是李渔最重要的小说。在《肉蒲团》德译本业已风行而英文转译本尚未面世的1961年，这无异于是在英语世界为《肉蒲团》打了一个影响很大的广告，同时也等于预先给李渔贴上了一道身份标签，使读者不知他还有《无声戏》《十二楼》《闲情偶寄》等脍炙人口的小说和散文巨著，也使后来者除非找出铁证来证伪，否则很难撇开情色元素和《肉蒲团》来谈李渔了。1970年代的茅国权和柳存仁(Mao & Liu, 1977:90-112)、松田静江(Matsuda, 1978:150-189)等人在缺乏新证据的情况下，还是选择了肯定李渔作者身份的立场，杨力宇等人(Yang *et al.*, 1978:60-70)甚至未就作者身份问题作任何说明和讨论就把《肉蒲团》与李渔相提并论。在这类评论和研究的引导下，学界在《肉蒲团》作者问题上的态度越来越明确，乃至越来越"傲慢"。到1980年代，何谷理一方面承认"没有找到无可辩驳的新证据"(Hegel, 1981:181)来证明李渔的作者身份，另一方面却又武断地宣称李渔

---

① 按海陶玮的文章发表于《远东学报》1961年第2期，该杂志为半年刊，因此发表时间应为下半年，很可能比高罗佩的书晚出。后者的参考文献里未见海陶玮这篇文章，即为一证。

就是作者,"没有什么理由继续争论下去了"(*op. cit.*:183);雷威安(Lévy,1986:460-461)则把矛头指向最早提出质疑的海陶玮,认为后者以出版年代和作者年龄等理由否定李渔作者身份的观点不成立,并指出《肉蒲团》的内容和批注等与李渔的风格非常相近,因此"作者之争应尘埃落定,回归李渔即作者的传统观点"。至1990年代,随着韩南译本及其音像版的出版,李渔的作者身份被进一步强化,"情色作家"这顶帽子短期内已很难脱掉。整个过程中我们可以看到,前有高罗佩的标签,后有马丁译本和韩南译本的两波冲击,加上学界和传播媒介的各种引导暗示和推波助澜,即便是有海陶玮、夏志清、Ingalls等学者的不同声音,以及张春树和骆雪伦等人的据理力争,李渔及其作品在英语世界的形象,却似乎已经深入人心、积重难返了。在这场"是"与"不是"的论争中,由于证伪(即找出《肉蒲团》小说的真正作者)的难度远大于跟风响应多数派观点(即基于现有的内外部证据推测"可能系李渔所作"),许多持反对意见的学者在找不到铁证的情况下,为了避免无谓的争论使更多原本不了解李渔的读者产生误会、扩大作者身份问题带来的负面影响,只能选择沉默,从而导致现实中赞同李渔作者身份的人数量远多于反对者,对于引导和固化英语世界的李渔形象产生了不小的影响。

当然,以上讨论的目的并不是要为李渔的《肉蒲团》作者身份"翻案"(因为即使在中国文学界这也是一个悬而未决的问题①),而是试图从翻译史的角度说明,李渔在英语世界的形象是译入语文化一步一步建构起来的,在此过程中,既有因选材偏颇导致的宏观偏离和因翻译改写(包括文本操控和跨媒介传播)造成的歪曲放大,也有因评论引导产生的舆论效应,而所有这一切,实质上都是译入语文化自身的需要在原作及其作者身上的投射:《十二楼》在19世纪被选择译入英语,是因为作品真实地反映了中国明清时期的社会生活,符合英国人了解中国的需要;《肉蒲团》在1950—1960年代译入德语、法语和英语,则反映和迎合了西方自身性解放运动的时代背景。由此可见,英语世界对李渔的形象建构是一个历史的、系统的过程,它反映的是英语世界自身的需求,与真实的李渔无关。在21世纪的今天,李渔在英语世界

---

① 国内学界自1980年代以降,虽然倾向于主张李渔为《肉蒲团》作者的居多,包括崔子恩(1989)、黄强(1996)、沈新林(1997)、李时人(1997)、冯保善(2010)、俞为民(2011)等,但一直存在争议,并无定论。2011年李渔诞辰400周年暨首届李渔国际学术研讨会上,孙福轩和孙敏强在梳理了历史上的相关文献及论点之后指出:"我们认为把《肉蒲团》的作者定为李渔为时还尚早一点,因为有些疑团还没有真正解开;……一些学者的论证也并没有真凭实据,都是旁敲侧击,大多是一些推测性的想象而已,……"并从前人论述、作品细节、劝惩主题、写作模式、语言风格乃至作品版本及年代等多个方面一一否定了李渔作为《肉蒲团》作者的可能性。参见孙福轩,孙敏强.李渔三论.//李彩标.李渔四百年:首届李渔国际学术研讨会论文集.北京:中国戏剧出版社,2012:166-172.

乃至整个西方的形象有可能因为西方对中国传统文化、思想等深入研究的需要而产生新的变化，因而当前既是一次向西方全面推介李渔、改变其扭曲形象的良机，同时也提醒我们应避免重蹈覆辙，警惕因作品取舍、翻译改写和舆论引导等做法而使作家形象遭遇矫枉过正的重新建构。

## 第三节 "投射"李渔：操控与建构的影响

由以上研究可知，李渔在进入英语世界的过程中遭遇了明显的操控和建构，后者按照自身不同时期的需要，通过文本选择、翻译改写、评论引导等方式，历时两个世纪，系统地完成了对李渔的形象建构。但这个被"投射"出来的李渔与中国文化和文学语境中的那个李笠翁已经相去甚远；由此造成的英语读者对李渔时代中国文学的总体印象也与实际情况存在较大出入。这是我们开展李渔的当代对外传播实践和研究时需要洞察并设法改变的局面。笔者认为，两个世纪以来英语世界对李渔的"投射"，至少造成了以下两方面的影响。

### 一、对李渔作家身份和形象的影响

这一点前文已多有介绍。其中对作家声誉影响最大的当属翻译选材的偏颇，因为文本选择决定着读者可以读到的内容。李渔最大的成就在戏曲及其理论，但现实中译入英语最多的却是他的小说，其中知名度最高的还是一部作者身份尚无定论的《肉蒲团》！随着该小说音像版的推出，加之评论与研究的推波助澜，可说 1990 年代之后笠翁在英语世界已形象尽毁矣！但如前所述，在 19 世纪乃至《肉蒲团》译入西方前的 20 世纪前半叶，翻译选材对李渔形象的影响并不大。恒慕义的《清代名人传略》一书对李渔身份的描述是"戏曲家、诗人、散文家"（Hummel，1943/2010：495），虽然也提到了《无声戏》《十二楼》《连城璧》等短篇小说集以及《肉蒲团》和《回文传》这两部"被归入李渔名下的长篇小说"（*op. cit.*：496），但只字未提"小说家"的身份。这说明在 1940 年代，英语世界还没有把李渔当成一位小说家来看待，至少还不认为他的主要成就在小说。① 应该说，在《肉蒲团》译入欧洲之前，西方对李渔的作家形象总体上还是比较客观公允的。

---

① 这也许与林语堂著作中对李渔小说提得不多有关。应该说林的意见代表了中国文学界对李渔主要成就的传统印象，不过与林同时代的孙楷第早在 1930 年代就指出李渔是清代最重要的一位小说家。

但随着 1960—1970 年代《肉蒲团》和《十二楼》译入英语,情势发生了很大的变化。

首先是李渔小说家的身份为越来越多的学者所认同。松田静江是较早关注李渔小说创作的学者之一,早在茅国权《十二楼》译本出版前的 1973 年就撰文探讨过李渔短篇小说中的才子佳人式爱情主题(Matsuda,1973:271-280),后来完成的博士论文更是李渔小说研究的专论,其中专辟第三章讨论《肉蒲团》(Matsuda,1978:150-189)。香港中文大学翻译研究中心主办的《译丛》杂志 1973 年创刊号刊登茅国权《鹤归楼》英译文时,编者按语对李渔的描述是"清初剧作家,热衷于通俗艺术,常被人(不太确定地)认为是情色小说《肉蒲团》的作者"(Mao,1973:26)。茅国权在两年后出版的《十二楼》英译本序言中,称李渔"是一位卓有成就的剧作家,也是最优秀的小说家之一,本该在中国文学界占有重要的地位,但很不幸,他的作品既不受同时代人的待见,也得不到现代学者的承认"(Mao,1975:ix);他认为李渔"很早以前就应该被公认是清代最优秀的小说家之一","其作品大多未译(入英语),亦未获认可"(*ibid.*)。在茅国权和柳存仁合著的李渔研究专论中,李渔是"一位多才多艺的诗人、散文家、小说家、戏曲家、文学批评家"(Mao & Liu,1977:7)。即便是专门研究李渔戏曲的 Henry,在其《中国娱乐》一书的前言中也认为"把他(李渔)作为一位散文家、戏曲理论家、小说家、园艺师,或是作为一位出版商-编辑来研究,都会和作为剧作家来研究一样合情合理,也都一样会回报颇丰"(Henry,1980:ix)。当然,1970 年代也还是有对李渔的小说家身份避而不谈的,例如《译丛》1978 年春季号所刊赖恬昌节译的袁枚《随园食单》和李渔《闲情偶寄·饮馔部》有编者按语,称李渔为"戏曲家、诗人、散文家","撰写了大量美文和披阅内容,就剧本创作、表演方法、女性魅力等发表自己的见解,在建筑、旅游、休闲、饮馔及卫生方面也多有心得记录";谈及李渔的创作特点和风格,只说他"极富创造力和幽默感",其作品"表述大胆自由,语言简单平易"(Lai,1978:58),却闭口不提他的小说。从中可以看出这位编者对李渔作家身份的立场,要么是拒不承认李渔的小说家身份,要么是出于某些考虑(譬如担心提到小说就不得不牵扯出情色元素来)而小心翼翼地回避着这个话题。不过这只是为数不多的做法,因为到 1970 年代,李渔的小说家身份在英语世界已经基本确立;不管这一身份与中国文学界对他的认同是否一致,也不管我们能否接受这样一个经过跨文化投射的李渔,他在西方人眼中已成明清小说家的代表之一,都已是既成事实。

其次是李渔头上的情色"光环"挥之不去。如前所述,由于《肉蒲团》从一开始译入西方时就注明作者是李渔,也由于 1990 年代之后这部小说及其衍生文本的跨媒介传播所带来的放大效应,情色元素成为英语读者和受众短期内难以摆脱的对李渔的原型印象。哪怕库恩和韩南再三强调作品的文学和社会价值并反复提醒读者要透过小说的表面情节和内容欣赏背后的道德主题和文化内涵,但作品中露骨的性描写还是产生了广泛的社会影响。在作者问题上,尽管大多数研究者在提及这部作品时都谨慎地使用了"attributed to Li Yu"(归在李渔名下)这样的表述,但对于无法理解中国传统小说作者问题复杂性的英语世界普通读者来说,作者只不过是一个名字而已,用不用"attribution"也差不多,既然有人说了是李渔,大家便也乐见"情色作家"这顶帽子扣在他头上,鲜有较真之人。于是,李渔在戏曲、散文、诗赋、园艺建筑、休闲养生乃至短篇小说等方面的辉煌成就,经过跨文化投射之后,在《肉蒲团》这道"光环"的映照下尽皆失色;在英语读者那里,李渔成了名副其实的登徒子,其作品惟有《肉蒲团》尔!

## 二、对中国传统小说总体形象的影响

在中国文学史上以戏曲名世的李渔,进入英语世界之后摇身一变成了小说家,又因《肉蒲团》被归入他名下而成了情色作家,被拿来与英语世界创作《芬妮·希尔》的克莱兰和创作《查泰莱夫人的情人》的劳伦斯相"媲美",翻译操控对作家的异域形象建构之影响不可谓不大。勒菲弗尔指出,重写是推动文学演进的重要力量,其能量足以"创造作家、作品、文学史时期、文学流派乃至整个文学系统的形象"(Lefevere,1992:5)。在李渔译入英语世界的过程中,操控与重写除了影响作家的形象和声誉之外,对中国文学总体形象也有一定的影响。

中国传统小说在中国文学史上的发展起步较晚,滥觞于唐传奇,勃兴于宋元话本,元明之际走向繁荣,至清中叶艺术成就达到顶点。李渔生活在一个中国小说的黄金时代,前有问世于元末明初的《三国演义》《西游记》等经典,后有乾隆时期(18世纪中叶)刊行的《儒林外史》和《红楼梦》等巨献;即便是在他所生活的17世纪,也不乏像《水浒》《西游补》《隋唐演义》《隋史遗闻》这样的优秀作品。当然,17世纪在中国文学史上也是一个情色小说盛产的时代,作品"鄙秽不堪寓目者居多"(刘廷玑《在园杂志》语,转引自孙福轩、孙敏强,2012:166),《金瓶梅》《隋炀帝艳史》《肉蒲团》,等等,均在这一时期成书。从作品本身的经典性和在中国文学史上的影响来看,这些艳情小说基本无法与以上所列的作品相提并论(或许与它们后世屡遭禁毁有关),但译入英语之后,其影响却比非情色题材的小说要大得多,极有可能影响英语读者对中国传统小说的总体印象和评价。就算是在这几部艳情小说中,尽管夏志清(1988:227)认为《肉蒲团》无论"如何的怪诞和淫秽",都是"一部比《金瓶梅》更为明晰紧凑、更有艺术性、也远为生动的作品",但《金瓶梅》在中国文学史上的经典地位一般都认为比《肉蒲团》更高一些,而后者除了露骨的性描写给读者带来的视觉冲击和猎奇体验,其深层次的教化寓意和目的等英语读者恐怕是很难领会的。这种在译出语里地位和评价原本不高的作品译入英语之后,由于题材特殊以及迎合了译入语的时代需求,其社会效应遂被几何级放大,甚至被当成了译出语文学形象的代言作品,从而拉低了中国传统小说在英语世界的整体形象。这样的现象在典籍外译历史上常有发生,也是当代典籍外译实践和研究领域需要引起高度重视的一个问题。

# 本章小结

本章基于操控学派的理论和思想分析了英语世界对李渔的形象建构及其影响。研究发现,在两个世纪的时间里,英语世界按照自身在不同历史时期的需要,通过文本选择、翻译改写和评论引导等三种途径,从宏观选材到微观操控,一步一步地完成了对李渔及其作品的形象建构。因此英语世界里的李渔形象,更多地反映了英语世界自身的需求,已不再是中国文学语境中那个真实的李渔了。我们认为,这种跨文化投射不仅使李渔的作家形象受损,对中国传统文学在英语世界的总体形象也产生了一定的影响,是李渔在英语世界的当代传播需要重点解决的问题,对于其他典籍外译也有重要的启发和借鉴意义。

# 第四章　李渔作品英译策略的历时演变

李渔在英语世界的传播已逾两个世纪,而且随着近年来国内外学界在李渔研究领域热情高涨,相关译介和研究如火如荼地展开,相信在不久的将来会有更多有影响的翻译和研究成果面世。因此,当前李渔英译与传播正处在一个承前启后、方兴未艾的新时代,有必要对以往的翻译策略作一系统的研究和归纳,从中总结经验、吸取教训,为李渔在英语世界的当代传播探索更有效的策略和方法,做好新时期中国典籍外译这篇大文章。

近年来,国内一些学位论文开始涉及或针对李渔作品的英译问题。例如,夏洁(2009)对德庇时与中国经典早期翻译的研究就涉及德庇时翻译李渔《十二楼》的策略及其文化原因。郭盈(2012)则对《十二楼》的三个主要英译本(即德庇时译本、茅国权译本和韩南译本)开展了对比研究,认为德庇时的《十二楼》译本"更接近一种东方轶事,一段充满异国风情的东方纪录"(*op.cit.*;7),它"描绘了中国古代美好的道德操守和与西方迥异的风土人情,……介绍中国现象和制造道德想象称为(*sic.*,疑应作"成为")译本功能的一体两面"(*op.cit.*;16);茅国权译本追求的是一种情节至上的"复述",[①]"实际是针对故事情节的缩写,……在尊崇以人物命运和事件发展为中心的故事情节的同时,茅译本丧失了原书潜藏的讽刺艺术。……《十二楼》也从游戏文章改换面目,成为一个颂扬真善美的市民故事集"(*op.cit.*;34);韩南的译本则是一篇语言、叙事和文化等各方面都精雕细琢的"才子文章"。因而从德庇时到茅国权再到韩南,三位译者的关注点从文本外部向文本本身转移,由译者中心向作者中心转移。李渔的地位,从可有可无的逸事记录者演变为叙事和悬疑高手,进而成为文体家;三部完成于不同历史时期的译本,也因译者的翻译观和翻译策略差异而分别呈现出故事、小说和散文的风格(*op.cit.*;69)。郭盈对于《十二楼》三个译本总体特点的描述和对翻译策略演变轨迹的归纳应该说是比较客观的,但研究对象囿于一部小说,难以概括两个世纪以来李渔全部作品英译的全貌。

基于前两章的梳理和分析,我们认为,李渔作品英译的策略在两个世纪

---

① 茅国权的"retelling"本书译为"译述"。——笔者注

的时间里发生了较大的变化,其中语言方面的总体变化趋势是由粗放到精细,文学方面是由通俗到雅致,文化方面是由译入语为中心到译出语为中心,副文本策略则是由浮泛到专深。以下逐一进行论述。

## 第一节　语言翻译策略:由粗而精

综观李渔作品的英译史,我们发现,在 1990 年代之前,无论是小说还是散文的翻译,也不管是德庇时、林语堂、茅国权、文世昌还是赖恬昌的译文,原作的语言一直都不是译者首要考虑的因素。于是可以看到,原文很多形象而精彩的语言表述形式在译文里要么变成了淡而无味的"白开水",要么被改得面目全非乃至完全抛弃。我们先以德庇时译本为例:

(7)穿的是缟衣布裙,戴的是铜簪锡珥,与富贵人家女儿立在一处,偏要把他比并下来。旁边议论的人,都说过缟布不换绮罗,铜锡不输金玉。

(《夺锦楼》,李渔,1991/9:38)

(7a)Their dress and ornaments were (from their station in life) coarse and ordinary, but yet, when these two girls were compared with the daughters of more wealthy and dignified persons, it was allowed by all, that they need not change their homely dress, and metal ornaments, for the silks and jewels of the others.

(Davis, 1822:111)

(8)他拿定这个主意,所以除了置产之外,不肯破费分文。心上如此,却又不肯安于鄙啬,偏要窃个至美之名,说他是唐尧天子之后,祖上原有家风,住的茅茨土阶,吃的是太羹玄酒,用的是土硎土簋,穿的是布衣鹿裘,祖宗俭朴如此,为后裔者,不可不遵家训。

(《三与楼》,李渔,1991/9:53)

(8a)He laid fast hold of this notion, and was determined to take care of his money. But not contented with being niggardly, he wished to assume credit to himself for it, and said that he was descended from one of the most ancient emperors, and that his ancestors were celebrated for their economy.

The father being thus parsimonious, his son was bound to obey his precepts.

(Davis,1822:156-157)

如前所述,德庇时译本总体上还算比较贴近原文,但从以上两例可以看出,原文的语言风格到了译文里踪迹全无:例(7)的"穿的是缟衣布裙,戴的是铜簪锡珥"和"缟布不换绮罗,铜锡不输金玉"、例(8)的"茅茨土阶""人羹玄酒""土䅏土簋""布衣鹿裘"等,不仅有具体的形象,还有整齐的音韵和形式特征,而在德庇时译文中,这些具体的形象几乎都被舍弃,泛化处理成了"coarse and ordinary""homely dress and metal ornaments""silks and jewels""celebrated for their economy"等平淡无奇的表述,原文的音韵之美也荡然无存。除此以外,例(7)中的"偏要把他比并下来"一句,德庇时的理解并不正确;例(8)中的"所以除了置产之外"未译,"唐尧天子"作了泛化阐释,"祖宗俭朴如此,为后裔者,不可不遵家训"一句理解亦有误……。仅此二例就有这么多问题,可见赵长江评价德庇时译本"比较朴素,没有冗词,也不夸张"的说法只对了一部分:德译素则素矣,语言风格与原文相比已是相当粗糙,而且漏译、错译数不胜数。

与德庇时译本相比,1970年代的茅国权译本因系华人译者所为,在对原作的理解方面还是比较到位的,错误较少,但另一方面,茅译本旨在提高可读性的"译述"策略,不仅使原作的内容遭到大幅调整和删削,而且译文语言的艺术水准也较原作有明显下降:

> (9)这位小姐既有秾桃艳李之姿,又有璞玉浑金之度,虽生在富贵之家,再不喜娇妆艳饰,在人前卖弄娉婷。终日淡扫蛾眉,坐在兰房,除女工绣作之外,只以读书为事。詹公家范极严,内外男妇之间最有分别。家人所生之子,自十岁以上者就屏出二门之外,即有呼唤,也不许擅入中堂,只立在阶沿之下听候使令。
>
> (《夏宜楼》,李渔,1991/9:76)

> (9a) Hsien-hsien was a beautiful and graceful girl. Though born into a wealthy family, instead of spending her time on cosmetics, she read and did needle work. Moreover, she had strong moral principles, the result of her father's strict family discipline. One of the rules of the family was that no male member over the age of ten was allowed into the women's apartments.
>
> (Mao, 1975:29)

对比原文和译文可以看到,茅译本只是传达大意,基本不顾原文的细节刻画和语言艺术。"秾桃艳李之姿"和"璞玉浑金之度"被简单处理成了"beautiful and graceful","娇妆艳饰"和"卖弄娉婷"也被简化成了"spending her time on cosmetics"（"淡扫蛾眉"亦与此相联）。如此处理，原文的大意虽在，译语的表述却是血肉全无、止余骨架矣！

（10）只见进门之际，大家堆着笑容，走近身来相见。及至一见之后，又惊疑错愕起来，大家走了开去，却像认不得的一般。三三两两立在一处，说上许多私话，绝不见有好意到他。这是甚么原故？只因贝去戎身边有的是奇方妙药，只消一时半刻，就可以改变容颜。起先被众人扯到，关在空房之中，只说是祸事到了，乘众人不在，正好变形。<u>就把脸上眉间略加点缀，却像个杂脚戏子，在外、末、丑、净之间，不觉体态依然，容颜迥别。</u>那些姊妹看见，自然疑惑起来。这个才说："有些相似。"那个又道："甚么相干。"有的说："他面上无疤，为甚么忽生紫印？"有的道："<u>他眉边没痣，为甚么陡起黑星？当日的面皮却像嫩中带老，此时的颜色又在媸里生妍</u>。"大家唧唧哝哝，猜不住口。

（《归正楼》，李渔，1991/9：113）

（10a）The broad smiles on the women's faces, when they entered the room, quickly vanished when they realized that the man in front of them did not really look like Pei, but was someone who only remotely resembled him. With doubts growing by the second, one woman voiced the complaint of all, "Pei did not have scars, as this one does. This is not Pei but someone else. Where are our useless servants?" Why couldn't the women identify Pei? Because, as master of the use of makeup, Pei had changed his appearance during those few moments when he was left alone.

（Mao, 1975：44-45）

本例译文对原文的改动比较大。内容方面，对原文细节多有删削和调整，例如见面时众妓女的反应、关于易容术的解释等。而改动更大的则是原文的语言：作者用了自己熟悉的"杂脚戏子""外、末、丑、净"等戏曲语汇来描写贝去戎易容之后的形象，生动而俏皮，众妓女七嘴八舌的对话也颇有形式特色。遗憾的是译文并未试图再现这样的语言艺术，甚至还把大段的文字内容全部删去了。

（11）后面有进大楼，题上一个匾额，叫做"萃雅楼"。结构之精，铺设之雅，自不待说。每到风清月朗之夜，一同聚啸其中，<u>弹的弹，吹的吹，唱的唱，都是绝顶的技艺，闻者无不销魂。没有一部奇书不是他看起，没有一种异香不是他烧起，没有一本奇花异卉不是他赏玩起。手中</u>

摩弄的没有秦汉以下之物,壁间悬挂的尽是宋唐以上之人。

(《萃雅楼》,李渔,1991/9:130-131)

(11a) They also rented a spacious building immediately behind these shops and called it "Ts'ui-ya lou," The Hall of Elegance. It was exquisite on the outside and beautifully decorated inside. Because of the trio's cultural interests, "Ts'ui-ya lou" quickly became a center of cultural activities. On clear nights, skilful musicians and singers displayed their talent there. It acquired the reputation of being a very refined and elegant place. It boasted of having the rarest books, plants, sandalwood and antiques, as well as outstanding interior decoration with the walls even adorned with some of the best pre-T'ang scrolls.

(Mao, 1975:53)

原文采用重复的句式描写萃雅楼之精美雅致,其中"弹的弹,吹的吹,唱的唱"一句,热闹场面跃然纸上;紧随其后的"没有一部/种/本/……不是他看/烧/赏玩起"也是重复并置的句型,意在渲染;末尾两句则以对仗句式,突出所收藏品之古雅。而到了译文里,原文热闹的现场感变成了平淡无奇的"才艺展示";一唱三叹地渲染的精致和品位,也沦为"最珍稀的书籍、植物、檀香";"没有秦汉以下之物"成了普普通通的"古玩"(antiques),"尽是宋唐以上之人"变成了"甚至还饰有一些唐代以前的最佳书画卷轴",不但意象尽失,连基本的强调意味都未能传达。

由以上几例可以看出,比德译本晚了一个半世纪推出的茅译本,虽然在理解方面比德译本有所进步,但在"译述"策略的主导下,对原作内容的删削调整力度过大,而语言方面甚至比德译本还粗糙。茅译本当初设定的目标读者群是英语国家的普通读者,从笔者手头掌握的出版信息来看,茅译本1975年出版,1979年修订再版,说明译本在一定程度上实现了译者的目标,在英语读者中有了一定的接受度。但从历史的角度来说,这种以译述为主导的译本由于忽视原作的语言艺术,往往会造成译作总体文学水准的下降,致使译文丧失长远的读者群。1930年代《水浒传》的两个英译本就是很好的例子:赛珍珠译本(Buck,1933)由于贴近原作语言风格,尽管颇多争议乃至诟病,但在美国一直都是中国文学选修课程阅读书目指定的水浒译本,而且近年来日益受到肯定;杰克逊译本(Jackson,1937)的做法则与茅国权《十二楼》译本非常相似,即舍弃细节、枉顾语言,结果就是今天几乎无人再读这样的译本。当然,译述策略在文化交流的初始时期还是有其积极意义的,茅译本在中西方隔阂乃至对立的冷战时期推出,对于推动东西方的沟通和交流发挥了重要的作用,其历史和文化价值应予充分承认。

1980 年代之前译入英语世界的李渔作品除了小说《十二楼》之外,还有《闲情偶寄》的部分内容。《闲情偶寄》是一部百科全书式文集,全书包含词曲部、演习部、声容部、居室部、器玩部、饮馔部、种植部、颐养部等八个部分。如前所述,林语堂在《生活的艺术》(1937)一书中多处引用或摘译过《闲情偶寄》的内容,涉及声容部、居室部、饮馔部、种植部、颐养部等部分,在《古文小品译英》(1960)中更是直接选译了声容部和颐养部的大段内容,译文篇幅达14 页。林语堂的译文总体上比较灵巧,很多时候并不拘泥于原文的字面表达或句式结构,而是根据英文的习惯遣词造句,因而译文相对原文来说删削改编比较普遍。试举一例:

> (12)穷人行乐之方,无他秘巧,亦止有退一步法。我以为贫,更有贫于我者;我以为贱,更有贱于我者;我以妻子为累,尚有鳏寡孤独之民,求为妻子之累而不能者;我以胼胝为劳,尚有身系狱廷,荒芜田地,求安耕凿之生而不可得者。以此居心,则苦海尽成乐地。如或向前一算,以胜己者相衡,则片刻难安,种种桎梏幽囚之境出矣。一显者旅宿邮亭,时方溽暑,帐内多蚊,驱之不出,因忆家居时堂宽似宇,簟冷如冰,又有群姬握扇而挥,不复知其为夏,何遽困厄至此! 因怀至乐,愈觉心烦,遂致终夕不寐。一亭长露宿阶下,为众蚊所啮,几至露筋,不得已而奔走庭中,俾四体动而弗停,则啮人者无由厕足;乃形则往来仆仆,口则赞叹嚣嚣,一似苦中有乐者。显者不解,呼而讯之,谓:"汝之受困,什佰于我,我以为苦,而汝以为乐,其故维何?"亭长曰:"偶忆某年,为仇家所陷,身系狱中。维时亦当暑月,狱卒防予私逸,每夜拘挛手足,使不得动摇,时蚊蚋之繁,倍于今夕,听其自啮,欲稍稍规避而不能,以视今夕之奔走不息,四体得以自如者,奚啻仙凡人鬼之别乎! 以昔较今,是以但见其乐,不知其苦。"显者听之,不觉爽然自失。此即穷人行乐之秘诀也。不独居心为然,即铸体炼形亦当如是。譬如夏月苦炎,明知为室庐卑小所致,偏向骄阳之下来往片时,然后步入室中,则觉暑气渐消,不似从前酷烈;若畏其湫隘而投宽处纳凉,及至归来,炎蒸又加十倍矣。冬月苦冷,明知为墙垣单薄所致,故向风雪之中行走一次,然后归庐返舍,则觉寒威顿减,不复凛冽如初;若避此荒凉而向深居就燠,及其再入,战粟又作何状矣。由此类推,则所谓退步者,无地不有,无人不有。想至退步,乐境自生。予为两间第一困人,其能免死于忧,不枯槁于迍邅蹭

蹬者,皆用此法。又得管城一物,相伴终身,以扫千军则不足,以除万虑
则有余。然非善作退步,即楮墨亦能困人。想虞卿著书,亦用此法,我
能公世,彼特秘而未传耳。

（《闲情偶寄·颐养部》行乐第一"贫贱行乐之法",李渔,1991/3:312-314)

(12a) The art of being happy though poor consists in one phrase,
to think "it could be worse." I am poor and humble, but there are
people poorer and more humble than myself. I have a big family to
support, but there are people living alone and without children, and
widows and orphans. I have to work hard on a farm, but there are
people without a farm, or who would rather work hard on their farm like
me but cannot because they are sitting in jail. It is a way of thinking, or of
looking at it. The same situation may look like hell to one and like
paradise to another. On the other hand, always to want to compare
oneself with one's betters will breed a state of mind conducive only to
one's own misery.

I remember the story of a high official who was traveling abroad.
It was summer and his bed was full of mosquitoes inside the net. He
thought of his own spacious hall at home, where the summer mat was
cooling to the body and many maids would attend to his comforts. The
more he thought, the more miserable he felt. He was not able to sleep
a wink. Then he saw a man walking about in the court of the inn,
seemingly quite happy with himself. He was puzzled and inquired how
he seemed to be so happy with the mosquitoes around and was not
bothered at all. The man replied, "I once had an enemy and was put in
jail. It was summer and the jail was full of vermin. But my hands and
feet were tied to prevent me from escape. It was terrible to be bitten
by insects and mosquitoes and not be able to do anything about it.
There are mosquitoes now. But I move about and they can't touch me.
In fact, it makes me happy to feel just the freedom of the limbs
alone." The man saw one side of it and the other man saw the other
side. The rich man felt quite lost when he heard the story.

(Lin, 1960: 216-217)

本例是从颐养部"行乐第一"的"贫贱行乐之法"中摘译的,原文共有千余字,

分为两段,林语堂只选译了第一段的主要内容,且其中有两处划线部分 300 余字未译。显而易见,达旨是林译的首要目的,在原文的立论和例证业已译出、文本内容相对已经比较完整的情况下,后面划线部分的进一步阐发在译者看来已属多余,删省是必然的选择;译文只在亭长讲完话之后加了一句 "The man saw one side of it and the other man saw the other side.",算是对所删内容的一点补偿。微观层面的改编也不少,例如,显者讲话用的是直接引语,译文处理成了间接引语;此外,"维时亦当暑月,狱卒防予私逸,每夜拘挛手足,使不得动摇,时蚊蚋之繁,倍于今夕,听其自啮,欲稍稍规避而不能,……"一句顺序多有调整(包括"蚊蚋之繁"移至"亦当暑月"后、句内主语由"狱卒"变为"手足"并使用被动语态等)。可以看到,林译在文本选择上比较认真,选的都是原文最核心的内容,微观层面则是删繁就简,灵巧地摆脱了原文形式的束缚,但翻译效果止于传意达旨,同时也有"译述"之嫌,可以推动文化之间的早期交流,但后续推动力和文化价值有限。

《闲情偶寄》词曲部和演习部代表了李渔在戏剧创作和表演方面的核心思想,通常被称为"李笠翁曲话",单行本刊行无数。如前所述,文世昌的硕士论文(Man,1970)是笠翁曲话专论,对李渔的戏曲理论作了比较全面和深入的分析,也选译了其中不少内容;文世昌后来发表于《译丛》的笠翁曲话节译(Man,1974:62-65),大部分取自他硕士论文中征引和翻译的李渔戏剧理论,个别之处在发表时作了微调和修改。总体上,文译从学术研究的需要出发,在思想内容上还是比较忠实于原文的,但细究之下却不难发现刀砍斧凿的痕迹,语言表达方面多粗糙敷衍,传达原义亦有隔靴搔痒之感:

(13)总而言之,传奇不比文章;文章做与读书人看,故不怪其深,戏文做与读书人与不读书人同看,又与不读书之妇人小儿同看,故贵浅不贵深。

(《李笠翁曲话》词曲部词采第二"忌填塞",李渔,1962:18-19)

(13a) All in all, drama is not the same as other forms of literary writing which are meant for the scholars and literate class and so justify a certain degree of abstruseness. Drama is meant to be performed before the literate and the illiterate alike, and for the enjoyment of uneducated women and children. Therefore immediate comprehensibility is preferred to intellectual profundity.

(Man, 1970: 51)

本例总体比较达旨,其中个别语句的译文还不无可圈可点之处,例如"故不怪其深"采用"justify"来处理、"贵浅不贵深"采用"be preferred to"的结构，就使译文灵巧地避开了原文"怪""贵"二字蕴含的由客体向主体的转换给译语句式结构造成的累赘问题，符合英文视点固定的造句习惯。但有些表述的处理则显得粗糙，似未仔细斟酌，例如"不读书人"译为"illiterate"就失之简单和绝对：原文的"不读书人"与"读书人"放在一起对比时，应是指教育程度一般的人，但并非文盲；其后的"不读书之妇人小儿"才是真的文盲，用"illiterate"和"uneducated"皆可。此外，"戏义做与读书人与不读书人同看"和"又与不读书之妇人小儿同看"两句间应是递进关系，这样才能在逻辑上推论出后面的"贵浅不贵深"，但文译只是简单地处理成了并列关系，致使前后两部分之间的因果关系被弱化。

(14)然一味显浅而不知分别，则将日流粗俗，求为文人之笔而不可得矣。元曲多犯此病，乃矫艰深隐晦之弊而过焉者也。极粗极俗之语，未尝不入填词，但宜从脚色起见。如在花面口中，则惟恐不粗不俗，一涉生旦之曲，便宜斟酌其词。无论生为衣冠仕宦，旦为小姐夫人，出言吐词，当有隽雅从容之度；即使生为仆从，旦作梅香，亦须择言而发，不与净丑同声，以生旦有生旦之体，净丑有净丑之腔故也。元人不察，多混用之。

（《李笠翁曲话》词曲部词采第二"戒浮泛"，李渔，1962：17)

(14a)If we strive for simplicity without discretion, it will eventually degenerate into crude vulgarity, unworthy of the workmanship of a literary writer. Many plays of the Yuan dynasty suffered from this defect. It was the result of too consciously avoiding the difficulty and obscurity of language.

The crudest and basest language can be used in drama, but it must fit the characters who speak it. It is imperative for the dialogue of a 'hua-mien' or painted face to be crude and vulgar whereas the words of the songs of the 'male' and the 'female' roles must be more carefully couched and refined. A 'male' role (sheng), whether it be a gentleman or an official, and a 'female' role (tan), be it a young lady or an elderly mistress, must as a rule use language of cultured refinement and leisurely elegance. Even if the 'male role' is a servant or the female role is a maid, he or she must choose words with some care, in order to be distinguished from the words and tone of the 'painted face' (ching) and 'comic roles' (ch'ou). The male and female roles are distinctly different character-types from the painted and comic roles. The Yuan dramatists, however, often overlooked this rule and simply treated the different roles without discrimination.

(Man, 1970: 45-46)

此处原文的"小姐"和"夫人"固然包含年龄方面的因素,但更多是对未婚和已婚女性的不同称呼,译文只选前者,失之偏颇。句子层面,"无论生为……,且为……"一句,译文主体结构是把生和旦作为并列主语,以"and"连接,这样处理本身并无不妥,问题是紧随其后的"生为仆从"和"旦作梅香"这两个子句之间的连词又变成了"or",明显不一致。另外,"以生旦有生旦之体,净丑有净丑之腔故也"一句是解释前面"亦须择言而发,不与净丑同声"的原因的,译文将其断成了独立的句子,原有的逻辑关系不复存在,原句中最重要的两个字"体"和"腔"也不知所踪。

(15)若论填词家宜用之书,则无论经、传、子、史以及诗、赋、古文,无一不当熟读,即道家、佛氏、九流、百工之书,下至孩童所习"千字文"、"百家姓",无一不在所用之中;至于形之笔端,落于纸上,则宜洗濯殆尽。亦偶有用着成语之处,点出旧事之时,妙在信手拈来,无心巧合,竟似古人寻我,并非我觅古人。

(《李笠翁曲话》词曲部词采第二"贵显浅",李渔,1962:15)

(15a)A dramatist needs to be knowledgeable and well-read. Not only has he to be versed in the classics and their commentaries, philosophical works, history, poetry, parallel prose, ancient prose; he should also be familiar with works of Taoism, Buddhism, different schools of thought, all sorts of occupations and even the primers for beginning learners such as *A Thousand Characters* and *A Hundred Names*. Yet when a dramatist actually makes use of these materials in his writing, they should be so fused with their own ideas that no trace can be found of direct allusions. Occasionally he has to use conventional proverbial sayings and allude to ancient events; these have to be done with such art that it appears artless and completely uncontrived. It must seem as though the ancient characters are seeking out the dramatist, not being sought after.

(Man, 1970: 48)

原文围绕"宜用之书"造句，首先将其分为"无一不当熟读"和"无一不在所用"两类，然后强调在写作过程中对书中内容"宜洗濯殆尽""信手拈来"，达到"竟似古人寻我，并非我觅古人"的境界。而译文从　丌始就把主语确定为 dramatist，导致第一句重心完全偏离，后面"至于形之笔端"一句的译文受此影响，不得不在从句里也用 dramatist 作主语，但主句的主语只能是 these materials(they)，这样一来，这个句子的从句跟着上文跑，主句则另起一个主语且用了两个"曲径通幽"的被动语态。问题还不止于此，紧随其后的两句主语又是一"人"一"物"、各为其"主"的情况！这样的语篇衔接，效果可想而知。

> (15)戏场锣鼓，筋节所关，当敲不敲，不当敲而敲，与宜重而轻，宜轻反重者，均足令戏文减价。此中亦具至理，非老于优孟者不知。最忌在要紧关头，忽然打断。如说白未了之际，曲调初起之时，横敲乱打，盖却声音，使听白者少听数句，以致前后情事不连，审音者未闻起调，不知以后所唱何曲。打断曲文，罪犹可恕，抹杀宾白，情理难容。予观场每见此等，故为揭出。又有一出戏文将了，止余数句宾白未完，而此未完之数句，又系关键所在，乃戏房锣鼓早已催促收场，使说与不说同者，殊可痛恨！故疾、徐、轻、重之间，不可不急讲也。场上之人将要说白，见锣鼓未歇，宜少停以待之；不则过难专委，曲白锣鼓，均分其咎矣。

　　（《李笠翁曲话》演习部授曲第三"锣鼓忌杂"，李渔，1962：74）

　　(15a)The gongs and drums of the orchestra are the muscles and joints of a play. If they are hit at the wrong time or with the wrong degree of force, they may mar the merit of the play in a performance. There are also principles underlying their use, principles which only those well experienced in the acting profession may be aware of. The effect is particularly detrimental should unwarranted interruption come at such crucial moments as when a speech is not yet finished or a song has just started. . . . Therefore the rhythm of the gongs and drums, be it quick or slow in tempo, light or heavy in force, must be treated with care.

　　　　　　　　　　　　　　　　　　　　　　　　　（Man，1974：65）

原文系《闲情偶寄》演习部"授曲第三"之"锣鼓忌杂"，全文（含标点）279 字，介绍戏曲演出过程中锣鼓使用的忌讳，指出演员与锣鼓师之间应协同配合。译文只译出了划线部分约百字内容，就所译部分来看尚属达意，但对比原文不难看出,译者对原文哪些内容该译、哪些可舍弃,明显不如林语堂拿捏得准。原文提出"最忌在要紧关头,忽然打断"之后,举了两种情况,一是"说白未了""曲调初起"时横敲乱打,二是"宾白未完"时锣鼓"催促收场";译文只是简单地一笔带过了第一种情况,第二种情况一字未译,就直奔"疾、徐、轻、重……"一句,草草收了场。原文末尾关于演员和锣鼓师应彼此配合的建议实质上也是核心内容之一,却被不负责任地舍弃了,这是很大的损失。

《闲情偶寄》饮馔部由三部分组成:"蔬食第一"(笋、蕈、莼、菜、瓜茄瓠芋山药、葱蒜韭、萝卜、芥辣汁)、"谷食第二"(饭粥、汤、糕饼、面、粉)、"肉食第三"(猪、羊、牛犬、鸡、鹅、鸭、野禽野兽、鱼、虾、鳖、蟹、零星水族),此外还有一则附录"不载果食茶酒说"。赖恬昌的译文选材面比较窄,只涉及原作"蔬食第一"之笋、蕈、菜、葱蒜韭,"谷食第二"之汤,"肉食第三"之蟹,以及"不载果食茶酒说"等篇目,且多为节译或编译,语言表述错漏、偏颇之处不少,精雕细琢更无从谈起。试举一例:

> (16)吾观人之一身,眼耳鼻舌,手足躯骸,件件都不可少。其尽可不设而必欲赋之,遂为万古生人之累者,独是口腹二物。口腹具,而生计繁矣;生计繁,而诈伪奸险之事出矣;诈伪奸险之事出,而五刑不得不设。君不能施其爱育,亲不能遂其恩私,造物好生,而亦不能不逆行其志者,皆当日赋形不善,多此二物之累也。草木无口腹,未尝不生;山石土壤无饮食,未闻不长养。何事独异其形,而赋以口腹?即生口腹,亦当使如鱼虾之饮水,蜩螗之吸露,尽可滋生气力,而为潜跃飞鸣。若是则可与世无求,而生人之患熄矣。乃既生以口腹,又复多其嗜欲,使如溪壑之不可厌。多其嗜欲,又复洞其底里,使如江海之不可填。以致人之一生,竭五官百骸之力,供一物之所耗而不足哉!吾反复推详,不能不于造物是咎。亦知造物于此,未尝不自悔其非,但以制定难移,只得终遂其过。甚矣!作法慎初,不可草草定制。吾辑是编而谬及饮馔,亦是可已不已之事。其止崇俭啬,不导奢靡者,因不得已而为造物饰非,亦当虑始计终,而为庶物弭患。如逞一己之聪明,导千万人之嗜欲,则匪特禽兽昆虫无噍类,吾虑风气所开,日甚一日,焉知不有易牙复出,烹子求荣,杀婴儿以媚权奸,如亡隋故事者哉!一误岂堪再误,吾不敢不以赋形造物视作覆车。
>
> (《闲情偶寄·饮馔部》蔬食第一,李渔,1991/3:234-235)

(16a)Admittedly certain parts of the body are quite indispensable-the eyes, ears, nose, tongue, hands and feet and so on. But I consider that the mouth and the stomach do more harm than good. It was a mistake for nature to endow us with them. They make life complicated and give rise to crime. Laws and penalty were made because of them. Plants have no mouth or stomach but there is nothing to prevent them from growing. Rocks do not eat or drink but they perpetuate without any trouble. Why then should there be such organs as the mouth and the stomach? Granted that they must have their places, they should only serve such purposes as they do for fishes and shrimp or dragonflies. While we will do what we can to minimize the evil, we cannot but blame nature for her mischief. Since we are stuck with our mouth and stomach we will have them serve our purposes instead of serving them. Hence my thoughts on the subject of food.

(Lai,1978:58)

这是饮馔部"蔬食第一"的开篇,借口腹之患引出"为造物饰非"的写作目的。赖译删省了原文第一处划线文字,对第二处划线部分也作了很多节略和改编;从保留的部分来看,译文比较粗糙,最多只能算基本达意,很多细节都没能译出,原文"口腹具""生计繁""诈奸出""五刑设"等句之间颇有气势的层层递进,在译文里也荡然无存。试对照林语堂的译文:

(16b)I see that the organs of the human body, the ear, the eye, the nose, the tongue, the hands, the feet and the body, have all a necessary function, but the two organs which are totally unnecessary but with which we are nevertheless endowed are the mouth and the stomach, which cause all the worry and trouble of mankind throughout the ages. With this mouth and this stomach, the matter of getting a living becomes complicated, and when the matter of getting a living becomes complicated, we have cunning and falsehood and dishonesty in human affairs. With the coming of cunning and falsehood and dishonesty in human affairs, comes the criminal law, so that the king is not able to protect with his mercy, the parents are not able to gratify their love, and even the kind Creator is forced to go against His will. All this comes of a little lack of forethought in His design for the human body at the time of the creation, and is the consequence of our having these two organs. The plants can live without a mouth and a stomach, and the rocks and the soil have their being without any nourishment. Why, then, must we be given a mouth and a stomach and endowed with these two extra organs? And even if we were to be endowed with these organs, He could have made it possible for us to derive our nourishment as the fish and shell fish derive theirs from water, or the cricket and the cicada from the dew, who all are able to obtain their growth and energy this way and swim or fly or jump or sing. Had it been like this, we should not have to struggle in this life and the sorrows of mankind would have disappeared. On the other hand, He has given us not only these two organs, but has also endowed us with manifold appetites or desires, besides making the pit bottomless, so that it is like a valley or a sea that can never be filled. The consequence is that we labor in our life with all the energy of the other organs, in order to supply inadequately the needs of these two. I have thought over this matter over and over again, and cannot help blaming the Creator for it. I know, of course, that He must have repented of His mistake also, but simply feels that nothing can be done about it now, since the design or pattern is already fixed. How important it is for a man to be very careful at the time of the conception of a law or an institution!

(Lin, 1937: 42-43)

不难看出,林译除省略了"作法慎初,不可草草定制"之后的内容,其他方面(包括译文忠实程度、句子之间逻辑关系的处理、译文流畅性和地道性等)均可圈可点,赖译相形之下可谓云泥之别。再如:

(17)菜有色相最奇,而为《本草》、《食物志》诸书之所不载者,则西秦所产之头发菜是也。予为秦客,传食于塞上诸侯。一日脂车将发,见坑(sic.,疑应作"炕")上有物,俨然乱发一卷,谬谓婢子栉发所遗,将欲委之而去。婢子曰:"不然。群公所饷之物也。"询之土人,知为头发菜。浸以滚水,拌以姜醋,其可口倍于藕丝、鹿角等菜。携归饷客,无不奇之,谓珍错中所未见。此物产于河西,为值甚贱,凡适秦者皆争购异物,因其贱也而忽之,故此物不至通都,见者绝少。由是观之,四方贱物之中,其可贵者不知凡几,焉得人人物色之?发菜之得至江南,亦千载一时之至幸也。

(《闲情偶寄·饮馔部》蔬食第一"菜",李渔,1991/3:239)

(17a) Hair Vegetable

There is a strange kind of vegetable called hair-vegetable. When I was in Shansi I saw something on the table in my room at the inn, which looked like a tangled bunch of hair. I thought it was an oversight of the maid who left it there after her toilet, but she said, "No, it is a delicacy and much sought after by the rich people." One way of preparing hair-vegetable is, first to soak it in water and then cook it in ginger and vinegar. It has a neutral taste and goes well with anything rich because it absorbs the taste of the principal ingredient in a dish.

(Lai, 1978：59)

本例原文共 700 余字,赖恬昌只选译了其中的"头发菜"部分,计 200 余字;即便如此,赖译也未完全译出,只是简单介绍了一下偶遇头发菜的过程,其中产地还写错了(Shansi 更像是"山西"而非"陕西",而且不作任何说明,译犹不译),烹调方法"浸以滚水,拌以姜醋"译成了"先浸于水中,继而与姜醋同煮"!原文对头发菜的点评,译文除了胡乱发挥一句,其余悉数略去。据赖译的编者按语介绍,译文是从赖氏即出的一部介绍中餐菜肴的 *Chinese Food for Thought* 一书中节录的,还称赖"在美食等文化题材上颇有鉴赏品味"(Lai,1978:47)。然而以这样的译文,莫说鉴赏品味,就连"粗糙"都算不上,因为除了一点猎奇的色彩,译文从内容到细节可说完全枉顾原作,连原文作为饮馔部最重要内容的烹制方法都译错了!

从 1990 年代开始,李渔作品的英译在语言上走向精细,内容方面的删削明显减少,也日益注重微观层面的词汇表述和句式特征的忠实传达。我们从韩南《十二楼》《无声戏》译本和夏建新等人的《李渔小说选》译本中各举一例:

(18)从古及今,都把"梅香"二字做了丫鬟的通号,习而不察者都说是个美称,殊不知这两个字眼古人原有深意:梅者,媒也;香者,向也。梅传春信,香惹游蜂,春信在内,游蜂在外,若不是他向里向外牵合拢来,如何得在一处?以此相呼,全要人顾名思义,刻刻防闲;一有不察,就要做出事来,及至玷污清名,梅香而主臭矣。若不是这种意思,丫鬟的名目甚多,那一种花卉、那一件器皿不曾取过唤过?为何别样不传,独有"梅香"二字千古相因而不变也?

(《拂云楼》,李渔,1991/9:152)

(18a) The word *meixiang* (plum-blossom fragrance) has been in use since ancient times as a general term for maidservants. People who take it for granted assume that it is meant to be flattering, not realizing that the ancients had a profound purpose in coining it: *mei* (plum-blossom) stands for *mei* (matchmaker) and *xiang* (fragrance) stands for *xiang* (hither and thither).* The plum sends the message of spring and its fragrance drives the bees wild. But when the message of spring is inside the house and the bees are outside, how are the twain going to meet—unless she goes hither and thither and brings them together? The ancients gave maidservants this name to remind people of the danger and put them on their guard. A single slip, and trouble will ensue, trouble that will ruin the mistress's reputation but leave the maid's intact.

Suppose for a moment that that was not the ancients' intention. The names available for maids are legion—at one time or another every flower, every vessel you can think of has been drawn upon—so why is the term *meixiang* the only one to have been handed down unchanged from ancient times?

(* Pairs of homonyms. The characters are quite distinct.)

(Hanan, 1992/1998: 118)

本例原文对"梅香"的解释颇为有趣,其中的字面解释涉及同音字的问题,是公认的翻译难点,同时也是翻译过程中难以绕开的问题,因为这是构建整个篇章话语体系的基础。韩南的译文与原文非常贴近,对"梅香"的同音字字面解释也采用了国际通行的处理办法(音译+意译)。我们对照一下茅国权的译文:

(18b) From time immemorial, the term "Mei Hsiang" has been used commonly as a synonym for a maid or maids. Thoughtless people often consider the term complimentary without realizing that its origin was derogatory. "Mei" means "a slave girl" and "Hsiang" means "the inclination towards some activity." Maids, because of the nature of their work, are allowed to move about both inside and outside the women's apartments. Many of their activities are aimed at making themselves more popular, often at the cost of their mistresses' good reputations.

(Mao, 1975：63)

可以明显看出，茅译存在对原文的删削，原文"若不是这种意思"之后的内容未译；对"梅香"字面解释的翻译也存在问题，"媒也"译成"a slave girl"，显然偏离了原文的本义。

　　(19)话说忠孝节义四个字，是世上人的美称，个个都喜欢这个名色。只是奸臣口里也说忠，逆子对人也说孝，奸夫何曾不道义，淫妇未尝不讲节，所以真假极是难辨。古云："疾风知劲草，板荡识忠臣。"要辨真假，除非把患难来试他一试。只是这件东西是试不得的，譬如金银铜锡，下炉一试，假的坏了，真的依旧剩还你；这忠孝节义将来一试，假的倒剩还你，真的一试就试杀了。

(《女陈平计生七出》,李渔,1991/8:93)

　　(19a) Loyalty, filial piety, chastity and fidelity are terms of general approbation that everyone rejoices in. The trouble is that loyalty is regularly found on the lips of traitorous officers and filial piety in the mouths of incorrigible sons, while adulterous husbands are constantly holding forth about fidelity and wanton wives about chastity. As a result it is almost impossible to distinguish true virtue from false. However, as the proverb has it: "Fierce winds reveal the sturdy plant and troubled times the loyal subject." Generally, if you want to tell whether something is true or false, you subject it to a test. The trouble is that in this case there is no test applicable. When metals are tested in a furnace, for example, the false are destroyed and the true survive. But if the people who claim to possess these four virtues are put to the test, the false will survive and only the true will perish.

(Hanan, 1990b：77-78)

此处原文提及世人对"忠孝节义"的喜欢时用了四个结构相同的并列句"奸臣口里也说忠，逆子对人也说孝，奸夫何曾不道义，淫妇未尝不讲节"，韩南一一译出，只是根据英文造句习惯添加了几个连词；原文引用的古语，韩南也是从词汇到句式都照直翻译，几乎未作任何调整或发挥。

(20)……把纸锭捏了又看,中间隐隐跃跃却像有行小字一般,拿到日头底下仔细一认,果然有印板印的七个字道:

不孝男王竺生奉。

小山看了,吓得寒毛直竖,手脚乱抖,对众人道:"原原原来是王竺生的父亲怪我弄去他的家事,变做人来报仇的。这等看来,又合着原籍苏州的话了。"

(《受人欺无心落局 连鬼骗有故倾家》,李渔,1991/8:169-170)

(20a)Gripping it between his finger and thumb, he examined the ingot again, and noticed a few microscopic scripts printed thereon that were barely visible. He put it in the sunshine for a clearer view, and saw seven characters that read:

OFFERED HERETO BY YOUR UNFILIAL SON ZHUSHENG.

Xiaoshan was scared stiff at the sight of the characters, his hands and legs shivering.

"It-it-it... wath... Zhusheng's late father," he lisped, "who came to take revenge on me for having taken away his property! No wonder he said Suzhou was his ancestral home!"

(Trans. Tang Yanfang, in Xia *et al.*, 2011:69)

本例原文的"七个字"和"原原原来是……"都属于语言层面的特征,字面翻译并不容易,放弃语言特征而作模糊处理则又失真,致译文质量不高。此处唐艳芳译文在二者的处理上做了值得肯定的努力:保留原文的"七个字"(seven characters),将其译为 7 个英文单词;"原原原来是"除照字面译成"It-it-it..."之外,还生造了一个词"wath"(was),辅以动词 lisp,将说话者吓得说话时舌头僵硬的形象栩栩如生地呈现在读者面前。

由以上例证可以看到,在李渔作品英译的历史上,就语言方面的翻译策略来说,总体上是从粗放走向精细的。具体而言,1990 年代以前的翻译以传达基本意义、促进文化初级交流为主要目的,轻视原文的语言特征和文学性,普遍存在对原文的删削改编现象,译文语言总体比较粗糙,忠实度不高;1990 年代以来的翻译,以韩南、夏建新、卓振英等译者为代表,日益重视原作语言风格的传译,使李渔作品的英译文在语言和内容上越来越贴近原文,而英语读者藉此看到的也是越来越真实的李渔。

## 第二节　文学翻译策略：由俗而雅

与语言翻译策略对应的是文学翻译策略由通俗走向雅致。如前所述，在李渔英译史的前两个阶段，受时代和文化交流背景等因素的影响，译者总体上比较关注原作的故事性，满足于介绍原文的主要内容和情节，而较少顾及原作的文学性。"文学性"（literariness）是俄国形式主义代表人物之一雅各布森（Roman Jakobson，1896—1982）在1921年出版的《现代俄语诗歌》一书中提出的概念，雅各布森将其定义为"使作品成其为文学作品的东西"（what makes a given work a literary work）（Das，2005：78）①，认为这才是文学研究的对象。鲍迪克《牛津文学术语词典》（在线版）对文学性的解释是"将文学文本与非文学文本区分开来的所有语言和形式特征"（the sum of special linguistic and formal properties that distinguish literary texts from non-literary texts）（Baldick，2008）②。可见，文学性与语言艺术（包括修辞等）和形式特征密不可分，是区分文学和非文学作品的重要标志。而梳理1990年代之前的李渔作品英译不难看出，译者大都是在用非文学的策略来翻译李渔文学作品的，具体表现就是对原作语言特点以及非故事性、非情节性内容的普遍漠视和任意删削改编。

首先是对原作拟话本小说开篇诗词及"入话"的无视。李渔的《十二楼》《无声戏》等短篇小说集都是典型的拟话本小说，其显著特点之一是独立成篇，每篇均以诗词开头，之后引入一段数百字到数千言不等的"入话"，意在铺陈叙事或就故事寓意作说理阐发，然后才切入正题，介绍时间、地点、人物及故事情节等，正文根据篇幅长短的需要分一到多个回目展开。从李渔作品前两个阶段的英译情况来看，译者大都程度不一地低估了开篇诗词和入话的作用。以下我们以《十二楼》之《合影楼》《夺锦楼》和《三与楼》为例：

（21）词云：

世间欲断钟情路，男女分开住。掘条深堑在中间，使他终身不度是非关。堑深又怕能生事，水满情偏炽。绿波惯会做新娘，不见御沟流出

---

① "Literariness," 31 March, 2019, https://en. wikipedia. org/wiki/Literariness.

② 参见 Chris Baldick ed. , *The Oxford Dictionary of Literary Terms* (London:Oxford UP. , 2008), 31 Mar. , 2019, http://www. oxfordreference. com/abstract/10. 1093/acref/9780199208272. 001. 0001/acref-9780199208272-e-661? rskey＝ABgv1M&result＝661.

墨痕香？

右调《虞美人》

这首词，是说天地间越礼犯分之事，件件可以消除，独有男女相慕之情、枕席交欢之谊，只除非禁于未发之先。若到那男子妇人动了念头之后，莫道家法无所施，官威不能摄，就使玉皇大帝下了诛夷之诏，阎罗天子出了缉获之牌，山川草木尽作刀兵，日月星辰皆为矢石，他总是拼了一死，定要去遂心了愿。觉得此愿不了，就活上几千岁然后飞升，究竟是个鳏寡神仙。此心一遂，就死上一万年不得转世，也还是个风流鬼魅。到了这怨生慕死的地步，你说还有甚么法则可以防御得他？所以惩奸遏欲之事，定要行在未发之先。未发之先又没有别样禁法，只是严分内外，重别嫌疑，使男女不相亲近而已。

儒书云："男女授受不亲。"道书云："不见可欲，使心不乱。"这两句话极讲得周密。男子与妇人亲手递一件东西，或是相见一面，他自他，我自我，有何关碍，这等防得森严？要晓得古圣先贤也是有情有欲的人，都曾经历过来，知道一见了面，一沾了手，就要把无意之事认作有心，不容你自家做主，要颠倒错乱起来。譬如妇人取一件东西递与男子，过手的时节，或高或下，或重或轻，总是出于无意。当不得那接手的人常要画蛇添足：轻的说他故示温柔，重的说他有心戏谑；高的说他提心在手、何异举案齐眉，下的说他借物丢情、不啻抛球掷果。想到此处，就不好辜其来意，也要弄些手势答他。焉知那位妇人不肯将错就错？这本风流戏文，就从这件东西上做起了。至于男女相见，那种眉眼招灾、声音起祸的利害，也是如此，所以只是不见不亲的妙。不信，但引两对古人做个证验。李药师所得的红拂妓，当初关在杨越公府中，何曾知道男子面黄面白？崔千牛所盗的红绡女，立在郭令公身畔，何曾对着男子说短说长？只为家主公要卖弄豪华，把两个得意侍儿与男子见得一面，不想他五个指头一双眼孔就会说起话来。及至机心一动，任你铜墙铁壁，也禁他不住，私奔的私奔出去，窃负的窃负将来。若还守了这两句格言，使他"授受不亲"、"不见可欲"，那有这般不幸之事！

我今日这回小说，总是要使齐家之人，知道防微杜渐，非但不可露形，亦且不可露影，不是单阐风情，又替才子佳人辟出一条相思路也。

元朝至正年间，广东韶州府曲江县有两个闲住的缙绅，一姓屠，一姓管。姓屠的由黄甲起家，官至观察之职；姓管的由乡贡起家，官至提举之职。他两个是一门之婿，只因内族无子，先后赘在家中。……

（《合影楼》，李渔，1991/9：13-15）

(21a) During the reign of a certain Emperor of the Yuen dynasty, in a district of the province of Canton, there lived two persons of rank, who had retired from the toils of office. Their names were Too and Kwan; the former of whom had obtained the highest literary distinctions, and had exercised the office of an Inspector General of a Province; while Kwan had attained to a lower rank, and an inferior office. They had married two sisters, and as their common father-in-law had no son, they both lived with his family. ...

(Davis, 1822: 53)

(21b) *To stop the road to romance,*

*Man and woman must live separately.*

*Dig a ditch in between*

*So they will never cross the gate of right-and-wrong.*

*If the ditch is too deep, it might create hazards;*

*If the water is too full, passion might become rampant.*

*Green waves become used to acting as Hung Niang.* \*

*Hast thou not smelt the fragrance of ink flowing out of the imperial ditch?* \*\*

According to this poem nothing in this world can stop a man and a woman once they have fallen in love. The only way to deal with the matter is to keep it from happening. If one waits until after the man and woman have fallen in love, no family discipline, no governmental power, no decree from the Supreme Deity of Taoism, no death warrant from the Chinese Pluto, no transformation of mountains and grass into swords and soldiers and constellations into archery will stop them. The lover will risk his life to fulfill his wish. He feels that it is better to be condemned to spend a million years as a romantic ghost than to have his desire thwarted. But before love makes him desperate, are there ways to contain him? The meting out of punishment for sinful thoughts and preventing outbursts of uncontrollable passion must begin at the earliest possible moment in a man's life. One must draw sharp distinctions between the inner and outer quarters of a residence, be suspicious of everyone and prohibit the sexes from mingling. \*\*\*

During the Chih-cheng years (1341 – 1367) of the Yüan dynasty, there were two retired country gentlemen in the district of Ch'ü-chiang of Shao-chou-fu in the province of Kwangtung. One was named T'u and the other Kuan. They were the sons-in-law of a family which had no son, so they lived together with their wives' family.

(Mao, 1975: 1-2)

(* Hung Niang is the clever maid in the play *Hsi Hsiang Chi*, which was based on a short story by Yüan Chen [779 – 831]. The play is about the wooing and winning of the beautiful Ts'ui Ying-ying by the scholar Chang Chün-jui and the part played by Hung Niang as the go-between for the lovers. Her name now connotates one who acts as the liaison between two lovers. ) (*op. cit.* : 132)

(** At one time some imperial concubines described their loneliness and sorrow on paper, then threw the paper into a ditch and it floated into the outside world. ) (*ibid.*)

(*** A traditional Chinese residence would usually be divided into the inner and outer quarters. The inner would be the living quarters of members of the immediate family, whereas the outer would be used for social purposes. ) (*op. cit.* :1)

原文以一首右调《虞美人》开篇,然后是八百余字的入话。从两种译文来看,德庇时完全放弃了这些内容,开门见山就直奔"元朝至正年间"去了,而且对故事发生的时间和地点都作了模糊处理;茅国权虽然译出了开篇词,但与原词相比已属散体译法,形式上损失了不少诗歌的属性(包括押韵、音节、节奏等),入话也只大略译出了第一段(有所取舍),其余内容悉数删去了。两相对比,德译本可以说几无文学性可言,茅译本略好一些,但总体也不高。

(22)词云:

一马一鞍有例,半子难招双婿。失口便伤伦,不俟他年改配。成对,成对,此愿也难轻遂。

右调《如梦令》

这首词,单为乱许婚姻、不顾儿女终身者作。常有一个女儿,以前许了张三,到后来算计不通,又许了李四,以致争论不休,经官动府,把跨凤乘鸾的美事,反做了鼠牙雀角的讼端。那些官断私评,都说他后来改许的不是。据我看来,此等人的过失,倒在第一番轻许,不在第二番改诺,只因不能慎之于始,所以不得不变之于终。

做父母的,那一个不愿儿女荣华,女婿显贵?他改许之意,原是为爱女不过,所以如此,并没甚么歹心。只因前面所许者或贱或贫,后面所许者非富即贵,这点势利心肠,凡是择婿之人,个个都有。但要用在未许之先,不可行在既许之后。未许之先,若能勾真正势利,做一个趋炎附势的人,遇了贫贱之家,决不肯轻许,宁可迟些日子,要等个富贵之人,这位女儿就不致轻易失身,倒受他势利之福了。当不得他预先盛德,一味要做古人,置贫贱富贵于不论,及至到既许之后,忽然势利起来,改弦易辙,毁裂前盟,这位女儿就不能勾自安其身,反要受他盛德之累了。这番议论,无人敢道,须让我辈胆大者言之,虽系末世之言,即使闻于古人,亦不以为无功而有罪也。

如今说件轻许婚姻之事,兼表一位善理词讼之官,又与世上嫁错的女儿伸一口怨气。

明朝正德初年,湖广武昌府江夏县有个鱼行经纪,姓钱,号小江,娶妻边氏。夫妻两口,最不和睦,一向艰于子息。到四十岁上,同胞生下二女,只差得半刻时辰。……

（《夺锦楼》,李渔,1991/9:36-37）

(22a) Early in the reign of an Emperor, of the Ming dynasty, there dwelt, in a city of the province of Hoo-kwang, a merchant, named Siaou-kiang, who had the misfortune to live on very indifferent terms with his wife. They were for a long while without any family, until, after a lapse of many years, two daughters, twins, were born to them....

(Davis, 1822: 109)

(22b) The saying commonly attributed to Mencius, that "Marriages are made in heaven," is one of those maxims which unfortunately find their chief support in the host of exceptions which exist to the truth which they lay down. Not to go further for an instance than the Street of Longevity, in our notable town of King-chow, there is the case of Mr and Mrs Ma, whose open and declared animosity to each other would certainly suggest that the mystic invisible red cords with which Fate in their infancy bound their ankles together, were twined in another and far less genial locality than Mencius dreamed of.

With the exception of success in money-making, fortune has undoubtedly withheld its choicest gifts from this quarrelsome couple.

The go-between who arranged their marriage spoke smooth things to Ma of his future wife, and described her as being as amiable as she was beautiful, or, to use her own words, "as pliant as a willow, and as beautiful as a gem;" while to the lady she upheld Ma as a paragon of learning, and as a possessor of all the virtues. Here, then, there seemed to be the making of a very pretty couple but their neighbours, as I have been often told, were not long in finding out that harmony was a rare visitant in the household. The daily wear and tear of life soon made it manifest that there was as little of the willow as of the gem about Mrs Ma, whose course features, imperious temper, and nagging tongue made her anything but an agreeable companion; while a hasty and irascible temper made Ma the constant provoker as well as the victim of her ill-humours.

By a freak of destiny the softening influences of the presence of a son has been denied them; but *en revanche* they have been blessed with a pair of the most lovely twin daughters,...

(Douglas, 1893: 82-83)

(22c)*One saddle for one horse,*

*One daughter for one son-in-law.*

*Irresponsible promises are a breach of the five human relationships.* *

*None should change the promise of betrothal;*

*The wish to be paired is hard to fulfill.*

This poem was written specially for those parents who arrange their children's marriages casually and don't carefully consider their welfare. It was not infrequent that a daughter was first engaged to Chang San and later to Li Szu, ** which resulted in endless quarrels and turned a happy occasion into a morass of petty lawsuits. Most magistrates would decree that the blame lies with the parents. In my judgment, the parents' chief error lies in promising marriage too readily the first time. If parents are not meticulous and prudent in choosing their prospective sons and daughters-in-law, it is more than likely that they will change their minds later on.

Which parents would not want their children prosperous and

married to well-known and important people? If parents break their earlier promises of betrothal, it is because of their desire to have their daughters marry better. My purpose is not to condemn their snobbishness, but to urge that they use their critical faculties fully before making commitments. It is their right to reject impoverished or unqualified prospects. But once a commitment is made, they must abide by it.

The following story is about the making and breaking of marriage promises by inconsiderate and thoughtless parents who treated their daughters' marriages so casually and with such indiscretion that they abused the sacred privileges of parenthood. Fortunately, a wise magistrate redressed the wrongs done the daughters and arranged for them to marry a well-qualified bachelor.

During the early years of the Cheng-te period of the Ming dynasty (1506 – 1521) there lived in the district of Chiang-hsia a fish jobber named Ch'ien Hsiao-chiang. He and his wife were not known for their marital happiness. They quarreled frequently and bitterly because of their differences of opinion and their unwillingness to compromise. They had no children until their forties when Mrs. Ch'ien unexpectedly gave birth to twin girls.

(Mao，1975：13-14)

(* The five human relationships are between prince and minister, father and son, husband and wife, brothers and friends.)

(** Chang San and Li Szu are the Chinese equivalents of Tom, Dick and Harry.) (op. cit.：133)

《夺锦楼》是 1980 年代之前《十二楼》各篇目中唯一一篇有三位译者翻译过的小说,因而在一定程度上反映了从 19 世纪初到 20 世纪末李渔作品英译的变化过程。德庇时译本的处理方式与例(21)如出一辙,仍然是忽略开篇词和入话,直奔正题;道格斯译本不仅无视原文的开篇词和入话,连原文的内容也改得面目全非,只能从夫妻不睦、双胞胎女儿等几个要素里依稀看到原作的影子;茅国权译本也与例(21)相似,以散体翻译开篇词,入话第一段尚算比较贴近原文,到第二段就有明显的选译和发挥的痕迹了。

(23)诗云:

茅庵改姓属朱门,抱取琴书过别村。

自起危楼还自卖,不将荡产累儿孙。

又云:

百年难免属他人,卖旧何如自卖新。

松竹梅花都入券,琴书鸡犬尚随身。

壁间诗句休言值,槛外云衣不算缗。

他日或来闲眺望,好呼旧主作嘉宾。

这首绝句与这首律诗,乃明朝一位高人为卖楼别产而作。卖楼是桩苦事,正该嗟叹不已,有甚么快乐倒反形诸歌咏?要晓得世间的产业都是此传舍蘧庐,没有千年不变的江山,没有百年不卖的楼屋。与其到儿孙手里烂贱的送与别人,不若自寻售主,还不十分亏折。即使卖不得价,也还落个慷慨之名,说他明知费重,故意卖轻,与施恩仗义一般,不是被人欺骗。若使儿孙贱卖,就有许多议论出来,说他废祖父之遗业——不孝,割前人之所爱——不仁,昧创业之艰难——不智。这三个恶名都是创家立业的祖父带挈他受的。倒不如片瓦不留、卓锥无地之人,反使后代儿孙白手创起家来,还得个“不阶尺土”的美号。所以为人祖父者,到了桑榆暮景之时,也要回转头来,把后面之人看一看,若还规模举动不像个守成之子,倒不如预先出脱,省得做败子封翁,受人讥诮。

从古及今,最著名的达者,只有两位。一个叫唐尧,一个叫虞舜。他见儿子生得不肖,将来这份大产业少不得要白送与人,不如送在自家手里,还合着古语二句,叫做:

宝剑赠与烈士,红粉送与佳人。

若叫儿孙代送,决寻不出这两个受主,少不得你争我夺,搆起干戈。莫说儿子媳妇没有住场,连自己两座坟山,也保不得不来侵扰。有天下者尚且如此,何况庶人!

我如今才说一位达者、一个愚人,与庶民之家做个榜样。这两分人家的产业,还抵不得唐尧屋上一片瓦,虞舜墙头几块砖,为甚么要说两分小人家,竟用着这样的高比?只因这两个庶民一家姓唐,一家姓虞,都说是唐尧、虞舜之后,就以国号为姓,一脉相传下来的,所以借祖形孙,不失本源之义。只是这位达者便有乃祖之风;那个愚人,绝少家传之秘。肖与不肖,相去天渊,亦可为同源异派之鉴耳。

明朝嘉靖年间,四川成都府成都县有个骤发的富翁,姓唐号玉川。此人素有田土之癖,得了钱财,只喜买田置地,再不起造楼房,连动用的家伙,也不肯轻置一件。至于衣服饮食,一发与他无缘了。……

(《三与楼》,李渔,1991/9:51-53)

(23a) During the reign of the twelfth Emperor of the Ming dynasty, in a district of the province of Sze-chuen, there lived a rich man, who was likely in time to be still richer. This person, whose name was Tang-yo-chuen, had an immense quantity of land. Whenever he got any money, it was his delight to add to his landed possessions; but he would neither build houses, nor would he supply himself with any of the comforts or necessaries of life, beyond what was absolutely indispensable. . . .

(Davis, 1822: 155)

(23b) *The straw hut, now sold, belongs to another.*

*Carrying my lute and my books, I moved to another village.*

*I built and sold my lofty house,*

*Not to burden my descendants.* \*

These lines, written during the Ming dynasty by a man of superior moral attainments, \*\* deal with the sale of property which, as we all know, is, at best, an annoyance. Why did he choose to wax poetic about it? He realized that worldly properties do change ownership, that rarely does a house remain in one family's possession for more than a hundred years, and that there has been no dynasty which lasted over a thousand years.

If a piece of property will have to be sold anyway in the second or the third generation, isn't it better for the present owner to sell it himself even at a loss? If he does, people may at least compliment him for being generous. However, if his son has to sell it at a loss, he will be called a squanderer for having failed to preserve the family property. Grandparents and parents should therefore carefully consider the true character of their descendants, to judge whether they can manage their inheritance. If there is any doubt, it should be disposed of so that the inheritance doesn't result in their children disgracing the family name.

There have been only two famous and wise kings in China. They were King Yao of T'ang and King Shun of Yü. \*\*\* Realizing that their children were neither deserving nor able, they gave away their kingdoms before they died. These generous actions fit the ancient saying:

*Swords to be given to heroes;*

*And rouge to women of beauty.*

To return to our story. During the Chia-ching years (1522 – 1566) of the Ming dynasty in the Ch'eng-tu district of Szech'uan province, there was a rich and avaricious man named T'ang Yü-ch'uan who had an insatiable appetite for acquiring land. . . .

(Mao，1975：21)

(* The second introductory poem of eight lines has been omitted. )

(** The poet referred to in the poem is probably Li Yü himself. During his life，he often had the unpleasant experience of having to sell his property. See the Introduction for further details. )

(*** Yao of T'ang and Shun of Yü were two legendary Chinese kings. ) (*op. cit.*：133)

如前所述，德庇时的《三与楼》译文最早曾于 1815 年在广州出版过单行本，但发行效果不佳，1816 年刊于《亚洲杂志》，1822 年与《合影楼》《夺锦楼》结集出版时德庇时对译文作了不少修改，修改的理由是早期的译文"过于严格贴近汉语的表达习惯了"(Davis，1822：12)。修改后的《三与楼》德译本总体风格与(21a)(22a)相近，行文造句并不紧贴原文，而是大体上跟着原文的情节走。不过本例中皇帝年号的处理与前两者不同，"嘉靖"被翻译成了"the twelfth Emperor"(对照[21a]的"a certain Emperor"和[22a]的"an Emperor")，说明德庇时早期的翻译策略还是能略微顾及一下原文细节的。尽管如此，这种处理方式能传达的信息终究有限，对提高译文的文学性并无太大作用。茅国权译文省略了第二首开篇诗(提供了一个注释，但未解释删省原因)，入话第一段中关于"自寻售主"和"儿孙贱卖"各有一些文采斐然的表述，读来十分生动，茅译却简单地用了一个"generous"和"squanderer"来处理，从内容来说可谓言简意赅，但从文学性来看则失之谫陋，尤其是舍弃了"不孝""不仁""不智"这些与原文文学、文化密切相关的表述之后，译文成了淡而无味的简单记叙。入话中两句古语"宝剑赠与烈士，红粉送与佳人"后的内容开始铺陈正文叙事，茅译只用了一句"To return to our story."便直奔故事正文而去，简则简矣，却也少了许多文学韵味。

与前两个阶段相比，1980 年代之后的李渔作品英译，对诗词和入话的内容和形式都要重视得多。以下我们从韩南《十二楼》《无声戏》译本和夏建新等人《李渔小说选》译本中各取一例加以说明。

(24)诗云：

两村姐妹一般娇，同住溪边隔小桥。

相约采莲期早至，来迟罚取荡轻桡。

又云：

采莲欲去又逡巡，无语低头各祷神。

折得并头应嫁早，不知佳兆属何人。

又云：

不识谁家女少年，半途来搭采莲船。

荡舟懒用些须力，才到攀花却占先。

又云：

采莲只唱采莲词，莫向同侪浪语私。

岸上有人闲处立，看花更看采花儿。

又云：

人在花中不觉香，离花香气远相将。

从中悟得勾郎法，只许郎看不近郎。

又云：

姊妹朝来唤采蘋，新妆草草欠舒徐。

云鬟摇动浑松却，归去重教阿母梳。

这六首绝句，名为《采莲歌》，乃不肖儿时所作。共得十首，今去其四。凡作采莲诗者，都是借花以咏闺情，再没有一首说着男子。又是借题以咏美人，并没有一句说着丑妇。可见荷花不比别样，只该是妇人采，不该用男子摘；只该入美人之手，不该近丑妇之身。

世间可爱的花卉不知几千百种，独有荷花一件更比诸卉不同：不但多色，又且多姿；不但有香，又且有韵；不但娱神悦目，到后来变作莲藕，又能解渴充饥。古人说他是"花之君子"，我又替他别取一号，叫做"花之美人"。这一种美人，不但在偎红倚翠、握雨携云的时节方才用得他着，竟是个荆钗裙布之妻，箕帚蘋蘩之妇，既可生男育女，又能宜室宜家。自少至老，没有一日空闲、一时懒惰。开花放蕊的时节，是他当令之秋，那些好处都不消说得。只说他前乎此者与后乎此者。自从出水之际，就能点缀绿波，雅称"荷钱"之号；未经发蕊之先，便可饮啜清香，无愧"碧筒"之誉。花瓣一落，早露莲房。荷叶虽枯，犹能适用。这些妙处，虽是他的绪余，却也可矜可贵。比不得寻常花卉，不到开放之际，毫不觉其可亲，一到花残絮舞之后，就把他当了弃物。古人云："弄花一年，看花十日。"想到此处，都有些打算不来。独有种荷栽藕，是桩极讨便宜之事,所以将他比做美人。

　　我往时讲一句笑话,人人都道可传,如今说来请教看官,且看是与不是。但凡戏耍亵狎之事,都要带些正经,方才可久。尽有戏耍亵狎之中,做出正经事业来者。就如男子与妇人交媾,原不叫做正经,为甚么千古相传,做了一件不朽之事? 只因在戏耍亵狎里面,生得儿子出来,绵百世之宗祧,存两人之血脉,岂不是戏耍而有益于正,亵狎而无叛于经者乎! 因说荷花,偶然及此,幸勿怪其饶舌。

　　如今叙说一篇奇话,因为从采莲而起,所以就把采莲一事做了引头,省得在树外寻根,到这移花接木的去处,两边合不着笋也。

　　元朝至正年间,浙江婺州府金华县,有一位致仕的乡绅,姓詹,号笔峰,官至徐州路总管之职。因早年得子二人,先后皆登仕路,故此急流勇退,把未尽之事付与两位贤郎,终日饮酒赋诗,为追陶仿谢之计。中年生得一女,小字娴娴,自幼丧母,俱是养娘抚育。詹公不肯轻易许配,因有儿子在朝,要他在仕籍里面选一个青年未娶的,好等女儿受现成封诰。

(《夏宜楼》,李渔,1991/9:73-76)

(24a)Poems:

> *There are pretty girls in both these hamlets,*
> *With a bridge between and the river below.*
> *They've sworn to be early for the lotus-picking;*
> *Those who come late will have to row.*
>
> *About to begin, they hesitate*
> *And bend their heads in silent prayer.*
> *The one with a double will soon be wed;*
> *And who will receive a sign so rare?*
>
> *I wonder whose daughter that girl is,*
> *Who joins a boat along the way.*
> *Too lazy by far, to pull on an oar,*
> *But in flowers plucked she wins the day.*
>
> *Sing but the lotus-picking songs*
> *And tell no wild, indecent lies.*

*A man on the bank admires the lotus*
*And on the lotus-pickers spies.*

*Among the flowers you're unaware,*
*But at a distance their scent is clear;*
*She draws this lesson: to ensnare a man*
*Just let him look, not come too near.*

*The girls are summoned to the lotus early;*
*For grooming they have no time to spare.*
*Down fall their tresses and, home again,*
*They get their mothers to redo their hair.*

These six poems, entitled "Lotus-picking Songs," were composed by your humble servant in his youth. * Originally there were ten of them, of which four have been omitted. Now, anyone who writes a lotus-picking poem uses that theme to sing of women, not of men, and of beautiful women, not of ugly ones. Obviously the lotus differs from all other flowers in that it has to be picked by women rather than men, and by beautiful women at that.

I don't know how many thousand species of charming flowers there are in the world, but the lotus is unique among them. Not only does it abound in color and grace, it also possesses fragrance and charm in plenty. Not only does it delight the mind and eye, eventually it forms arrowroot to satisfy our hunger and thirst. The ancients dubbed it the prince of flowers, but I have another name for it: the beauty among flowers. And this beauty serves other purposes besides dalliance and lovemaking. It is also the frugal, diligent wife in the homespun dress, the sort of wife who is capable of bearing children as well as gracing her household. From youth to old age she knows not a single day of leisure, not one idle hour.

The flowering season is the lotus's heyday, and the blessings it confers then need not be recounted here. Instead I shall confine myself to the time before and after its flowering. From the moment it appears above the surface, it enhances the green waters with its *lotus coins*, to use the elegant term. And even before the buds have formed, you can drink in their pure scent; they deserve the accolade *azure cups*. Then no sooner have the petals fallen than the seed-pods appear, while the leaves, withered though they may be, are still not without their value. Although these marvelous features are mere addenda to the lotus's main contribution, they are admirable nonetheless. It differs markedly from ordinary flowers, which are not particularly attractive before they bloom and seem hardly worth saving once they fade. The ancients said, "Tend a flower for a year and enjoy it for ten days." From that point of view no flower is worth the bother. Only with the lotus do you get a real bargain, which is why I have likened it to a beautiful woman.

I once made a humorous remark that people at the time told me was worth preserving, and I propose to repeat it here, gentle readers, to see if you agree: "Frivolous and lewd behavior must have something serious and proper about it if it is to be perpetuated." And there *are* cases in which serious and proper results do emerge from frivolous and lewd behavior. For example, if sexual intercourse was not considered serious and proper in the very beginning, why has it been handed down from ancient times as a permanent part of life? Because out of the frivolity and lewdness of sex come sons to perpetuate the ancestral shrine and continue our lineage. How can anyone deny that the frivolity of sex supports a serious endeavor and that its lewdness is at least not inconsistent with propriety? This is the point to which my talk of lotus blossoms has brought me. I hope the reader will forgive me for rambling on so.

I shall now tell a remarkable story, and because I started off talking about lotus-picking, I shall take that subject as my lead-in, to avoid the danger of picking the wrong tree and finding that the graft doesn't take.

During the Zhizheng period** of the Yuan dynasty, there lived in Jinhua county of Wuzhou prefecture a retired official named Zhan Bifeng. He rose to be governor of Xuzhou, by which time his two sons, born while he was still quite young, were already launched on their own careers, so he retired at the top of his profession and transferred his remaining ambitions to them, spending his days on wine and poetry in imitation of Tao Qian and Xie Lingyun. ***

(* The ten poems appear in Li Yu's collected works, *Independent Words* [*Yijia yan*] 5, in a somewhat different order.)

(** 1341 – 1368)

(*** The poet Tao Qian [365 – 427] and Xie Lingyun [383-443] celebrated the joys of private life in the country.)

(Hanan, 1992/1998：3-6)

可以看到,原文开篇一口气列出了 6 首诗,韩南译文一一译出,而且偶数行还押韵,尽管音节和节奏存在一些出入,但与前两阶段的李渔作品英译文相比,已属差强人意了。入话的处理也与原文贴近,基本全部译出,而且其中"花之君子""花之美人""荷钱""碧筒""弄花一年,看花十日"以及"移花接木"等颇有中国文学韵味的表述均照直译入英文,大大提高了译文的文学性。

(25)诗云:

　　　从来尤物最移人,况有清歌妙舞身;
　　　一曲霓裳千泪落,曾无半滴起娇羞。

又词云:

　　　好妓好歌喉,擅尽风流。惯将欢笑起人愁。尽说含情单为我,魂魄齐勾。

　　　舍命作缠头,不死不休。琼瑶琼玖竞相投。桃李全然无报答,尚羡娇羞。

　　这首诗与这首词,乃说世间做戏的妇人比寻常妓女另是一种娉婷,别是一般妖媚,使人见了最易消魂,老实的也要风流起来,悭吝的也会撒漫起来。这是甚么原故?只因他学戏的时节,把那些莺啼燕语之声、柳舞花翻之态操演熟了,所以走到人面前,不消作意,自有一种云行水流的光景。不但与良家女子立在一处,有轻清重浊之分;就与娼家姊妹分坐两旁,也有矫强自然之别。况且戏场上那一条毡单,又是件最作怪的东西,极会难为丑妇,帮衬佳人。丑陋的走上去,使他愈加丑陋起来;标致的走上去,使他分外标致起来。常有五、六分姿色的妇人,在台下看了,也不过如此;及至走上台去,做起戏来,竟像西子重生,太真复出,就是十分姿色的女子,也还比他不上。这种道理,一来是做戏的人,命里该吃这碗饭,有个二郎神呵护他,所以如此;二来也是平日驯养之功,不是勉强做作得出的。是便是了，天下最贱的人，是娼优隶卒四种，做女旦的，为娼不足，又且为优，是以一身兼二贱了。为甚么还把他做起小说来？只因第一种下贱之人，做出第一件可敬之事，又如粪土里面长出灵芝来，奇到极处，所以要表扬他。别回小说，都要在本事之前另说一桩小事，做个引子；独有这回不同，不须为主邀宾，只消借母形子，就从粪土之中，说到灵芝上去，也觉得文法一新。

却说浙江衢州府西安县，有个不大不小的乡村，地名叫做杨村坞。这块土上的人家，不论男子妇人，都以做戏为业。梨园子弟所在都有，不定出在这一处，独有女旦脚色，是这一方的土产。他那些体态声音，分外来得道地，一来是风水所致，二来是骨气使然。只因他父母原是做戏的人，当初交媾之际，少不得把戏台上的声音、毡单上的态度做作出来，然后下种，那些父精母血已先是戏料了；及至带在肚里，又终日做戏，古人原有胎教之说，他那莺啼燕语之声，柳舞花翻之态，从胞胎里面就教习起了；及至生将下来，所见所闻，除了做戏之外，并无别事，习久成性，自然不差，岂是半路出家的妇人所能仿佛其万一？所以他这一块地方，代代出几个驰名的女旦。……

（《谭楚玉戏里传情 刘藐姑曲终死节》，李渔，1991/8：251-253）

(25a) Poem：

*Beauty's power to stir the heart*
*Is heightened by her acting art.*
*Though her singing make a thousand cry,*
*No tear will come to Beauty's eye.*

Lyric：

*A pretty bawd with a singing voice—*
*Charms, she has them all.*
*Her constant smile will banish care,*
*Till all men think she favours them,*
*Their hearts in thrall.*

*They risk their lives to make her gifts,*
*Not stopping till they die.*
*They shower her with precious gems,*
*And when they get no sweets in turn,* *

*They think—she's shy.*

Both poem and lyric make the point that when it comes to charm, actresses are in a different class altogether from the ordinary run of prostitutes. Men lose their hearts to actresses, the strait-laced turning into romantics and the tight-fisted into big spenders. Why should this be? Because in training to become actresses, these women have practiced those warbling, dulcet tones and that delicate, willowy grace of theirs to perfection. There is no need for them to affect such things in company, for they come naturally. When actresses are placed beside girls of good family, their impurity outshines the latter's purity; when put beside prostitutes, their naturalness highlights the others' affectedness. In addition, that carpet on the stage is a most peculiar thing, for it hurts the ugly woman as it helps the beauty. When an ugly woman comes on stage, she appears even uglier, but when a beautiful woman does so, her beauty is enhanced. It is common for a woman of middling attractiveness off-stage to look like the reincarnation of Xishi or Yang Guifei** as soon as she sets foot on stage and begins her performance, at which point even a perfect beauty cannot compare with her. There are two reasons for this. Firstly, actors and actresses are predestined for their trade and have a god, Erlang, who watches over them. And secondly, the impression they make is the result of long training, not something that can be produced by a mere act of will.

However that may be, the four lowliest classes in society consist of prostitutes, entertainers, lictors and slaves. *** Thus actresses, as both prostitutes and entertainers, combine two of the four classes. Why, then, should an actress be made the subject of a story? Because when a person from the lowliest class of all performs the noblest deed of all, it is fully as remarkable as a magic mushroom growing out of a dunghill, and it deserve to be publicized.

Whereas other stories relate an anecdote as a prologue to the story proper, this one will follow a different course. It has no need to play the host ushering in the guest, for it will generate the child from the mother. To begin with the dunghill and go on from there to tell of the magic mushroom—that is something entirely new in literary composition.

Let me tell how in Xi'an county of Quzhou prefecture in Zhejiang there was a township of moderate size named Yang Village in which all of the inhabitants, men as well as women , took up acting as a career. Now, actors are produced in every part of the country, not just this one, but actresses were the specialty of this area, because the singing and acting here were remarkably authentic. If geomancy was one factor, genetic inheritance was certainly another. Because an actress's parents were actor and actress themselves, they brought into play during the sexual act, before the seed was sown, the very same voices and movements that they employed on stage. Thus the essential ingredients of an acting career were already present in the father's semen and the mother's blood. Moreover, during the mother's pregnancy, she would continue to act full time. The ancients held the theory that a child's education begins *in utero*;**** thus the mother's dulcet tones and willowy grace would have been instilled in the child before birth. And once she was born, everything she saw or heard had to do with the theatre. Custom eventually turned into instinct, and she proved a natural performer. How could anyone who took up acting at a later stage even begin to compare with her? Which explains why this locality produced several outstanding actresses in every generation.

(* The allusion is to the love song "Mugua" in the *Poetry Classic*: "She threw a tree-peach to me; / As requital I gave her a bright greenstone," etc. See Arthur Waley, trans. , *The Book of Songs* [New York: Grove Press, 1987], p. 31. )

(** Of the Zhou and Tang dynasties, respectively, they came to personify ideals of beauty. )

(*** Sons born to people in any of these occupations were excluded from the civil service examinations. )

(**** I. e. , *taijiao*, by which the embryo is held to be morally influenced by the mother's behaviour. )

(Hanan, 1990b: 161-163)

本例原文开篇诗词各有一首,韩译在传达原诗词内容和意境的同时,也尽力再现了其形式特征,其中诗的押韵采用了"aabb"韵脚,词的上下阕都是第

二、五行押韵。入话的处理与例(24)一样,内容忠实、完整,一些有文化渊源的专有名词(西子、太真、二郎神等)均采用了直译加注的办法,富于文学性的表述(如"莺啼燕语之声""柳舞花翻之态""为主邀宾""借母形子""粪土里面长出灵芝来""父精母血"等)也都是按字面直译。通过语篇层面保留开篇诗词和入话及微观层面对原文语言、修辞、专名等元素的直译,译文不仅展现了原作拟话本小说的完整面貌,而且读来给人精致、生动、自然的印象,原作的文学性得到了最大程度的保留,译文读者也得以在了解故事内容的同时欣赏到中国文学本身之美。

(26)诗云:

世间何物最堪仇,赌胜场中几粒骰。

能变素封为乞丐,惯教平地起戈矛。

输家既入迷魂阵,赢处还吞钓命钩。

安得人人陶士行,尽收博具付中流。

这首诗是见世人因赌博倾家者多,做来罪骰子的。骰子是无知之物,为甚么罪他? 不知这件东西虽是无知之物,却像个妖孽一般,你若不去惹他,他不过是几块枯骨,六面钻眼,极多不过三十六枚点数而已;你若被他一缠上了,这几块枯骨就是几条冤魂,六面钻眼就是六条铁索,三十六枚点数就是三十六个天罡,把人捆缚住了,要你死就死,要你活就活,任有拔山举鼎之力,不到乌江,他决不肯放你。如今世上的人迷而不悟,只要将好好的人家央他去送。起先要赢别人的钱,不想到输了自家的本;后来要翻自家的本,不想又输与别人的钱。输家失利,赢家也未尝得利,不知弄他何干?

(《受人欺无心落局　连鬼骗有故倾家》,李渔,1991/8:148-149)

(26a)Poem:

*The most accursed thing in th' world , I see ,*

*Is th' gambling dice that one can hardly flee.*

*By turning th' rich in no time to beggars ,*

*It does beat ploughshares soon into daggers.*

*The losers b'witched , a doorless maze's their fate.*

*The winners hooked , like foolish fish for bait.*

*If only all could be Tao Kan in th' past ,* [*]

*And th' evil device be banished at last* !

This poem is composed to condemn the dice used for gambling, in view that most gamblers have ended up ruining their families and losing their fortunes. But why denounce the dice? The reason is that, lifeless as it is, a dice is like a real demon: if you have no interest in it, it's no more than a skull-like cube, with spots on its six sides, at most thirty-six of them; but if you indulge in gambling, it'll become a horrible ghost, the six spotted sides being like six iron chains and the spots themselves the thirty-six fierce and powerful Heavenly Stars, ** and you'll be tied up to face your doom, just like Xiang Yu who met his on the bank of the Wujiang River, in spite of how strong and powerful he was. *** Many people today remain, nevertheless, obstinately fixed in the delusion, managing to bankrupt themselves through gambling. They intend to win other people's money, only to find their own totally lost; and then, eager to win it back, they lose more. While the losers do deserve their losses, the winners are scarcely beneficiaries thereof. Why, then, are they so enthusiastic about the game?

(* Tao Kan [259 – 334] was a famous general and senior official during the Eastern Jin dynasty [317 – 420], known for his filial piety, rectitude, diligence, and self-discipline. He was also Great-grandfather of the great poet Tao Yuanming [ca. 365 – 427])

(** It was a Taoist belief in ancient China that the handle of the Big Dipper consisted of thirty-six Heavenly Stars and seventy-two Earthly Stars, each representing a god responsible for expelling various evil spirits from the secular world. )

(*** Xiang Yu [232 BC – 202 BC] was one of the greatest military commanders in the peasant uprising that put an end to the Qin dynasty [221 BC – 206 BC], known as Xiang Yu the Conqueror. A warrior of herculean strength and unmatched courage, he was, nonetheless, finally defeated by his rival Liu Bang [256 BC – 195 BC], the founder of the succeeding dynasty, owing to his political and tactical mistakes. He committed suicide by the Wujiang River shortly after his last remaining troops were routed by his enemy. )

(Trans. Tang Yanfang, in Xia *et al.*, 2011: 41-42)

原文以一首七言律诗开篇,偶数行押韵,比较工整,唐译与原文一样,都是八行,每行10个音节,全诗押"aabbccdd"韵。入话方面,本例只取了原文的一部分内容,从中可以看到,译文比较完整,内容和形式上也比较贴近原文,其中涉及原文文化的"陶士行""三十六天罡""拔山举鼎""乌江"等表述,译文都作了注释,帮助读者了解原作的文化背景。

除了开篇诗词,李渔的小说中还有不少与作品情节相关的诗词歌赋、谚语对句等,主要起推动叙事、烘托气氛等作用,也是原作文学性的重要体现。但早期的英译文对这类内容基本不译,实在绕不过去的也多舍形趋义。例如:

(27)珍生听见,惊喜欲狂,连忙走下楼去,拾起来一看,却是一首七言绝句。其诗云:

"绿波摇漾最关情,何事虚无变有形?
非是避花偏就影,只愁花动动金铃。"

珍生见了,喜出望外,也和他一首,放在碧筒之上寄过去,道:

"借春虽爱影横斜,到底如看梦里花。
但得冰肌亲玉骨,莫将修短问韶华。"

玉娟看了此诗,知道他色胆如天,不顾生死,少不得还要过来,终有一场奇祸。又取一幅花笺,写了几行小字去禁止他,道:

"初到止于惊避,再来未卜存亡。吾翁不类若翁,我死同于汝死。戒之慎之!"

珍生见他回得决裂,不敢再为佻达之词,但写几句恳切话儿,以订婚姻之约。其字云:

"家范固严,杞忧也甚。既杜桑间之约,当从冰上之言。所虑吴越相衔,朱陈难合,尚俟徐觇动静,巧觅机缘。但求一字之贞,便矢终身之义。"

玉娟得此,不但放了愁肠,又且合他本念,就把婚姻之事一口应承,覆他几句道:

"既删郑卫,当续《周南》。愿深窈窕之求,勿惜参差之采。此身有属,之死靡他。倘背厥天,有如皎日。"

珍生览毕,欣慰异常。

(《合影楼》,李渔,1991/9:20-22)

(27a) As soon as he heard her, he ran down joyfully from the summer-house, and took up the roll; in which he found the verses, of which the purport was, "That the troubled face of the water was the image of her mind: that she had been greatly surprised by his coming over to that side; but that in running away from him with such haste, she had been prompted only by the fear of discovery and punishment." When Ching-seng had read this, he was delighted beyond measure, and speedily writing some verses in reply, placed them in the roll, and threw them across. In these he observed that "their present mode of communication was nothing more than gathering flowers in a dream; and that they must endeavor to make it more unfettered, as well as more intimate for the future." Having perused this, Yu-kiuen was immediately aware that he was determined to come over at all hazards, let what would happen, and that it must certainly end in some terrible catastrophe. She therefore wrote him back one or two lines, in which she said, "that his first adventure had ended in nothing worse than a severe fright on her part, but she could not tell what might be the consequence of another visit. That *her* father was not like *his*, but would certainly put them both to death: and that therefore he ought to be considerate and prudent." Chin-seng, finding that she gave him this determined answer, did not venture to repeat his former words, but wrote back a formal proposal of marriage, in which "he bewailed the unhappy circumstances which at present opposed their union; but advised that they should wait to see how things turned out, and seize some more favourable opportunity. He only stayed for one word in reply, to render inviolable their contract for life." Yu-kiuen was not only set at ease by this, but readily consented to his proposal, and answered him in a few lines, in which she expressed her willingness, and declared "that she considered herself as devoted to him alone, and that death only should absolve them from this vow, which was made in the face of heaven." Chin-seng, on the receipt of this answer, was greatly rejoiced, as well as consoled for the misery of separation.

(Davis，1822：67-70)

类似本例这样的诗赋在《十二楼》早期译入英语的篇目中不在少数。从德庇时的译文来看，无论诗歌还是书信，原文的形式特征基本上都被放弃了，内容也只传达了最基本的一些元素，原文所涉及的专名、典故等完全舍弃（连注释也没有一个），而且如前所述，德庇时采用了一种把间接人称置于直接引语之中的话语表述形式，读来不无怪异之感。对照一下茅国权的译文：

(27b) What ecstasy it was to hear his beloved's voice! Chen-sheng quickly ran down from the pavilion and took out of the water the flower petals which enclosed the following poem:

> *The rippling green waves are most suggestive of love.*
> *What assumes a form out of nothingness?*
> *'Tis not that I avoided the flower for the reflection;*
> *I worried about the movement of the flower which might shake the golden bell.*

Yü-chüan's poem explained that she had run away because she had been afraid of being exposed, and suggested that her affection for her beloved continued. Needless to say, Chen-sheng was exuberant when he read it, and wrote a poem in reply:

> *To be fond of spring, one loves the shadow in the sun;*
> *But it remains like viewing flowers in a dream.*
> *If I could only touch thy white skin and feel thy jade-like bones,*
> *It would matter not whether my life were long or short.*

Yü-chüan was deeply flattered by Chen-sheng's love for her, but his impulsive nature worried her. So she hastily wrote yet another poem, this one to forestall any more rash moves on his part:

> *When you came the first time, it ended in fear and shock.*
> *The result, if you come again, is hard to predict.*
> *My father is unlike your father;*
> *But my death would be like your death.*
> *Refrain! Be discreet.*

Realizing that Yü-chüan was a cautious and timid maiden, Chen-sheng dared not disobey her and wrote a brief note asking her to marry him:

> Your family rules are strict and the worries of the man of Ch'i are proportionately great.* If we stop the "Sang-chien" meetings,** then you must accept my proposal of marriage. You

worry about the states of Wu and Yüeh*** being so hostile, and the feud of the families of Chu and Ch'en,**** but let us just wait. As for now, give me one true word, and I will remain forever yours.

Her worries were considerably lightened by Chen-sheng's note, and Yü-chüan replied affirmatively: "As we have expunged the lewd songs of Cheng and Wei,***** we will continue with the Kuan-ch'ü odes.****** As for me, my body and soul belong to you until death." What more could one ask from a lovely maiden like Yü-chüan?

(Mao, 1975: 5-6)

(* "The man of Ch'i" was a man full of needless worries.)

(** A place noted for profligacy.)

(*** Two rival feudal states; in present day Kiangsu and Chekiang.)

(**** A village in Kiangsu. Residents were named either Chu or Ch'en.)

(***** Two feudal states. Cheng occupied the present K'ai-feng in Honan Province; Wei occupied what is now Eastern Honan and Southern Hopei. Many of their lewd songs were alleged to have been expunged by Confucius, but some are still extant in the *Book of Odes*.)

(****** Wedding songs.) (*op. cit.*: 133)

两相对照,可以看到茅国权译文对原文诗赋的重视程度明显比德庇时高,也尽力保留了原文的一些形式特征(包括诗歌形制、中古英语表述如 thy 等),因此文学性总体上高于德译本;但细究之下,茅译本与前引各例一样,将原诗的主要特征(音节、节奏、押韵等)基本舍弃了。此外,第一首诗后面添加了一小段原文没有的内容,作为诗歌内容的补充说明,这样做是否有画蛇添足之嫌,似不能简单下定论,但难免让人觉得译者对自己的诗歌译文并不是很有信心。因而与 1990 年代之后的译本比起来,茅译本的文学性就要稍逊一筹了:

(28)你道是件甚么东西? 有《西江月》一词为证:

非独公输炫巧,离娄画策相资。微光一隙仅如丝,能使瞳人生翅。

制体初无远近,全凭用法参差。休嫌独目把人嗤,眇者从来善视。

(《夏宜楼》,李渔,1991/9:82)

(28a) What do you suppose the object was? A lyric to the tune "Moon Over West River" describes it best：

> *It equals Lu Ban's dazzling sleight*
> *And adds to Lilou's range.* \*
> *Its infinitesimal thread of light*
> *Will let the eye take flight.*
>
> *When new，it has no near or far*
> *And needs to be set right.*
> *Don't mock；the single-eyed*
> *See with the keenest sight.*

(\* Zhou dynasty figures. Lu Ban was the great artificer；Lilou had superhuman eyesight. The terms *microscope* and *telescope* in parentheses are the translator's additions.）

(Hanan，1992/1998：16)

拟话本小说中每遇情节扣人心弦之处或新奇之物，往往会以诗词加以描摹。本例即是《夏宜楼》中描写"千里镜"（即望远镜）的一首词，原文在这首词前后还有 2000 字左右的内容，介绍包括千里镜在内的"诸镜之式"以及男主瞿吉人获得千里镜的来龙去脉，但被茅国权译本悉数删去了。韩南译本完整保留了这部分内容，对本例这首状物词的翻译也很注意诗歌形式特征的保留——原词各行大部分由 6 字组成，译文也大部分还以 6 个音节；用韵方面，原词采用衣支韵，上下阕都在二三四行押韵，译文采用的是/aɪt/韵，上阕押一二四行，下阕押二四行，虽有出入，但总体上再现了原词的形式特征。再如：

(29) 只见五条玉笋捏着一管霜毫，正在那边誊写。其诗云：
　　"重门深锁觉春迟，盼得花开蝶便知。
　　不使花魂沾蝶影，何来蝶梦到花枝？"

(《夏宜楼》，李渔，1991/9：87)

(29a) He found Hsien-hsien busy writing a poem which he could read through the telescope. It went as follows：

> *The doors are locked；spring has arrived late.*
> *I hope for the flowers to bloom and the butterflies to come.*

*Not allowing the flower to be tainted by the butterfly,*

*How is it possible for the butterfly to dream about the flower?*

(Mao, 1975: 32)

(29b) He saw her slender fingers grip the brush and copy out a poem:

*Deep within the double gates, spring comes slow.*

*She longs for the buds to open and the butterflies to know.*

*If the flower isn't touched by a butterfly's shade,*

*Why do butterfly dreams to the flowery branches go?*

(Hanan, 1992/1998: 24-25)

(30) 想到此处,就手舞足蹈起来,如飞转到书房,拈起兔毫,一挥而就。其诗云:

"止因蝶欠花前债,引得花生蝶后思。

好向东风酬凤愿,免教花蝶两参差!"

(《夏宜楼》,李渔,1991/9:88)

(30a) Realizing that the poem was unfinished, Ch'ü took out a piece of paper and wrote these lines to complete it:

*The butterfly owes the flower a previous debt,*

*Causing the flower to think of the butterfly.*

*Let them complete their life of bliss.*

*Don't ever let them go astray.*

(Mao, 1975: 32)

(30b) At this thought he jumped for joy and rushed down to his study, where he seized his brush and dashed off a conclusion to the poem:

*All because the butterfly owes the flower a debt,*

*The flower has come to think the butterfly is slow.*

*Let me thank the east wind for our predestined bond—*

*For now no chance remains we won't together grow.*

(Hanan, 1992/1998: 26)

这两例之所以放在一起来讨论,是因为例(29)是《夏宜楼》女主娴娴写的一首七绝,而例(30)则是男主瞿吉人通过千里镜看到该诗之后写给女主的应和诗,因此两首诗在内容、意境和形式上是有关联的。对比两种译文可以看到,(29a)和(30a)秉承茅译本一贯的自由体诗歌翻译风格,两首诗的译文既不工整也不押韵;而(29b)和(30b)尽管音节和节奏并不是十分整齐和严格,但二者均押/əʊ/韵(原文两首诗也均押衣支韵),如果把原文的两首诗合在一起作为一首七言律诗来看就会发现,韩译的押韵位置与原诗是完全相同的。两种译文的文学性,由诗词的翻译立见高下。

(31)立定主意,走到京中,拜过二詹之后,即便央人议婚。果然不出所料,只以"榜后定议"为词。吉人就去奋志青云,到了场屋之中,竭尽生平之力。真个是文章有用,天地无私,挂出榜来,巍然中在二中。此番再去说亲,料想是满口应承,万无一失的了。不想他还有回覆,说:"这一榜之上同乡未娶者共有三人,都在求亲之列。因有家严在堂,不敢擅定去取。已曾把三位的姓字都写在家报之中,请命家严,待他自己枚卜。"

吉人听了这句话,又从新害怕起来,说:"这三个之中,万一卜着了别个,却怎么处? 我在家中还好与小姐商议,设些计谋,以图万一之幸。如今隔在两处,如何照应得来?"就不等选馆,竟自告假还乡。《西厢记》上有两句曲子,正合着他的事情,求看官代唱一遍:

"只为着翠眉红粉一佳人,误了他玉堂金马三学士。"

丢了翰林不做,赶回家去求亲,不过是为情所使;这头亲事,自然该上手了。不想到了家中,又合着古语二句:

莫道君行早,更有早行人。

原来那两名新贵,都在未曾挂榜之先,就束装归里。因他临行之际曾央人转达二詹,说:"此番下第就罢,万一侥幸,望在宅报之中代为缓频,求订朱陈之好。"所以吉人未到,他已先在家中,个个都央人死订。

(《夏宜楼》,李渔,1991/9:91-92)

(31a)Soon Ch'ü went to the capital. As expected, Hsien-hsien's two brothers said that they would not consider any proposal of marriage until after the examination. Days later, Ch'ü passed the examination, but his score was not good enough to be among the senior scholars. He thought that the two brothers might accept his marriage proposal anyway, but they told him that there were two others from their district who had also passed the examination and asked to marry Hsien-hsien. Consequently, the brothers had sent the names of all three to their father who would decide which suitor would marry their sister.

Ch'ü hurried home. When he got there he learned that the other two had been trying to persuade Mr. Chan, each pointing out his capabilities and his future prospects.

(Mao, 1975: 34)

(31b) Arriving in the capital, he paid his respects to the Zhan brothers and then sent in his proposal of marriage. As he feared, they replied that they were postponing their decision until the results were out.

Jiren set his heart on gaining the highest honors and poured all of his efforts into the examination. As the proverb says, When a man's writing is good enough, the gods play fair. Jiren ranked high on the list of successful candidates, in the second honor group. Renewing his proposal, he assumed it would now be eagerly accepted; in fact he thought there was no longer any chance of failure. But the brothers replied: "There are three unmarried local candidates on the list, all of whom have proposed marriage. Father is at home, and we can't make the decision by ourselves, so we've sent him the three names and suggested he decide by lot."

Once again Jiren grew alarmed. What if he draws someone else's name? he asked himself. It's lucky I worked out a plan with his daughter for such an event! But if we're separated, we won't be able to coordinate our efforts. Without waiting for the election to the Hanlin Academy, he petitioned for leave to return home. There are two lines from *The West Chamber* that fit his situation perfectly, lines that I offer to the reader to sing in his place:

> For a painted eyebrow and a powdered cheek,
> He gave up the Hall of Jade and the Golden Horse. *

Driven by love, he sacrificed his chance of an Academy appointment and rushed home to urge his suit, confident of success. But as the proverb says, No matter how early you set off, someone is sure to have left before you. The other suitors had packed and set off for home before the results were even posted, leaving his message for their friends to pass on to the Zhan brothers: "If we fail, no matter, but if we are lucky enough to succeed, we ask that in your letter home you commend us to your father and seek a marriage for one of us with this daughter." Both men were already there when Jiren arrived.

(* Written about 1300, *The West Chamber* is the most famous Chinese play. The lines, slightly misquoted, come from part 3, scene 1, where they are sung by the maid Hongniang. Jade Hall and Golden Horse refer to a hall of fame for eminent statesmen.)

(Hanan, 1992/1998: 29-31)

本例原文共有三处对句:熟语"文章有用,天地无私"、出自《西厢记》的"只为着翠眉红粉一佳人,误了他玉堂金马三学士"、古谚"莫道君行早,更有早行人",茅译本无一译出,此外,细节删省甚多、直接引语变成间接引语等,这些做法使得译文的文学性比原文逊色不少。对比之下,韩译本的处理明显更贴近原文,不仅三处对句完整译出,而且对《西厢记》唱词还作了注解(本章第四节另述),最大程度地保留和传达了原作的文学性。

(32)那些当道见他说得近情,料想没有他意,就一面写荐书,一面兑银子,当下交付与他。书中的话不过首叙寒温,次议衷曲,把卖笔之事倒做了余文。随他买也得,不买也得,那里知道,醉翁之意原不在酒,单要看他束贴上面该用甚么称呼,书启之中当叙甚么情节,知道这番委曲,就可以另写荐书。至于图书笔迹,都可以摹仿得来,不是甚么难事。

(《归正楼》,李渔,1991/9:110)

(32a) Impressed by Pei's "sincerity," the officials gave him cash for the brushes and wrote letters of recommendation, in which there were personal greetings to officials in Nanking and elsewhere. In reading the letters, Pei's major interest was to learn how officials addressed one another. For once he learnt how this was done, he re-wrote all the letters, it being easy to imitate the penmanship and to duplicate official seals. In the re-written letters, Pei created still another identity for himself, one which made him a man of importance.

(Mao, 1975: 43)

(32b) So convincingly did he speak that the officials assumed he had no ulterior motive and wrote out their letters of recommendation and also paid up the money they owed. The letters opened with the usual formalities and went on to talk of personal matters, the brushes being mentioned only in a postscript.

But whether the recipients actually bought any brushes was a matter of supreme indifference to Bei, for "the Old Tippler's mind was on something other than the wine."* All he wanted was to know how to address his hosts on visiting cards and what to mention in letters; armed with that information, he could write his own letters of introduction. As for the writing, that was no problem; he could imitate anybody's hand.

(* A common expression drawn from Ouyang Xiu's "The Old Tippler's Pavilion.")

(Hanan, 1992/1998: 58)

"醉翁之意不在酒"一语出自北宋著名文学家欧阳修《醉翁亭记》名句"醉翁之意不在酒,在乎山水之间也",原指亭中饮酒、意不在酒而在美景,后用于表示本意在他或别有用心,已是脍炙人口的成语,其出处《醉翁亭记》亦被尊为中国古代散文名篇。从两种译本来看,茅译在"译述"策略的主导下,目光只在故事主要情节,对原文细节多有删改,也在不经意间放弃了成语的翻译,损害了原作的文学性;而韩译不仅按字面译出了成语,而且为其加上引号并作注解释了引文出处。韩译这样做的最大好处,是使读者在作品内容的阅读间隙稍作停顿时,能注意到原作的形式之美并欣赏其作为文学作品的魅力——须知一部只有情节的作品,带给读者的一般只有紧张、新奇、兴奋等一过性的阅读体验,而文学作品(尤其是经典文学)能给世人留下恒久印象的,却往往是其中那些看似与内容并无直接关联的元素(如形式、修辞、副文本等),即文学性。

(33)又替他取个法号,叫做"净莲",因他由青楼出家,有出污泥而不染之意,故此把莲花相比。

(《归正楼》,李渔,1991/9:117)

(33a)... and changed Sister Su's name to "Pure Lotus," comparing her *hui-t'ou* to the purity of the lotus flower.

(Mao, 1975: 47)

(33b)He also chose a name in religion for her, Pure Lotus, likening her to a lotus blossom because she had joined the order from a brothel unsullied by all the filth around her.

(Hanan, 1992/1998: 67)

"出污泥而不染"语出北宋思想家周敦颐《爱莲说》"予独爱莲之出淤泥而不染，濯清涟而不妖"一句，多用于赞扬在污浊环境中保持高尚品行的人，并无太多典故或深奥内涵，采取韩译本那样的字面直译即可传达原意。茅译将其等同于佛教的"回头"，原因可能是《归正楼》入话部分曾就"回头"作过阐发："到了水穷山尽之处，恶又恶不去，善又善不来，才知道绿水误人，黄泉招客，悔不曾遇得正人君子，做个中流砥柱，早早激我回头也。//《四书》上有两句云：'虽有恶人，斋戒沐浴，亦可以事上帝。''斋戒沐浴'四个字，就是说的回头。"（李渔，1991/9：100）茅国权译本在正文该处将"回头"音译为"*hui-t'ou*"（Mao，1975：37），并提供了一个尾注解释："Literally, the expression means to turn the head. Used as a metaphor, it means to change one's mode of life, as is stated later in the story."（*op. cit.*：134）。但本例原文并未提"回头"二字，译成"*hui-t'ou*"既不准确也失之牵强，而且英语读者碰到这种音译的专名往往一头雾水，只能回过头去找原先的注释来帮助理解（但茅译采用的又是尾注），这样一来二去，接受效果就会大打折扣，阻碍读者欣赏原文的文学之美。

另外，李渔小说的文学性还表现在作为"说书人"的叙事者与作为"听书人"的读者之间常见的"现场对话"式交流。这种"面对面"的话语沟通，是话本、拟话本小说的典型特征之一，在篇首入话、正文以及回末等处均可见到，既是语篇衔接的需要，也是营造现场气氛、增加叙事生动性的有效手段。试举二例：

（34）汝修睡了半个时辰，忽然惊醒，还在药气未尽之时，但觉得身上有些痛楚，却不知在那一处。睁开眼来把沙太监相了一相，倒说："晚生贪杯太过，放肆得紧，得罪公公了。"沙太监道："看你这光景，身子有些困乏，不若请到书房安息了罢。"汝修道："正要如此。"

沙太监就唤侍从之人扶他进去。汝修才上牙床，倒了就睡，总是药气未尽的缘故。正不知这个长觉睡到几时才醒，醒后可觉无聊？看官们看到此时，可能勾硬了心肠，不替小店官疼痛否？

（《萃雅楼》，李渔，1991/9：143）

（34a）Ch'üan woke up in pain, but still drugged was unable to locate its source. He asked permission to retire. "You look exhausted," Eunuch Sha replied with mock consideration. "Go to my study and rest a while."

（Mao，1975：60）

(34b)After sleeping for an hour, Quan awoke with a start, but although he felt some pain, he was still under the influence of the drug and did not know where the pain came from. With a conscious effort he focused his gaze on Eunuch Sha.

"I'm afraid I drank too much and took liberties that offended Your Grace."

"You look a little tired," said Eunuch Sha. "You'd better go into the library and rest."

"Just what I feel like doing."

Eunuch Sha told his staff to help Quan into the library where, because of the lingering effects of the drug, he fell asleep as soon as his head touched the pillow.

We do not know when he will awaken from his long sleep and what despair he will feel. Having read this far, gentle readers, are you able to steel your hearts and feel no pain on behalf of the little shopkeeper?

(Hanan, 1992/1998：104-105)

原文描述萃雅楼的小店官权汝修被沙太监药酒迷倒、惨遭阉割后的情形，划线部分即是回末说书人与读者之间的模拟对话，采用设问的方式，形象、生动而且现场感十足，读来令人怜悯之情油然而生。由两种译本可见，茅译仍然遵循"译述"策略，简化内容、调整风格，因而译文已无原作那样的话本小说特征；韩译则不仅在内容上忠实于原文，也原汁原味地再现了原文的话本小说风格，使原作的文学性得以成功保留和传达。

(35)……算计定了，就随着朋友去查访佳人的姓字。访了几日，并无音耗。不想在无心之际遇着一个轿夫，是那日抬他回去的，方才说出姓名。原来不是别个，就是裴七郎未娶之先与他许过婚议的。一个是韦家小姐，一个是侍妾能红，都还不曾许嫁。

<u>说话的，你以前叙事都叙得入情，独有这句说话讲脱节了。既是梅香、小姐，那日湖边相遇，众人都有眼睛，就该识出来了，为何彼时不觉，都说是一班游女，两位佳人，直到此时方才查访得出？</u>

<u>看官有所不知。</u>那一日湖边遇雨，都在张皇急遽之时，论不得尊卑上下，总是并肩而行；况且两双玉手同执了一把雨盖，你靠着我，我挨着你，竟像一朵并头莲，辨不出谁花谁叶。所以众人看了，竟像同行姊妹

一般。……

(《拂云楼》,李渔,1991/9:159-160)

(35a)He and his friends went to work immediately trying to identify the two beauties. After several unsuccessful efforts, they met a sedan-chair coolie who said they were a Miss Wei and her maid Neng Hung.

(Mao,1975:67)

(35b)He joined his friends in their efforts to identify the women. Days of searching brought no result, until he happened to hire the same bearer who had taken the women home. They proved to be none other than the girl to whom Septimus had once been betrothed, Miss Wei, and her maid Nenghong, neither of whom was engaged.

*Storyteller, your previous narrative was plausible enough, but not this last point. If the women were maid and mistress, the people at the lake that day would surely have been able to discern the fact. Why did they leap to the conclusion that the girls were sisters on an outing and not discover their mistake until now?*

Gentle reader, there is a point here that you have failed to grasp. When the storm first struck the lake, panic reigned, and all thought of social status was cast aside as the two women raced along together. Moreover they were holding the same umbrella and their bodies touched; they were a double lotus blossom and you couldn't tell flower from leaf. That was why people assumed they were sisters.

(* A passage of simulated address to the narrator. )

(Hanan,1992/1998:130)

本例原文划线部分模拟的是听书人对说书人的诘问以及后者的回应。对比两种译文可知,(35a)用了两句话将原文如此丰富的内容一笔带过,细节根本无法顾及,遑论原作的话本小说风格了;(35b)则不仅全文照译,而且还将整段诘问文字以斜体标出并加注解释,有效地再现了原作的文学性。

本节以大量例证说明,李渔小说的开篇诗词和入话、正文中的诗词歌赋和熟语对句以及拟话本小说的"说书体"风格等在译入英语的过程中,经历了"完全不译→部分删改→全面再现"的演变过程,说明原作的文学性从最初全然不入译者"法眼"到中期开始引起注意再到当代获得充分尊重,经历了一个从无到有、从低到高的发展过程。简言之,翻译策略的由俗而雅,说明英语世界越来越把李渔的作品当成文学作品来翻译和接受了。这既是时代进步使然,也是李渔在英语世界译介多年之后逐步获得认同的结果。

## 第三节　文化翻译策略:由 TCC 而 SCC

语言是文化的载体,二者密不可分,因而在语言之间的翻译转换过程中,文化几乎是一个绕不过去的环节,尤其是在与文化联系十分紧密的文学作品的翻译中更是如此。文化包罗万象,涉及一个民族的历史地理、人物典故、政治经济、制度习俗,等等。文化的翻译过程则是一个十分复杂的博弈过程:译出文化的影响力、两种文化的力量对比、译入文化对外来文化的接受态度等,都是可能影响文化翻译效果的重要因素;问题的复杂性还在于,这些因素都是因时、因势、因人而异的变量。因此,两种文化之间的翻译如果从历史的角度来看,我们常常会发现不同时代的译者对原文文化的处理存在较大的历时差异,其策略往往在译出文化和译入文化之间游移,有时偏向译入文化,有时则又偏向译出文化。

在李渔英译史上,不同时代的文化翻译策略也各不一样,但总体趋势是从译入文化为中心(target-culture centeredness,TCC)向译出文化为中心(source-culture centeredness,SCC)演变,演变的规律与中西方文化力量的消长以及文化交流程度的变化大致对应。在 1980 年代以前,由于中英文化交流不多,规模也不大,英语世界对中国文化的整体了解较少,接受意愿也不强烈,因此对李渔作品的英译在文化策略上是以译入文化为中心的,较少顾及译出文化的形象和要素,即使偶尔采用注释,也大都止于基本达意,并不以引导读者进入译出语文化语境为目的。试举几例:

(36)观察无可奈何,只得负荆上门,预先请过了罪,然后把儿子不愿的话,直告路公。

(《合影楼》,李渔,1991/9:24)

(36a)Poor Too had no help for it, but was obliged to go as a self-condemned* criminal to Loo-kung. He first entreated pardon for his mistake, and then informed him of his son's determination.

(*Literally, "carrying on his head the instrument of his punishment.")

(Davis,1822:77-78)

(36b)With much reluctance, Mr. T'u went to see Mr. Lu again, apologized and explained why the engagement had to be broken.

(Mao，1975：8)

原文"负荆请罪"语出战国时期赵国廉颇和蔺相如"将相和"的典故。德庇时译文"to go as a self-condemned criminal"并不准确，所提供的注释也只是大略解释了一下该表述的字面意义，完全未涉及原作的典故出处。这样的译文无助于读者了解原作的文化，注释也成为摆设，没能发挥应有的文化阐释作用；茅国权译本则只用了一个"apologized"，不仅忽视了原文的典故，连字面意思都未纳入考虑，从文化翻译角度来说还不如德庇时译本所做的努力。

(37)锦云道："小妹今日之来，不是问安，实来报喜。《合影编》的诗稿，已做了一部传奇，月下就要团圆快了。只是正旦之外又添了一脚小旦，你却不要多心。"

(《合影楼》，李渔，1991/9：30)

(37a)Kin-yun answered，"The purpose of my coming to-day is not so much to inquire after your health，as to communicate to you some joyful intelligence. The poem concerning the rencontre of the shadows has already been converted into a romance，and it is right that we bring it to a finale. In addition to the principal female performer* in the Drama，an inferior one has been added；—but you need not be anxious about the result."

(* For the names of the usual characters in the Chinese dramas, see Morrison's Dictionary, [according to the sounds,] under the word *He*,"a theatrical performance.")

(Davis，1822：97-98)

(37b)...Chin-yün said，"The reason I came today is to bring you good news. I have heard about the 'Ho-ying Volume,' and that you are about to be united with your beloved. But you two will have to put up with a minor character like me. I hope you won't mind."

(Mao，1975：11)

"正旦"和"小旦"均为中国戏曲的女性角色名称，在本例中用作比喻，分别指故事的女主角和女配角。德庇时将其意译为"principal female performer"和"inferior one"，舍弃了原文的名称及其背后的戏曲文化联想，注释也只是让读者去找一部语焉不详的文献作进一步了解，注释本身既未介绍中国戏曲角色的信息，也不解释"正旦""小旦"的文化内涵和修辞意义，基本上没有起到注释的作用。茅国权译本大体差不多,只译了一个"小旦"的意思(minor character),而且没有提供注释,相比之下在文化翻译方面未做任何努力。需要指出的是,由于李渔对戏曲的熟稔,他的小说中经常利用戏曲的角色名称来作比喻,从而使叙述更加形象生动;而像德译本和茅译本这样轻易放弃文化翻译的做法,不仅剥夺了读者了解原作文化元素的权利,同时也是对译出文化的不尊重。相比之下,1990年代的韩南译本对原作戏曲角色名称的翻译策略更值得肯定。试举《拂云楼》一例:

(38)裴七郎自从端阳之日见妻子在众人面前露出许多丑态,令自己无处藏身,刻刻羞惭欲死。众人都说:"这样丑妇,在家里坐坐罢了,为甚么也来游湖,弄出这般笑话!总是男子不是,不肯替妇人藏拙,以致如此。可惜不知姓名,若还知道姓名,倒有几出戏文好做。妇人是'丑',少不得男子是'净',这两个花面自然是拆不开的。况且有两位佳人做了旦脚,没有东施、嫫姆,显不出西子、王嫱,借重这位功臣点缀点缀也好。"内中有几个道:"有了正旦、小旦,少不得要用正生、小生,拼得费些心机去查访姓字,兼问他所许之人。我们肯做戏文,不愁他的丈夫不来润笔。这桩有兴的事是落得做的。"又有一个道:"若要查访,连花面的名字也要查访出来,好等流芳者流芳,贻臭者贻臭。"

七郎闻了此言,不但羞惭,而且惊怕,惟恐两笔水粉要送上脸来。所以百般掩饰,不但不露羞容,倒反随了众人也说他丈夫不是。被众人笑骂,不足为奇,连自己也笑骂自己!及至回到家中,思想起来,终日痛恨,对了封氏虽然不好说得,却怀了一片异心,时时默祷神明,但愿他早生早化。

(《拂云楼》,李渔,1991/9:158)

(38a)The unpleasant experience at the West Lake made Ch'i-lang feel that he had been humiliated beyond words. He remembered what some of the youths said about his wife, "A woman as ugly as she should stay home. Why does she go out? It's her husband's fault for not stopping her. If we knew who he was, we would write a play about the ugly wife and her indulgent husband." Ch'i-lang could not forget the events of that day, the memories of which became a terrible burden for him to bear. He secretly wished that his wife would have an early death, and thus spare him more embarrassment.

(Mao, 1975:66)

(38b) When Septimus saw his wife exposing her numerous failings in public at the Dragon Boat Festival and leaving him with no place to hide, he was mortally ashamed. Among his friends, however, the consensus was as follows: "A woman as ugly as that ought to stay home. Why incur all this ridicule by visiting the lake? It's really her husband's fault for not helping her hide her shortcomings. What a pity we don't know his name! If we knew it, we'd have the makings of a play here. She'd be the clown and he the villain, of course; the two painted-face roles are all set. In addition we'd have the two beauties for the heroine roles, and since you need someone monstrously ugly to highlight a great beauty, we'd use this tower of strength to round the thing out."

"Now that we have our heroines, all we need are the heroes," said someone. "Let's try our best to find out their fiancés' names as well as their own. If we show an interest in writing the script, the fiancés will undoubtedly pay us for our work. Such fascinating material— it's practically asking to be written up!"

"If you're going to find out their names," put in another, "you ought to find out who the painted faces are, too, so that you can give discredit—as well as credit—where it's due."

At this point Septimus felt more than ashamed, he felt afraid, afraid of those two streaks of white paint that would be daubed on his villain's face,* and he tried by every means he knew to conceal his connection. He not only hid his own embarrassment, he even joined the others in condemning the woman's husband. Dissatisfied with their ridicule, he in effect ridiculed himself.

Reflecting on the incident after his return, he was consumed with loathing. Although he could not express the feeling to his wife, he began to feel estranged from her and prayed constantly for her early demise.

(* The role-types on the Chinese stage are distinguished by facial makeup as well as by costume.)

(Hanan, 1992/1998: 127-129)

如上，原文的"丑""净""花面""旦脚""正旦""小旦""正生""小生"等戏曲角色名称,在茅译本的"译述"中消失得无影无踪;在韩译本中的译名"clown" "villain""painted-face roles""heroine roles""heroines""heroes"尽管不是十分精确,却也算得上是基本到位了,而且原文"惟恐两笔水粉要送上脸来"的比方,在韩译本中也加注作了解释,可以看出已经是竭尽全力在传达原文的文化内涵。但文学翻译毕竟不同于学术翻译,不能像文世昌译笠翁曲话那样对角色名称完全采用音译的处理办法,否则以一篇音译满天飞的小说译文,其可读性会大大降低;原文的"东施""嫫姆""西子""王嫱"等专名未作音译加注处理,译者可能正是考虑到这些人名虽有文化典故,但与上下文情节并无直接关联,重要性也不如上下文的戏曲角色名称,而只是几个孤立的比喻,因此不必一一作文化阐释。

(39)那些未娶的少年,一发踊跃不过,未曾折桂,先有了月里嫦娥,纵不能勾大富贵,且先落个小登科。

(《夺锦楼》,李渔,1991/9:45-46)

(39a)The young men who were unmarried were extremely rejoiced at having a chance of obtaining a handsome bride, together with their literary honours.

(Davis,1822:138)

(39b)... to the bachelors, it would be their chance to win a real prize, a flesh and blood beauty, a much more gratifying and practical prize than the award of a degree.

(Mao,1975:17-18)

本例原文"折桂"和"月里嫦娥"均有一定的文化典故或意蕴。前者系"蟾宫折桂"(或月中折桂)的简称,关于典故出处有多种说法(包括《晋书·郤诜传》、"吴刚伐桂"神话传说等),后指科举及第;后者源于中国传统神话,一般喻指人间难觅的美女。从译文来看,两位译者均采用了意译的方法,以解释代替原文的比喻和典故:对比德译本的"literary honours""a handsome bride"和茅译本的"the award of a degree""a flesh and blood beauty"可见,二者本质上并无高下之分,因为在放弃原文文化的传达这一点上,两位译者选择了相同的立场,所不同者仅在解释的方式而已。实际上西方文化里也有用月桂树来象征最高荣誉的神话传说以及比喻夺冠的说法,两种译文却不约而同地放弃了建立文化对等的尝试,只能说明译出语的文化元素并未引起译者的注意,或至少不是译者优先考虑的因素。

(40)要晓得水流不返,还有沧海可归;人恶不悛,只怕没有桃源可避。到了水穷山尽之处,恶又恶不去,善又善不来,才知道绿水误人,黄泉招客,悔不曾遇得正人君子,做个中流砥柱,早早激我回头也。

(《归正楼》,李渔,1991/9:100)

(40a)You must bear in mind that although the river never turns back, it still has the sea to end up in, but I very much doubt that there is any Peach Blossom Spring there for the wicked man who fails to repent. When he has exhausted the hills and waters, when his sins can get no worse nor his virtues any better, he will at last understand how deceptive the green waters are, and, when the Yellow Springs beckon, will regret that he has never met an upright man to stand like the Grindstone Pillars amidst the flood and inspire him to turn back.

(Hanan, 1992/1998: 42)

本例原文属正文开始前的入话,因此茅国权译本未译。由韩南译本可见,原文涉及典故或其他文化背景的表述,包括"桃源""黄泉""中流砥柱"等,都采用专有名词形式作了直译处理,且未提供注解或文内解释。处理成专有名词,可使英语读者意识到原文表述作为地理范畴可能具备的文化性,从而引导读者进入原作的文化语境;而不加注解则可"迫使"读者通过上下文或寻求文外支持(如互联网)来解读原文的文化内涵。本例译者不加注解,很可能是因为这几个语汇并无过于专深的文化典故,读者通过上下文一般都能找到文化解码的线索;即使需要诉诸文外支持,利用互联网的一般资源(例如维基百科等)也都能很快检索到相关解释。

(41)金、刘二人听到这句说话,甚是惊骇,说:"叫我准备茶汤,这是本等。为甚么说到陪坐之人也叫他收拾起来? 他又不是跟官的门子,献曲的小唱,不过因官府上楼没人陪话,叫他点点货物,说说价钱。谁知习以成风,竟要看觑他起来! 照他方才的话,不是看货,分明是看人了。想是那些仕宦在老严面前极口形容,所以引他上门,要做'借花献佛'之事。此老不比别个,最是敢作敢为,他若看得中意,不是'隔靴搔痒'、'夹被摩痒'就可以了得事的,毕竟要认真舞弄。难道我们两个家醋不吃,连野醋也不吃不成!"私自商议了一会,又把汝修唤到面前,叫他自定主意。汝修道:"这有何难! 待我预先走了出去,等他进门,只说不在就是了。做官的人只好逢场作戏,在同僚面前逞逞高兴罢了,难道好认真做事,来追拿访缉我不成?"金、刘二人道:"也说得是。"就把他藏过一边,准备茶汤伺候。

(《萃雅楼》,李渔,1991/9:134)

(41a)Being simple and honest, Chin and Liu could not understand why it was specified that the person serving the refreshments must be neat and handsome, unless His Excellency was more interested in a handsome young man than in the lovely things they had to sell. After a heated and panicky discussion, they decided that Ch'üan should absent himself during Yen's visit.

(Mao, 1975:55)

(41b)Jin and Liu were alarmed. "Seeing to the tea-that's our job. But why this talk about the person who keeps him company? Why should *he* have to spruce himself up? He's not some official's pet doorman or singing-boy! When officials go upstairs and have no one else to talk to, we send him up to list what we have in stock and discuss prices. By now it's evidently become *de rigueur*, and they *expect* to see him! From what they say in their message, it's obviously him, not our goods, that they're interested in. I imagine those officials gave old man Yan a glowing account to tempt him here-worshipping Buddha with borrowed flowers, as it were. But this old man is different from others; he's bold and ruthless, and if he likes what he sees, he won't be content to scratch the itch through his boot, he'll do his damndest to fool around with the lad. We may not be jealous of each other, but we'll certainly be jealous of an outsider!"

After talking it over privately, they called Quan in and asked him to decide.

"I don't see any problem," he said. "Let me leave before he gets here, then just tell him I've gone out. Officials get carried away and boast about their pleasures in front of their colleagues, that's all. He'll hardly go so far as to arrest me!"

"You're right," said Jin and Liu, hiding him away and getting on with their preparations.

(Hanan, 1992/1998:91-92)

此处原文"借花献佛""隔靴搔痒""吃醋"等成语和俗语均以具象之物引出内

涵丰富的文化比喻。茅译本不仅完全忽略了这些喻体，而且是把整个情节用两句话匆匆带过，原文的对话、细节等内容和形式几无保留。韩南译本相比之下则要负责得多，前两个成语中的比喻均按字面完全译出，后一个俗语的翻译，由于"醋"的文化联想在译出文化和译入文化中差别太大，韩译作了意译处理，"吃家醋"译为"be jealous of each other"，"吃野醋"为"be jealous of an outsider"，原文文化形象虽难再现，内涵则应该说是比较准确地抓住了。值得一提的是，"醋"的翻译，在韩南的译本中并非一成不变，而是根据具体情境有所区别：

(42)所以不等开口，就预先说破他，正颜厉色之中，原带了三分醋意。如今知道那番屈膝全是为着自己，就不觉改酸为甜，酿醋成蜜，要与他亲热起来，好商量做事。

(《拂云楼》，李渔，1991/9：167)

(42a)When Dame Yü arranged to meet her in private, Neng Hung thought that the old woman wanted to use her as a go-between, a role she deeply resented. But when she learned that Ch'i-lang had actually kowtowed on her account, and not for her mistress, it made her happy. She would have liked to accept his love, though not without some reservation,...

(Mao, 1975：71)

(42b)That was why she had exposed the scheme before the other woman could open her mouth. But her stern expression had also concealed a good deal of envy, and now, on learning that Septimus had bent the knee for *her*, the envy turned to sweetness and the vinegar to honey, and she was eager to get on good terms with Mother Yu and discuss what steps to take next.

(Hanan, 1992/1998：140)

本例两种译文长度相当，但对比之下可以看出，茅译在文化元素的处理上明显是以译入语为中心的，原文的"醋意""酸""甜""醋""蜜"等表述完全不译，译文准确性方面也不如韩译，例如把"要与他亲热起来"理解为能红接受裴七郎的爱(实际上是指能红改变对俞阿妈的态度)等。韩译此处对"醋"的处理分成三个步骤进行：首先是将"醋意"译为"envy"，舍弃了醋的字面表述；到"改酸为甜"时继续将"酸"译为"envy"，但"甜"按字面译出；最后将"酿醋成蜜"中的"醋"和"蜜"均按字面直译——通过这三个循序渐进的步骤，读者不知不觉就被带入了原文的文化语境，"醋"的文化内涵也在不经意之间得到了理解和接受。

(43)东楼见说他不转，只得权时打发。到第四日上，就把一应货物取到面前，又从头细阅一遍，拣最好的留下几件，不中意的尽数发还。除货价之外，又封十二两银子送他，做遮羞钱。汝修不好辞得，暂放袖中，到出门之际就送与他的家人，以见"耻食周粟"之意。回到店中，见了金、刘二友，满面羞惭，只想要去寻死。金、刘再三劝慰，才得瓦全。

(《萃雅楼》，李渔，1991/9:139-140)

(43a)Failing to achieve success immediately, Yen temporarily left Ch'üan alone. On the fourth day, Yen gave instructions that all the goods he had bought at "Ts'ui-ya lou" should be returned except for a few things that he really liked. He gave Ch'üan the money for these items and an additional twelve ounces of silver for the "services rendered" during the three nights. Unable to refuse the money, Ch'üan "pocketed" it in his sleeves but gave it to Yen's servants before leaving for "Ts'ui-ya lou." Mortified by what he had had to go through, Ch'üan was going to commit suicide, but his friends persuaded him not to.

(Mao, 1975: 57-58)

(43b)... Unable to persuade him, Yan had to send him away-at least for the present. On the fourth day he had the goods brought before him and looked them over once more, then chose a few of the best pieces for himself and sent the rest back. In addition to the cost of the pieces that he kept, he paid Quan twelve taels in personal compensation.

Quan could scarcely refuse. He tucked the money in his sleeve and, as he went out the gate, he handed it to Yan's servants. He was ashamed to betray his friends by accepting it. *

On meeting Jin and Liu, he was indeed overcome with shame, and his only thought was to kill himself. His partners had to plead with him again and again before he reluctantly agreed to go on living....

(* The text alludes to the Shang dynasty loyalists Bo Yi and Shu Qi.)

(Hanan, 1992/1998: 99)

原文"耻食周粟"涉及历史人物及掌故，完全译出并不容易，也无必要，因而茅译本选择舍弃不译。韩译本在正文里对此亦未过多解释，只以脚注形式提示读者原文用典，而注释又只简单提了一下两位历史人物伯夷、叔齐的名字和身份，刻意将读者引入原作的文化语境对此作深入了解。译者用心何其良苦！

(44) 韦小姐道："父母相逼，也要他肯从，同是一样天伦，难道他的父母就该遵依，我的父母就该违拗不成？四德三从之礼，原为女子而设，不曾说及男人，如今做男子的倒要在家从父，难道叫我做妇人的反要未嫁从夫不成？一发说得好笑！"

(《拂云楼》，李渔，1991/9:163)

(44a) "If Ch'i-lang was right to obey his parents, shouldn't I also obey mine? The principle of 'three obediences and four virtues'* was designed for women. Ch'i-lang obeyed his parents but expects me to disobey mine. Have you ever heard of anything more ridiculous?"

(Mao，1975:69)

(* A woman should obey her father before marriage, her husband after marriage and her eldest son after the death of her husband. The four virtues are right behavior, proper speech, proper demeanor and proper employment.) (*op. cit.*: 134)

(44b) "His parents could never have forced him into it if he hadn't been willing. The same moral laws apply to both of us, so why should I disobey *my* parents while he obeys his? The Four Virtues and Three Obediences were instituted for women,* not men, but in this case it's the man who is apparently supposed to obey his father before marriage. Am I as a woman expected to obey my *husband* before I marry! That's even more ridiculous!"

(* The virtues were in respect of conduct, speech, demeanor, and accomplishment. The obediences were to one's father at home, to one's husband in marriage, and to one's son in widowhood.)

(Hanan，1992/1998:134-135)

原文的"四德三从"通称"三从四德"，其中"三从"语出《仪礼·丧服·子夏传》，要求妇人"未嫁从父，既嫁从夫，夫死从子"；"四德"语出《周礼·天官·九嫔》，指女子应具备"妇德、妇言、妇容、妇功"等四种品行。本例中两位译者均很重视这一表述的文化阐释,除了字面传译之外,都通过注释对原文的文化内涵作了介绍,这是值得肯定的。但对照之下还是可以看出一些细微的差别,例如对成语本身的翻译处理方式,茅译用的是引号,韩译则是实词首字母大写;用法上,茅译把三从四德作为一个整体,在前面加了一个范畴词"principle",后面的谓语动词采用的是第三人称单数,韩译则是将其作为复数概念来使用;"四德"与"三从"的顺序,茅译与原文相反,韩译则完全一致,等等。以上这些差别本身并无优劣之分,只是反映了两种译本各自不同的文化翻译立场:前者采用引号并添加范畴词的做法,削弱了原文成语的文化属性,使读者不必进入原作的文化语境就能大致领会原文的交际意义,因而属于典型的以译入文化为导向的翻译策略;后者采用实词首字母大写的译法,本质上是以专有名词的呈现方式给译入语读者造成一种"压力",迫使其进入原作文化语境来理解原文的内容和形式、实现"知其然知其所以然"的文化翻译目标,因而是以译出文化为导向的翻译策略。历史地看,后者代表了李渔作品英译策略的发展趋势和方向。

以上例证显示,在李渔英译史上,文化翻译策略的总体演变规律是由译入文化为中心向译出文化为中心发展,其中前两个阶段的文化翻译多以降低文化难度、迁就读者理解能力等做法为主,具有明显的译入文化导向;进入第三个阶段,特别是 1990 年代以后,文化翻译策略转向以译出文化为中心,译者不再无限照顾译入语读者的文化理解力,而是有意无意地通过逐字对译等方式把一些文化语汇直接抛给读者,引导乃至"逼迫"后者进入译出语的文化语境来理解其内涵。文化翻译策略的这一演变,既与全球化大背景下翻译的文化转向有重要的渊源,同时也反映了中西文化实力及影响力对比的历史性变化,值得当代典籍翻译实践者和研究者的注意和重视。

## 第四节　副文本策略:由泛而专

"副文本"(paratext)是法国当代文学批评家热拉尔·热奈特(Gérard Genette,1930—2018)在 1980 年代提出的一个概念。热奈特在其《副文本:文学解读的门槛》(*Paratexts*:*Thresholds of Interpretation*,1997)①一书里

---

① 该书法文原版由巴黎 Editions du Seuil 出版社于 1987 年出版,原书名是《门槛》(*Seuils*)。本书参考的是剑桥大学出版社 1997 年出版的英译本,由 Jane E. Lewin 翻译,约翰·霍普金斯大学的 Richard Macksey 撰写前言。

开宗明义地指出,文学作品很少有只以文本示人而全然不具作者姓名、书名、序言、插图等语言或非语言伴生物的(Genette,1997:1);他认为这些围绕在文本周围并使文本得到延伸的元素,其目的是保证文本可以存世(presence in the world),亦即"能以书本形式获得世人'接受'及消费"(ibid.)。因此,副文本就是"使文本成其为书本并以此种形式提供给读者和更多受众"的东西(ibid.);它超越了边界或封闭的界限,成为一道门槛、一个博尔赫斯所谓出入房屋的"门厅"(vestibule)、一个文本内外之间"界限不明的区域"(undefined zone),或者是勒热纳(Phililppe Lejeune)所谓"现实中支配读者阅读文本全过程的印刷文本的边缘地带"(op. cit.:1-2)——总而言之,副文本就是文本(text)与非文本(off-text)之间的一个过渡(transition)和"交易"(transaction,原文斜体)区,它以提升文本接受效果和阅读相关性为己任(op. cit.:2)。热奈特将副文本分为文内副文本(peritext)和文外副文本(epitext)两大类,前者指书本装帧范围内除正文之外的语言和非语言要素,包括封面、作者姓名、书名及章节名、排版、印刷、致谢、题词、序跋、注释等(op. cit.:16-343),后者则指与文本相关但不在书本装帧范围内的其他文本,包括公开出版和发表的出版商、经纪人及作者自己的各类声明、评述,以及不公开发行的通信、日记、口述内容等(op. cit.:344-403)。两种副文本相辅相成,运用得当可以形成证据链,从侧面为分析和解读文本提供有用信息和有力证据,因而是对传统文学文本解读的有效补充。一般来说,文内副文本可随作品传世,相对易得,也比较直观;文外副文本则因与作品文本不在一起、出版和发表不同步,或因作品流传年代久远、相关评论和记录等材料散佚,完整获取的难度相对较大,而且与文本的关联往往并不那么直接,有时甚至需要做一些分析、甄别和推理才能用来解读文本。

　　副文本同样适用于翻译研究,尤其是用于侧面分析译本的翻译策略、传播定位以及接受情形等信息,可以有效补充译文分析本身的不足,使译本读者和翻译研究者对译本的认识更客观、全面,避免片面和偏颇的评价。在李渔作品的英译史上,除了以上所述语言、文学、文化等方面的文本翻译策略,不同时期的副文本也表现出鲜明的时代特征,为我们认识和理解当时的文化力量对比及交流状况、文本翻译策略、译本定位与接受等提供了虽非直接但却非常重要的线索。其中许多文外副文本(包括书评、相关研究文章等)本书前两章已有介绍,文内副文本主要表现在三方面:一是书名(以及回目名)和作者姓名的呈现方式;二是译序;三是注释。由于李渔的作品中只有《十二楼》在三个时期都有译本(即第一阶段的德庇时译本和道格斯译本、第二阶段的茅国权译本和第三阶段的韩南译本),因此以下我们仍然选取这部小说,就三个时期英译本的以上三种文内副文本作一历时对比分析。

首先看书名和作者姓名的呈现方式。如前所述,德庇时译本的书名是《中国小说》,道格斯译本是《中国故事》,二者展示方式如图 4-1 和图 4-2 所示:

## CHINESE NOVELS,

TRANSLATED FROM THE ORIGINALS;

TO WHICH ARE ADDED

### PROVERBS AND MORAL MAXIMS,

COLLECTED FROM

THEIR CLASSICAL BOOKS AND OTHER SOURCES.

THE WHOLE PREFACED BY

### OBSERVATIONS

ON THE

LANGUAGE AND LITERATURE OF CHINA.

BY JOHN FRANCIS DAVIS, F.R.S.

LONDON:
JOHN MURRAY, ALBEMARLE STREET.
1822.

图 4-1 德庇时译本扉页

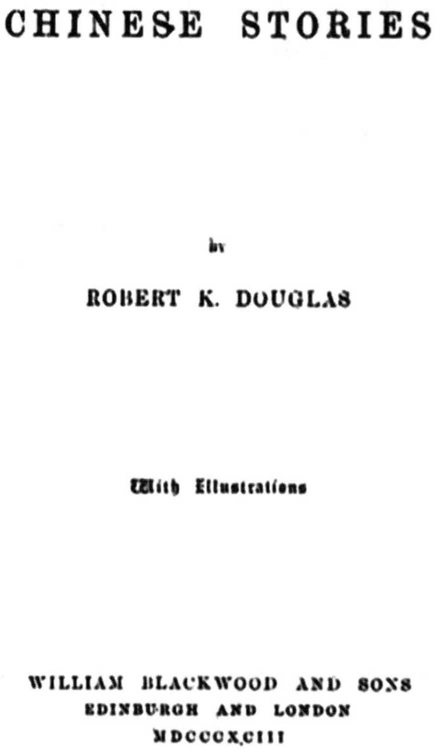

# CHINESE STORIES

by

ROBERT K. DOUGLAS

With Illustrations

WILLIAM BLACKWOOD AND SONS
EDINBURGH AND LONDON
MDCCCXCIII

图 4-2　道格斯译本扉页

　　可以看到,两种译本对原作的书名和作者姓名均付之阙如。不仅如此,二者对所选篇目的名称以及每篇小说里的回目名,处理方式要么是意译,要么就是略去。例如德本《合影楼》《夺锦楼》和《三与楼》分别译为"The Shadow in the Water"(Davis,1822:51)、"The Twin Sisters"(*op. cit.*:107)和"The Three Dedicated Chambers"(*op. cit.*:153)①;道本所选《夺锦楼》译名是"The Twins"(Douglas,1893:82)。回目名称上,《合影楼》和《三与楼》各分三回,每回都有一个由对句组成的题目(如"堕巧计爱女嫁媒人 凑奇缘媒人赔爱女""造园亭未成先卖 图产业欲取姑予"等);《夺锦楼》只有一回,但也有题目。而德本只保留了"Section I.""Sections

———————————

　　① 《三与楼》1822 年收入《中国小说》时,德庇时对标题和内容作了较大修改,参见本书第二章相关介绍。

II. "这样的序号,标题内容悉数删去不译。类似德本和道本这样的做法,在 19 世纪英语国家可能是比较普遍的现象,但这种对原作书名和作者姓名 的漠视或随意处置,暴露了译者对异域文化和文本的傲慢。通过图 4-3 和 图 4-4 对照一下茅国权译本的做法:

**Li Yü's TWELVE TOWERS**

Retold by Nathan Mao

**Twelve Towers**

Short Stories by Li Yü
Retold by Nathan Mao

The Chinese University of Hong Kong

中文大學出版社
**The Chinese University Press**

图 4-3　茅国权译本扉页
（1975 年版）

图 4-4　茅国权译本扉页
（1979 年修订版）

可以看到,茅译本初版是把作者李渔的名字放在书名里的,虽然有所区 分("Li Yü"首字母大写,"TWELVE TOWERS"所有字母都大写),却终不 免混为一谈之嫌。修订版的书名只取"十二楼",作者姓名则以副标题形式 呈现。这一变化一方面反映了译者对原作书名的重视和对作者的尊重,另 一方面还有可能说明,译者在译本初版时对作者在英语读者中的认知度并 无把握,把作者姓名放在书名里可起宣传推广的作用,而到修订版推出时这 一点看起来已经不成问题了,故而从书名中将其删去。篇目名称的翻译,茅 译本采取的是"意译＋音译"的处理方式,如"The Jackpot (*Tuo-chin lou*)" (《夺锦楼》)、"The Magic Mirror (*Hsia-yi lou*)"(《夏宜楼》)等;但在回目名 称的翻译上,茅译本则又与 19 世纪译者的做法一样,只用"I""II""III"标 序,不译标题内容。因此似乎可以说,茅译本虽然在语言、文学、文化等方 面偏向译入语,但就副文本策略而言,至少在书名和作者名的处理上对原 作和作者还是足够尊重的,只是在回目名称的翻译上还保留着 19 世纪的做法,其中可能既有翻译思想和操作难度等原因,也有过渡阶段承前启后的时代原因。

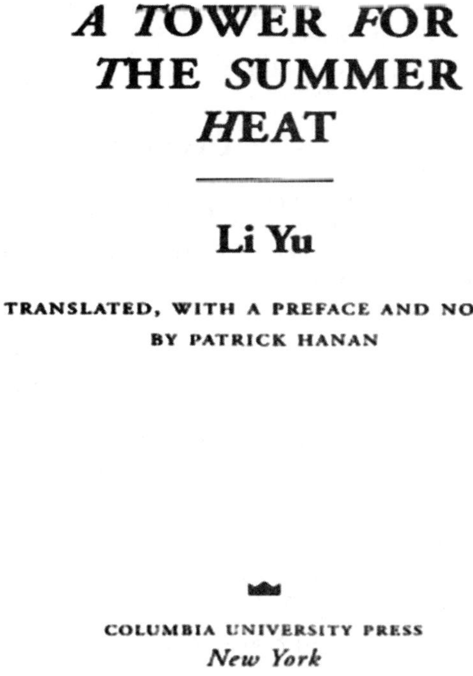

## A TOWER FOR THE SUMMER HEAT

## Li Yu

TRANSLATED, WITH A PREFACE AND NOTES,
BY PATRICK HANAN

COLUMBIA UNIVERSITY PRESS
New York

图 4-5 韩南译本扉页

由图 4-5 可见,韩南译本的扉页中,书名、作者、译者按字体和字号各得其所,主次分明,是当代翻译界的标准做法。书名的翻译,由于韩译并非全译本,故用所选篇目之一《夏宜楼》的篇名而未取"十二楼"之名,也是合理的选择。篇名的翻译则是采取字面对译的处理方式,如"Return-to-Right Hall"(《归正楼》)、"House of Gathered Refinements"(《萃雅楼》)等;此外,对每篇小说里的回目标题,韩译本也是尽量全部译出,表 4-1 显示了《夏宜楼》的三个回目标题。

表 4-1　韩南《夏宜楼》回目标题英译文

| 第一回<br>浴荷池女伴肆顽皮<br>慕花容仙郎驰远目<br>（李渔，1991/9：73） | **CHAPTER 1**<br>*In which girls play pranks while bathing in the lotus pond,*<br>*And an immortal's eyes roam far in admiring their charms.*<br>（Hanan,1992/1998：3） |
|---|---|
| 第二回<br>冒神仙才郎不测<br>断诗句造物留情<br>（同上：81） | **CHAPTER 2**<br>*A man of talent springs a surprise by impersonating an immortal;*<br>*The Creator of Things does a favor by interrupting a poem.*<br>（op. cit. ：15） |
| 第三回<br>赚奇缘新诗半首<br>圆妙慌密疏一篇<br>（同上：89） | **CHAPTER 3**<br>*Half a poem fabricates a predestined bond;*<br>*A secret message gives rise to a brilliant lie.*<br>（op. cit. ：26） |

像韩南《十二楼》英译本这样的做法在当代并非孤例，事实上，1990 年代以来的李渔小说英译也大都是遵循名从主人原则、对书名（包括章节名）和作者名体现了充分尊重的，例如韩南组织翻译的《无声戏》（Hanan,1990b）、夏建新等人翻译的《李渔小说选》（Xia *et al.*,2011）等，莫不如此。

其次是译序。如前所述，德庇时《中国小说》总共 250 页，正文包括《合影楼》《夺锦楼》《三与楼》等三篇小说的译文以及 126 条中国格言谚语，除此以外还有一篇题为《中国语言文学观察》的导言，然而这篇长达 50 页的导言主要篇幅都用于中国语言文学的宏观介绍，真正与所选三篇小说有关的内容只有三段（Davis,1822：10-12）。道格斯《中国故事》导言（Douglas,1893：xi-xxxvii）也是关于中国小说的总论，几乎不涉及具体的故事内容。可见 19 世纪李渔作品英译本的译者序，其着眼点更多是泛泛的介绍，与具体篇目内容的关联度并不高，自然也谈不上专深的研究。相比较而言，1960 年代以后的译者序在题材和内容的相关性和深度方面做得更好。例如茅国权译本的初版就分序言（Mao,1975：ix-x）和导论（*op. cit.*：xi-xv）两部分，前者回顾了过去两个世纪以来中国文学在西方的译介概况及其不足，引出李渔及其作品在中国文学史上受到的冷遇和偏见，并介绍了《十二楼》译述的原因、读者对象、文本处理说明及鸣谢等；后者主要介绍李渔生平及其作品。到 1979 年修订再版时，更是在原序之后加了一则再版序，为其"译述"法正名和辩护（Mao, 1979: xiii-xv），同时根据茅国权、柳存仁合著的《李渔》（1977）一书第一、四章的内容对导论内容也作了大幅改动和添加（op. cit.: xvii-xxxvi），重点介绍李渔其人、其生活艺术等，修订版的导论在专业性和深度两方面均远胜初版导论。1990年代韩南译本的译者序，并不做中国语言文学等宏大背景的铺陈，而是开门见山地指出李渔短篇小说在题材、语言、体制等方面的特征，并就篇目选择、原作成书时间和版本信息等作了简明扼要的介绍（Hanan, 1992/1998: vii-xi）。与茅国权译本相比，韩南译本的译者序更加简洁，但其专业性和深度毫不逊色，尤其是与所选文本的相关性更是远胜于茅译，例如，为了说明李渔小说的语言风格，韩南甚至在译序里直接引用《生我楼》中的原话："谁想造物之巧，百倍于人，竟像有心串合起来等人好做戏文小说的一般，把两对夫妻合了又分，分了又合，不知费他多少心思！这桩事情也可谓奇到极处、巧到至处了，……"（Who would ever have expected the Creator's ingenuity to be a hundred times greater than man's? It is as if he had deliberately combined these events so that they could be turned into a play or a story-uniting the two couples and then separating them, separating and then uniting them, at a prodigious cost in mental effort. This plot rates as novel and ingenious to an extraordinary degree!）（op. cit.: viii; 原文见李渔, 1991/9: 267）。对比之下，茅译本修订版的导论中也有一些引用，但引用的大多不是所选文本的内容，而是取自李渔的《笠翁一家言文集》《笠翁一家言诗词集》及《闲情偶寄》等著作，与所翻译的文本并无直接关联。由上可见，在李渔作品英译史上，译序的总体发展规律是由浮泛走向专深，译序内容与翻译文本之间的关联度也由最初的几乎不相关演变至后来的联系日益紧密。这些变化既反映了中英之间文化交流的历史发展脉络，也提示了当代英语读者对深度译介中国文学的需求和兴趣，值得典籍翻译者思考和探索。

　　最后我们重点探讨一下《十二楼》英译本注释的历时变化。① 按照热奈特的定义，注释是"与文本中大致确定的一部分内容有关联（或相反或相成）、长度不一（短至一词亦可）的陈述"（"a statement of variable length [one word is enough] connected to a more or less definite segment of text and either placed opposite or keyed to this segment". Genette, 1997: 319）。热奈

---

　　① 这部分研究的主要内容已公开发表。参见唐艳芳. 李渔《十二楼》英译注释历时对比研究. 燕山大学学报, 2018(5): 34-42.

特明确指出注释属于副文本的范畴,其区别于序跋等其他副文本的最明显特征就是只针对部分文本,因而内容上总是表现出局部性和褊狭性(*op. cit.*:319-320)。对于注释的分类,热奈特虽然提到了译者的注释,将其归入"真代注"(authentic allographic notes)之列(*op. cit.*:322),但他的关注点主要在原创作品的注释问题,分类也主要是按注释主体身份(如著者、代注者、注释对象等)和注释时间先后(如原注、后注、延注等)划分注释功能的(*op. cit.*:322-343)。然而,对于翻译注释来说,这样的分类并无实质意义,因为译本注释本质上是一种由第三方(译者、点校人、出版商等)完成的"代注",它主要负责向译入语的当下读者提供有助于理解原文文本内容的副文本信息,并不试图介入或影响读者对原作及原作者的评价或接受过程。

翻译界关于注释的分类一直存在着不同的标准和方法。例如有学者就按性质将注释分为知识性(包括解释性、指示性、对比性)注释和研究性(包括发现性和质疑性)注释(周领顺、强卉,2016:106)。但笔者认为,翻译注释与原文文本之间的联系主要是通过注释内容这条纽带实现的,因此按内容来分类似乎更具可操作性、更便于分析。根据笔者对《十二楼》德庇时译本、茅国权译本和韩南译本的完整调查,三个译本的注释总数共有 190 个,其中德译本 28 个、茅译本 69 个、韩译本 93 个;从全部注释的内容来看,大致可归为 7 类,其中有些包含两种以上内容的复合型注释,则按其主要内容归类。为方便辨识和讨论,以下各例采用前文部分带注释译例的做法,将英译文分成两部分:第一部分是与原文对应的正文,注释处用"*"号标出,第二部分注释内容另起一行,用括号列出;正文与注释在相同页码范围内的只在注释末尾标注文献信息,不在相同页码的则分别标注。该 7 类注释如下:

(A)语言类注释:解释原文语言文字现象或字面意思的注释。例如:

(45)观察无可奈何,只得负荆上门,……

(《合影楼》,李渔,1991/9:24)

(45a)Poor Too had no help for it, but was obliged to go as a self-condemned* criminal to Loo-kung.

(* Literally, "carrying on his head the instrument of his punishment.")

(Davis,1822:77-78)

(46)"斋戒沐浴"四个字,就是说的回头。

(《归正楼》,李渔,1991/9:100)

(46a)Controlling the thoughts, fasting and praying mean to *hui-t'ou*.*

(Mao,1975:37)

(*Literally, the expression means to turn the head. Used as a metaphor, it means to change one's mode of life, as is stated later in the story.) (*op. cit.*: 134)

(B)文学类注释:提供文学背景知识或文学创作手法等信息的注释。例如:

(47)只为着翠眉红粉一佳人,误了他玉堂金马三学士。

（《夏宜楼》,李渔,1991/9:92）

(47a)For a painted eyebrow and a powdered cheek, / He gave up the Hall of Jade and the Golden Horse. *

(*Written about 1300, *The West Chamber* is the most famous Chinese play. The lines, slightly misquoted, come from part 3, scene 1, where they are sung by the maid Hongniang. Jade Hall and Golden Horse refer to a hall of fame for eminent statesmen.)

（Hanan, 1992/1998:30）

(C)文化类注释:提供原文典故、历史、地理、习俗等信息的注释。例如:

(48)"……如今虽列衣冠,不久就要逃儒归墨,所以不敢再误佳人,以重生前的罪孽。"

（《夺锦楼》,李渔,1991/9:48）

(48a)He should never consent to ruining the life of still another girl, and he was seriously thinking of living a life of self-denial as recommended by Micius. *

（Mao, 1975:19）

(*Micius is the Latinized name of Mo-tzu (4th – 5th centuries B.C.). His doctrines were attacked by Mencius.) (*op. cit.*: 133)

(D)翻译类注释:解释原文内容删减、增补、调整等情况的注释。例如:

(49)"贵连襟心性执拗,不便强之以情,只好欺之以理。小弟中年无子,他时常劝我立嗣,我如今只说立了一人,要聘他女儿为媳,他念相与之情,自然应许。等他许定之后,我又说小女尚未定人,要招令郎为婿,屈他做个四门亲家,以终凤昔之好。他就要断绝你,也却不得我的情面,许出了口,料想不好再许别人。待我选了吉日,只说一面娶亲,一面赘婿,把二女一男并在一处,使他各畅怀抱,岂不是桩美事?"

（《合影楼》,李渔,1991/9:28）

(49a)"Your relative, Mr. Kuan, is the stubbornest of men. As you know, I have no son, and Mr. Kuan has often advised me to adopt one. I plan to tell him that I have adopted one and wish to have his daughter as my new son's wife. Most likely he will accept the proposal. After he agrees, I will tell him that my daughter will marry your son on the same day and that the wedding will take place in my house."*

(Mao, 1975: 11)

(* The last part of the story describes how everything was carefully explained to Kuan. Since the details are anticlimactic, they have been briefly summarized. ) (*op. cit.*: 133)

(E)文献类注释:提示引文出处或延伸阅读文献等信息的注释。例如:

(50)这首新诗要劝世上的人个个自求上达,不可安于下流。

(《归正楼》,李渔,1991/9:99)

(50a)This newly written poem urges each and every one of us to aspire to higher things, not content ourselves with what lies below us. *

(* Cf. D. C. Lau trans. , *The Analects*, p. 128: "The gentleman gets through to what is above; the small man gets through to what is down below. ")

(Hanan, 1992/1998: 42)

(F)知识类注释:介绍译出语社会生活等相关知识的注释。例如:

(51)那里知道这位姑娘并无歹意,要做个瞒人的喜鹊,飞入耳朵来报信的。

(《合影楼》,李渔,1991/9:30)

(51a)She was not aware that Kin-yun, far from having any bad intentions, wished to imitate the bird* which is the messenger of glad tidings, and fly to her ear with the secret intelligence.

(* *Hy-tsiŏ*, a poetical name for the swallow. )

(Davis, 1822: 95-96)

(G)其他补充类注释:解释原作词句内涵,或难以归入前6类的注释。例如:

(52)男儿膝下有黄金,一屈岂堪再屈!

(《拂云楼》,李渔,1991/9:179)

(52a)Since there's gold at a man's knee,* how can I kneel again?

(* I. e. , a man's kneeling is a precious gift that is not to be casually bestowed. )

(Hanan，1992/1998：159)

统计显示，上述 7 类注释在三个英译本中的数量和占比情况存在明显差别，详见表 4-2。

表 4-2 《十二楼》英译本注释类型与数量占比一览

| 注释类型 | 注释数量及占比 | | |
| --- | --- | --- | --- |
| | 德庇时译本 | 茅国权译本 | 韩南译本 |
| 语　言　类 | 2(7.14%) | 14(20.29%) | 8(8.60%) |
| 文　学　类 | 1(3.57%) | 0(0.00%) | 7(7.53%) |
| 文　化　类 | 2(7.14%) | 26(37.68%) | 46(49.46%) |
| 翻　译　类 | 4(14.29%) | 5(7.25%) | 1(1.08%) |
| 文　献　类 | 1(3.57%) | 0(0.00%) | 14(15.05%) |
| 知　识　类 | 14(50.00%) | 20(28.98%) | 9(9.68%) |
| 其他补充类 | 4(14.29%) | 4(5.80%) | 8(8.60%) |
| 合　　计 | 28 | 69 | 93 |

表中各译本的注释数可用图 4-6 这样的柱状图直观呈现。

图 4-6 《十二楼》英译本各类注释数量对比

但因各译本篇目数不等,这种简单的数量呈现容易给人错觉,很难反映每个译本注释策略的真实面貌。例如,德本的知识类注释和茅本的语言类注释数均为 14 个,但前者是基于 3 篇小说、注释总数 28 个的局部样本,后者则是基于 12 篇小说、注释总数为 69 个的完整样本,因此这两个 14 的数值不具可比性。又如,三个译本的知识类注释单从数值看似乎是茅本最多、德本和韩本依次递减,但实际上如果把占比因素纳入考量就能看到图 4-7 那样明显的递减效果,更能反映真实的情况:

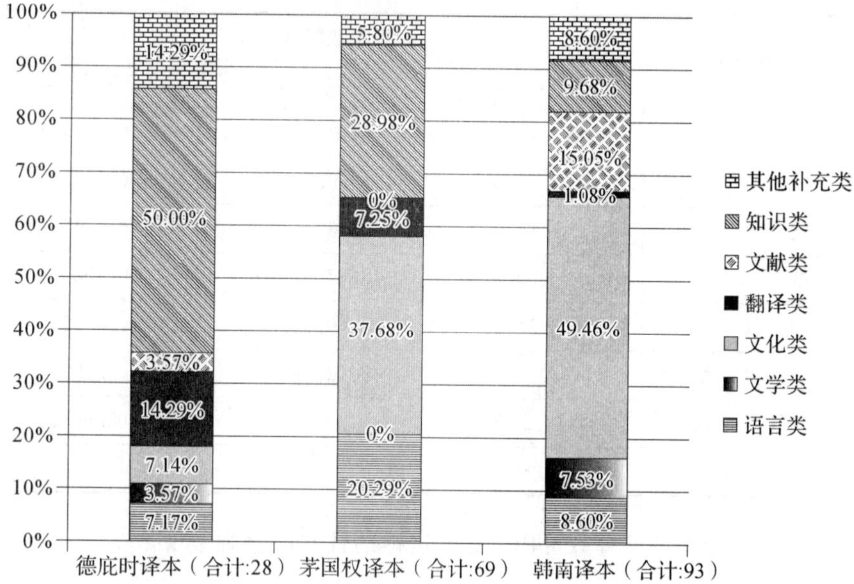

图 4-7 《十二楼》英译本各类注释占比情况对照

由以上统计图表可以看到:

1. 从德本到茅本再到韩本,知识类和翻译类注释呈递减趋势(50.00%→28.98%→9.68%;14.29%→7.25%→1.08%),文化类注释呈递增趋势(7.14%→37.68%→49.46%)。

2. 其余几类注释中,茅本语言类注释占比(20.29%)明显高于德本(7.14%)和韩本(8.60%),成为后两者之间的"驼峰";文学类和文献类注释数则均为 0,明显低于后两者,补充类注释的占比也略低一些,成了后两者之间的"马鞍"。

我们先分析一下各类注释中增减幅度较大的类型。从最早的德本到最晚的韩本,减幅明显的是知识类注释(50.00%→9.68%)和翻译类注释(14.29%→1.08%),增幅明显的则是文化类注释(7.14%→49.46%)和文献类注释(3.57%→15.05%)。这些数据反映了 19 世纪初至 20 世纪末不同历史时期的译者对原作不同方面内容重视程度的显著变化,具体一点说,就是关于原作社会生活方面的一般介绍和翻译行为本身的解释越来越少,针对原文典故、史地、习俗等文化现象以及学术性的深度阅读和探究越来越多。以知识类注释为例,我们从德本随取几例:

(53)这两个孩子又能各肖其母,在襁褓的时节,还是同居,辨不出谁珍谁玉。

(《合影楼》,李渔,1991/9:16)

(53a)While they still rode about on the backs of their nurses,* (which was previous to the separation of the families,) it was not easy to discover which was the pearl, and which the gem.

(* The Chinese mode of carrying children. )

(Davis,1822:56-57)

(54)若把别位官儿,定要拘牵成格,判与所许之人,这两条性命就要在他笔底勾消了!

(《夺锦楼》,李渔,1991/9:44)

(54a)Had you gone to another officer, he would have adhered to the usual track, and awarded them to one or other of the suitors; and thus the happiness of these two young women would have been destroyed by a single stroke of his pencil.*

(* The Chinese write with a hair pencil. )

(Davis,1822:132-133)

(55)玉川思想做封君,只得要奉承儿子,不知不觉就变起常性来,回覆他道:……

(《三与楼》,李渔,1991/9:54)

(55a)As the father had an object* in humouring his son, he deviated on this occasion from his usual maxims. He replied,...

(* When a man in China attains to high literary rank, certain honours are conferred on his *father*. A Hong merchant at Canton, whose son was a member of the Imperial College, had the privilege of erecting certain poles or masts in his grounds, indicative of the favour of the emperor. )

(Davis,1822:158)

(56)他有这个见解列在胸中,所以好兴土木之工,终年为之而不倦。

(《三与楼》,李渔,1991/9:55)

(56a) Having these ideas in his breast,* he went on with his work, and laboured at it in an indefatigable manner.

(* The Chinese suppose that the abdomen is the seat of ideas.)

(Davis, 1822:162)

(57)继武唤他上船,取文契一看,原来是他丈夫的名字,要连人带产投靠进来为仆的。

(《三与楼》,李渔,1991/9:63)

(57a) Ke-woo told her to come into the boat,* and taking the document from her, looked at it. It turned out to be a deed, or bond, in the name of her husband, who desired, with his family and effects, to come under his protection, and become his slaves.

(* Almost all journeys are performed in China by water. The British Embassy of 1816, of which the translator was a member, travelled a distance of about 1200 miles, along canals and navigable rivers.)

(Davis, 1822:194)

由以上几例可见,德本的知识类注释可谓包罗万象,涉及中国人的衣食住行、思维与行为方式、经济与社会运行模式,等等,但多浅尝辄止,而且与作品内容的关联并不密切。对照一下韩本的知识类注释:

(58)正看到热闹之处,不想飓风大作,浪声如雷,竟把五月五日的西湖水变成八月十八的钱塘江,潮头准有五尺多高,盈舟满载的游女都打得浑身透湿。

(《拂云楼》,李渔,1991/9:154)

(58a)In the midst of the excitement, a hurricane struck the lake, the waves began pounding on shore like thunder, and the West Lake in the fifth month was suddenly transformed into the Qiantang River in the middle of the eighth.* Waves five feet or more in height came crashing in and drenched the boatloads of women sightseers to the skin.

(* The Qiantang River is noted for the thunderous tidal waves that occur at the equinox.)

(Hanan, 1992/1998:122)

(59)七郎闻了此言,不但羞惭,而且惊怕,惟恐两笔水粉要送上脸来。所以百般掩饰,不但不露羞容,倒反随了众人也说他丈夫不是。

（《拂云楼》,李渔,1991/9:158）

(59a) At this point Septimus felt more than ashamed, he felt afraid, afraid of those two streaks of white paint that would be daubed on his villain's face,* and he tried by every means he knew to conceal his connection. He not only hid his own embarrassment, he even joined the others in condemning the woman's husband.

(* The role-types on the Chinese stage are distinguished by facial makeup as well as by costume.)

（Hanan, 1992/1998: 128）

(60)这是甚么原故？只因宋朝的气运一日衰似一日,金人的势焰一年盛似一年,又与辽、夏相持,三面皆为敌国,一年之内定有几次告警,近边的官吏死难者多,要人诠补。

（《鹤归楼》,李渔,1991/9:207）

(60a) What lay behind this decree? The fortunes of the Song dynasty were steadily declining, while the power of the Jin was as steadily rising. * What's more, China was at loggerheads with both the Liao and the Xi Xia and so had enemies on three sides, a situation that produced several crises a year. Many of the officials stationed near the frontier had lost their lives, and replacements were urgently needed.

(* The Liao kingdom lay to the northeast, the Xi Xia to the northwest. The Jurched, also in the northeast, conquered the Liao and established the Jin empire.)

（Hanan, 1992/1998: 179）

可以看到,韩本的知识类注释无论专业程度还是关联程度都比德本高很多。造成两者之间这种反差的主要原因,一是中西方之间的语言文化交流经历了从19世纪初互不了解到20世纪末近乎知己知彼的发展历程,当年双方接触伊始十分重要的知识介绍和语言转换类问题,今天已经不再是译者首要考虑的因素了,取而代之的是译入语读者对原作文化深度阅读和了解的需求;二是随着1980年代以降中国国际影响力的扩大,西方读者了解和研究中国文化的热情日益高涨,译者审时度势,在译本中增加原作文化方面的注释(包括文献等延伸阅读信息)以满足读者需求,也是合理的选择。

其次,茅本在4类注释上与德本、韩本有显著区别,或者说打破了后两者间的变化规律。如前所述,茅本采用的是一种以译入语普通读者为中心的"译述"式翻译方法,旨在通过篇名改译、重复内容删省、句子结构调整等途径,为译入语读者降低阅读难度、扫清跨文化交流障碍。具体到注释上也可以看到,茅本的单篇注释数最少,仅5.75个(对比德本的9.33个和韩本的15.5个),而且文学类和文献类注释数还为零,此外注释形式也是对阅读干扰最小的尾注。至于茅本语言类注释数大于德本和韩本,那是因为茅本在对12篇小说题名作"意译+拼音"处理的同时,还不厌其烦地作注解释了每个标题的字面意思;如果去掉这12个题名的注释,则茅本语言类注释的占比就会跌至2.90%,那样就与文学类、文献类、补充类注释比其余两个译本(明显)偏低的情形一致了。由此似可推知,茅本是三个译本中最偏向可读性和最不重视注释的译本。当然,在东西方沟通不畅乃至对立的1970年代,这样的翻译策略可以有效推动双方的初步交流,因而也有其时代需要与合理性。

此外,德本和韩本有3类注释(语言、文学、其他补充)占比相对比较接近,但二者内容和侧重点差别较大。以文学类注释为例:

(61)俗语讲得好:

> 说不出的,才是真苦。
>
> 挠不着的,才是真痒。

(《合影楼》,李渔,1991/9:25-26)

(61a)It is very truly said, that "there is no grief like the grief that does not speak;* there is no pain like that which seeks not relief."

(* ——"The grief that does not speak

Whispers the o'er fraught heart, and bids it break."

*Macbeth*.)

(Davis,1822:83)

(62)却不知做小说者颇谙《春秋》之义:世上的月老,人人做得,独有丫鬟做不得;丫鬟做媒,送小姐出阁,就如奸臣卖国,以君父予人,同是一种道理。

(《拂云楼》,李渔,1991/9:153)

(62a) But what you may not realize is that this author is well versed in the principles of the *Spring and Autumn Annals* and knows that everybody in the world may serve as a matchmaker *except* a maidservant.* For a maidservant who plays the matchmaker in her mistress's marriage is obeying the same principle as the traitor who betrays his country and his lord.

(*A terse chronicle allegedly compiled by Confucius. Some of its commentaries specialize in finding moral judgments in the chronicle's terminology—a view that was generally believed in Li Yu's time.)

(Hanan，1992/1998：120)

(63)倒是半载易过,半夜难熬,正合着唐诗二句:

"似将海水添宫漏,并作铜壶一夜长。"

(《鹤归楼》,李渔,1991/9:221)

(63a)But that half night was harder to endure than half a year, as the Tang poem points out:

It seemed as if all the waters of all the seas

Had filled the water clock, so long was the night.*

(*Adapted from a poem by Li Yi [748–827].)

(Hanan，1992/1998：201)

例(61)是德本唯一的文学类注释,可以看到,它是引用英语读者熟悉的莎士比亚《麦克白》中的一句对白来阐释原作内容的,这反映了德本以译入语读者为中心、追求"通达""晓畅"的翻译立场。而其余韩译各例则是以更加专业的注释引导译入语读者进入原作的文学语境,体现了韩本以译出语为中心、追求"深度"的翻译思想。

由以上调查和统计可知:从最早的德本到最晚的韩本,注释的类型和内容发生了较大变化,变化的总趋势是专业性显著增强,其中文化类、文献类等专业型注释数明显增多;数量变化不大的注释(如语言类、文学类、补充类)和减少的注释(如知识类、翻译类),其内容的专业程度及与文本的关联程度也明显提高。三种译本注释内容和类型的差别,与中西方不同历史时期的接触程度、文化力量对比、文化交流形式等因素密切相关,也反映了三位译者根据对各自所处时代中西文化交流和读者接受状况等因素的判断而选择的阐释策略:德本偏重知识介绍、轻视文化阐释和延伸阅读,而且知识类注释的内容与文本关联度不高,反映了中英文化交流早期的译者希望通过翻译帮助读者初步了解一个陌生国度的翻译目的;茅本注释总数最少,其中文学类和文献类注释数为零,而且采用了对阅读干扰最小的尾注形式,反映了东西方隔阂乃至对立的冷战时期华人译者通过提高可读性来沟通中西的努力("译述"的翻译方法也证明了这一点);韩本注释的数量、长度、专业性、关联度等均明显高于前两个译本,说明在全球化时代和中国国际影响力提高的背景下,西方学者研究和翻译中国文化典籍的热情空前高涨,为帮助英语读者深入了解中国而主动选择了求深、求专的翻译策略。事实上,深度化已是当代典籍翻译大势所趋,仅就注释而言,韩南(Hanan,1990b)所译《无声戏》、卓振英(2011)所译李渔诗赋楹联、夏建新等(Xia,et al.:2011)所译《李渔小说选》等都已经采用了大量的评注和注释,为英语读者深度了解原作内涵或文化背景提供了有力的副文本支持。

副文本是侧面了解译本和翻译策略的重要窗口。本节以上通过《十二楼》英译本所呈现的原作/原作者/书名、译序以及翻译注释等副文本,揭示了李渔作品英译策略由浅而深、由泛而专的演变规律。这一规律对于当前李渔作品英译(或推及典籍翻译)中如何充分有效地利用各种副文本策略、将中国语言文学文化的精髓推向世界,有着重要的启示意义。

## 本章小结

本章对李渔英译史上翻译策略的历时演变开展了较为全面和深入的调查。大量例证和分析表明,李渔作品的英译策略在四个方面发生了比较明显的变化:(1)语言策略由粗放走向精细。1990年代之前的译本大多漠视原文的语言,删削改编现象比较普遍,忠实程度不高,质量稍好一点的译文(如林语堂)则又惜乎仅为少量节译;1990年代之后的译本相比较更加重视原作语言风格和特征的保留与再现。(2)文学策略由通俗走向雅致。原作的文学性(包括开篇诗词和入话、正文诗词歌赋与熟语对句、拟话本小说的说书体风格等)在早期的译本中被完全忽视,而在当代的译本中则受到了充分的尊重。(3)文化策略由以译入文化为中心(TCC)走向以译出文化为中心(SCC)。在李渔作品英译的前两个历史阶段,文化翻译以降低文化难度、迁就读者理解等做法为主;1990年代以后的译本则多见文化语汇逐字对译、引导读者进入译出文化语境的做法。(4)副文本策略由浮泛走向专深。通过《十二楼》三种英译本在书名/作者名、译序以及译本注释等方面的呈现方式和内容发现,李渔作品的早期英译本,原作的书名/作者名均遭忽视或隐去,译序与所选文本之间的关联度低,翻译注释的专业性和文本相关性也不强;当代译本无论在副文本的显示度、关联度还是专业性方面均明显超越了之前的译本。上述这些变化,既反映了李渔作品英译策略的历时发展规律,同时也为当前中国典籍翻译提供了重要的历史借鉴和方法论启示。

# 第五章　结　语

　　李渔在英语世界的传播历时两个世纪,仅凭这一点就已经超过了不少中国古代经典作家和文人。尽管国内外文学界对他的地位和评价一直不乏争议,但在中西文化交流史和翻译史的研究中,其作品恒久的生命力和对英语世界的影响是客观存在的事实,不应无视或低估。本书通过对李渔英译史的梳理以及李渔作品英译策略历时演变规律的调查,获得了一些有价值的发现。本章拟就研究发现及其启示、不足之处与后续研究展望等作一整理和探讨。

## 第一节　本书主要发现、结论及启示

### 一、主要发现及结论

　　本书在前人研究的基础上,通过文献梳理和译本调查与分析,主要在以下几个方面获得了一些发现或结论:

　　(一)李渔英译史的系统整理

　　本书在前人研究的基础上,对两个世纪的李渔英译史做了一次较为全面的整理。笔者根据各个时期的译本和相关研究情况,将李渔在英语世界的传播分为三个阶段,即 19 世纪的滥觞期、1960—1980 年代的复兴期、1990 年代以降的繁荣和成熟期,并分析了每个时期的主要译事及研究情况:

　　19 世纪的李渔作品英译以零散翻译为主要特点,译者多为来华传教士、商人、外交官等,选材集中在拟话本小说集《十二楼》,翻译策略删削改编居多,其中伯奇《生我楼》译文仅 6 页,只是原文的梗概,道格斯《夺锦楼》译文只保留了原文故事的母题,人物、情节、叙事方式等要素均面目全非,即便内容方面最忠实的德庇时《合影楼》《夺锦楼》和《三与楼》译文,细节方面也多有调整和删改,译文比较粗糙。这一阶段的系统研究付之阙如,所能看到的只有德庇时和道格斯译序对中国语言和文学的宏观介绍,较少涉及所译小说的内容、创作技巧等,而且译序中表达的语言和翻译观流露出明显的东方主义倾向。

从 1960 年代开始,英语世界的李渔译介与研究进入复兴期,主要表现在两个方面:一是作品翻译数量和种类激增。艳情小说《肉蒲团》的英译是这个阶段的一件大事,原本这部小说的作者是有争议的,但由于库恩德译本以及马丁转译本所署作者名字都是李渔,因此它在欧洲被先入为主地和李渔联系在了一起,对后者的文学声誉造成了较大的负面影响。茅国权的《十二楼》译本是李渔英译史上唯一的全译本,但采用的是译述法,删减调整幅度很大,损害了原作的文学性。除了小说的英译以外,这一阶段还有一些以简介或学术研究为目的的零散摘译,包括林语堂、文世昌、赖恬昌等,原文取材集中于李渔的百科杂论巨著《闲情偶寄》,其中林语堂的《古文小品译英》中就摘译了《闲情偶寄》声容部和颐养部 4 篇文章的主要内容;文世昌专治笠翁曲话,摘译了词曲部和声容部的部分内容;赖恬昌则是摘译了饮馔部的部分内容。二是相关学术研究蓬勃发展。研究的数量、范围和学术水平大大超过了前一阶段,也为后一阶段的李渔英译和研究打下了坚实的基础。

1990 年代以来,李渔英译和研究进入了稳定的繁荣期。美国哈佛大学著名汉学家韩南的数本译作均在 1990 年代出版,包括《肉蒲团》(直接从中文译入英语)、《十二楼》《无声戏》等;进入新世纪以后,卓振英的《李渔诗赋楹联赏析》和夏建新等人的《李渔小说选》先后出版,标志着大陆学者和翻译家开始登上李渔英译的历史舞台。相关研究方面也日趋成熟,表现在研究深度和范围稳步提升、学术观点日益多样、研究视角与方法走向多元等。

通过李渔英译史的爬梳,本书厘清了李渔在英语世界传播与接受的概况,包括作品题目、译本信息、传播情况以及相关研究等,为李渔作品英译及相关研究打下了坚实的史料基础。这也是近年来李渔英译研究方面最全面和深入的一次翻译史梳理工作。

## (二)英语世界对李渔形象的建构

"重写"是操控学派关注的焦点。本书从操控学派的理论切入,将翻译中的重写分为微观重写和宏观重写两类,指出操控学派关注的重写主要在微观层面,但在很大程度上,译前选材和译后传播等宏观层面的操控对作家和作品形象建构的影响更大。从 19 世纪以来李渔作品在英语国家的译介和传播情况看来,英语世界一直都在按照自身的需要操控着李渔形象的建构,其建构李渔形象的途径主要有三:

　　一是文本选择。李渔作品译入英语最多的是小说,而他在中国文学史上更负盛名的戏曲却没有一部完整译入过英语,他的百科杂论《闲情偶寄》也只有极少量用于介绍和研究的摘译,诗赋楹联直到新世纪才有了第一部选译本。他的小说中,最优秀的作品是《十二楼》和《无声戏》,其中英译最早、历史最长、译本最多的是《十二楼》,但在英语世界影响最大的却是一部作者身份尚无定论的《肉蒲团》。笔者认为,英语世界对李渔作品的选择,反映了译入语自身在不同时代的目的和需求,例如早期选择《十二楼》是为了了解中国社会的需要;1960 年代选择《肉蒲团》也是迎合西方当时性解放运动的时代背景;戏曲和散文少人问津,则可能与英国文学传统缺乏译介戏曲的兴趣和动力、《闲情偶寄》内容繁杂难以吸引读者等原因有关。而选材偏颇的直接后果就是使得英语读者对李渔作家形象的认知和评价局限于(艳情)小说家,全然不知他在戏曲、散文、建筑、园林、美食、养生等其他方面的造诣和成就。

　　二是翻译改写。李渔作品英译史上的文本改写形式多种多样,大到语篇层面的整体改写(例如伯奇之译《生我楼》,译文压缩成了一个 6 页的原作梗概;道格斯之译《夺锦楼》,译文只保留了原文的母题,人物、细节、对话、结局等要素均完全不同,成了典型的"豪杰译",等等),小到局部内容的删减和改编(例如德庇时对原作诗词、入话的删减以及对话形式的频繁转换等)。除此以外,文本的跨媒介传播(如《肉蒲团》录音版和改编拍摄的电影等)也是一种不容忽视的改写形式,因为有了多媒体和网络技术的助推,文本的跨界传播速度更快、影响更大;李渔在西方的"艳情"声誉,与《肉蒲团》的译介有很大关系,而小说的跨媒介传播则又在其中起了催化剂的作用。

　　三是评论引导。评论者的态度反映了译入语的意识形态和诗学标准,是影响甚至决定译本接受效果的重要因素。本书考察和梳理了《肉蒲团》英译过程中的各种评论之后指出,李渔在英语世界的形象是通过评论与译介之间的交互影响乃至"共谋"投射和建构起来的;首先是作品的译介对读者和评论者产生先入为主的影响,其次是评论和研究反过来固化由作品译介造成的印象,经过多番交互和博弈,最终造就了一个符合英语文学文化规范和需要的李渔形象。

　　但英语世界通过以上途径建构起来的李渔形象,与中国文学史上真实的李渔已经相去甚远,对李渔的文学声誉和中国传统小说的整体形象也产生了不利的影响。因而当代的李渔作品英译应最大限度地降低操控的负面影响,保证典籍翻译的文本真实性和传播效果。

### (三)李渔作品英译策略的演变

李渔在英语世界历时两个世纪的传播过程中,其作品的翻译策略发生了比较大的变化,主要表现在以下四个方面:

一是语言翻译策略由粗放走向精细。研究发现,1990 年代之前的译本普遍漠视原文的语言特征和内容细节,因此删削改编现象随处可见,尤以伯奇和道格斯译本为甚;德庇时译本删去了原文的诗词和入话,总体语言比较粗糙;林语堂译本比较精到,但都是节译,难以形成影响;茅国权译本篇目齐全,但只保留了主要情节,内容细节多有删改,诗词和入话也只保留了一部分保留,匆匆行文之间,原文语言艺术已难顾及;文世昌和赖恬昌的译文也都是摘译,质量不高。相比之下,1990 年代以来的译本更加重视原作语言风格和特征的保留与再现。

二是文学翻译策略由通俗走向雅致。早期的李渔小说英译本基本无视原作的文学性,原文作为拟话本小说的开篇诗词和入话、正文中的诗词歌赋与熟语对句、拟话本小说的说书体风格等,大部分都被删去,偶有少量保留的(如茅国权译本),文学性也已经大打折扣。晚近的译本,包括韩南、卓振英、夏建新等译本,均十分重视原文文学性的再现,在诗词、韵文、语篇风格等方面做了大量细致的努力,译本的文学性较前大有进步。

三是文化翻译策略由以译入文化为中心走向以译出文化为中心。研究发现,早期的李渔作品英译在文化方面比较迁就译入文化读者,想方设法地抹消原文的文化色彩,降低文化难度,求得读者对故事内容和情节的轻松理解和接受。而 1990 年代以来的译本在文化策略上明显转向译出文化,对原文的文化语汇多采取逐字对译(或直译加注)的办法,力求引导读者进入原文文化语境来理解文化。这一转变与 1990 年代之后翻译的文化转向有一定关系,也反映了中国文化影响力提高之后西方读者了解中国文化的主动性较前更为强烈。

四是副文本翻译策略由浮泛走向专深。副文本是侧面了解文本及其传播与接受等情况的一个重要窗口。本研究通过考察《十二楼》三种英译本在书名/作者名、译序、译本注释等副文本的呈现方式和内容,发现李渔作品早期译本的原作书名/作者名均被忽视或隐去,译序与所选文本之间的关联度比较低,注释的专业性和文本相关性也不强;而当代译本无论在副文本的显示度、关联度还是专业性等方面均明显超越了之前的译本。

翻译策略是文化交流的一面镜子。李渔作品英译策略的上述这些变化,是东西方不同历史时期文化交流状况投射于翻译的影子,从中可以看出不同时期双方文化力量对比与文化交流情况。同时,从翻译策略的历时演变也能总结出对我们今天的文化交流有助益的启示,为当代典籍翻译探索更有效的方法。

## 二、研究启示

本研究对于翻译理论研究和典籍翻译实践均有一定的启示。对翻译理论研究的启示是:(1)作家形象的跨语言文化建构是一个系统的过程,译入语受众(包括译者、专业评论者、出版商等)会按照自己的意识形态和诗学规范,通过原作选材、翻译改写、评论引导等操控手段,逐步将作品和作家塑(改)造成符合自身需要的形象。由于每个时代都有自己特定的翻译目的和要求,文化力量对比和操控的实施手段也各不相同,因而惟有通过对翻译过程的历时和全方位考察才有可能做到比较客观地评价各种主客体要素和环节在翻译和译本接受过程中发挥的作用或产生的影响,现实中也才能根据需要做出正确的策略选择。(2)成功的文学翻译从来都不是孤立的文本迻译,其背后必定是两种文化和文学系统之间的一场深度对话,这就意味着除了译者直接参与文本翻译之外,两种文化里的读者、翻译评论者和研究者、出版商等主体也在直接或间接地参与文明之间的沟通、交流乃至博弈。对于译出文化来说,如果希望自己的作品和作家在进入其他文化后不失真、不遭误读和改写,除了最大限度地做好文本本身的翻译之外,还应高度重视评论界的国际对话,积极推动国内主流权威的学术观点和研究结论走向世界,尽可能多地影响译入文化的读者(尤其是评论界),防止后者在解读和接受译本过程中可能出现的偏见。

对我国当代典籍翻译实践的启示是:(1)典籍翻译的原作选材应力求全面、准确。对于确定为某一作家名下的作品,应坚持"译无不尽"的原则,进行系统译介;而对作者身份、版本等存疑的作品则应"存疑不译",尽量避免推向国外,以免造成误读和偏见。(2)典籍翻译策略和方法应以忠实、完整为先。应坚持以译出语和译出文化为中心的导向,充分尊重译出语的语言、文学和文化,宏观层面尽可能采用全译,微观层面注重贴近原作语言特征,尤须摒弃无视原作文学性的、大刀阔斧的删削改写。应充分认识到副文本的重要作用以及当代典籍翻译的"深度"化趋势,善用序、跋、注释、插图、装帧印刷等各种副文本形式,通过各种学术式和语境化手段,将文本"置于丰富的文化和语言情境之中"(Appiah,1993:817),达到使译入语读者对译出语文化更加尊重、对其他民族思维和表述方式更加欣赏(Shuttleworth &

Cowie,1997/2004:171)的翻译目的。此外还应积极考虑利用跨媒介手段传播和展现原作中的积极元素,取得事半功倍的效果。

## 第二节　本书不足之处及后续研究展望

### 一、不足之处

受主客观条件所限,本书在以下几个方面还有一些不足之处:

(1)理论研究。由于本书以翻译史梳理和译本分析为主要目标,加上研究者理论水平有限,在理论探索方面着力不够,只是利用一些文化翻译理论(如操控学派)和文学批评理论(如副文本)分析和解释李渔在英语世界的传播和接受,理论创新不足。

(2)文本分析。本书在文本分析上着墨较多,但分析方法偏经验,缺乏明确的分析框架,系统性和科学性有待加强。

(3)传播评估。本书对李渔英译史的梳理应该说是比较全面和完整的,但在译本的传播效果方面缺乏有力的直接证据,尤其是 19 世纪的译本,很难获得第一手的传播信息;20 世纪的译本情况稍好,但传播效果评估依然是一个难题,所能仰仗的主要还是专业评论意见,普通读者中间的传播效果信息获取存在偶然性(例如通过图书借阅信息等),因而有可能影响对译本传播的正确评估。

### 二、后续研究展望

本书作为李渔英译研究领域的首次较为系统的整理和研究,虽然取得了一些成绩或进展,但还是存在诸如以上所列的种种问题和不足的。为推动该领域研究的可持续发展,笔者认为应在以下几个方面开展后续研究:

(1)挖掘资料,加大理论研究力度。对于翻译史研究来说,史料的收集只是第一步的基础性工作(即"史实"部分),更重要的工作在对史料的进一步整理和挖掘、形成分析性和理论性的创见(即"史论"部分)。本书在前人研究的基础上,完成了李渔作品英译史料的系统整理,也在史料分析和理论探索方面迈出了第一步;后续研究可以此为出发点,加大理论研究投入,将李渔在英语世界的传播与接受置于更宏大的语言、文学、文化和翻译理论语境下开展思辨性和批判性的研究,使研究结论更具理论普适性和科学意义上的可复制性,从而对相关研究形成启发和辐射效应。

(2)搭建框架,提高译本分析质量。本书尽管在文本分析的系统性和科学性方面有待加强,但一个重要的贡献是通过大量例证把不同时期李渔作品英译本的主要面貌以及历时演变情况勾勒了出来;在此基础上,研究者可以搭建科学的分析框架,为译本分析提供可以追溯的路径和模式,提高译本分析的质量。

(3)理实结合,重视当代传播事业。翻译研究除了考察真相、探索规律、启发理论思辨等目的之外,还有一个重要的使命就是为翻译实践提供寻找理论和实践依据。本研究对李渔英译史的梳理和各时期英译本的探查,归根结底是要为当下的典籍翻译事业探索行之有效的策略和方法。李渔的作品中还有相当一部分(包括戏曲作品和《闲情偶寄》)尚未译入英语,已经译入英语的也并非全无重译之必要,而本书针对李渔作品英译策略历时演变的调查,有些发现和结论是可以直接用于指导当代李渔作品的(重新)翻译的。因此,今后一段时期的李渔英译研究应重视理论与实践相结合,汲取前人经验、总结教训,将以往翻译实践的研究成果转化为当代李渔作品英译的智力支持,为李渔在英语世界的当代传播提供科学的依据和强大的动力。

# 参考文献

[1]Appiah, Kwame A. "Thick Translation." *Callaloo* 16, 4 (1993): 808-819.

[2]Baldick, Chris, ed. *The Oxford Dictionary of Literary Terms*. London: Oxford UP. , 2008. accessed 31 Mar. , 2019. http://www. oxfordreference. com/abstract/10. 1093/acref/ 9780199208272. 001. 0001/acref-9780199208 272-e-661? rskey=ABgv1M&result=661.

[3]Bassnett, Susan, and Lefevere, André, eds. *Translation, History and Culture*. London: Pinter Publishers, 1990.

[4]Birch, Samuel, and LI, Yü, pseud. *Yin Seaon Low, or the Lost Child. A Chinese Tale.* [*An Abstract of a Tale from the* Shih êrh Lou *of Li Yü. Signed B. , i. e. Samuel Birch.*] *Extracted from the* Asiatic Journal, *etc*. London, 1841. Web.

[5]Buck, Pearl S. , trans. *All Men Are Brothers (Shui Hu Chuan)*. By Shi Naian. 2 vols. New York: The John Day Company, 1933.

[6]Chang, Chun-shu, and Chang, Shelley Hsueh-lun, *Crisis and Transformation in Seventeenth-Century China: Society, Culture, and Modernity in Li Yü's World*. Ann Arbor: The University of Michigan Press, 1992.

[7]Das, Bijay K. *Twentieth Century Literary Criticism*. Rev. & Enl. Ed. New Delhi: Atlantic, 2005.

[8]Davis, John F. *Chinese Novels, translated from the originals; to which are added Proverbs and Moral Maxims, collected from their classical books and other sources*. London: John Murray, 1822.

[9]Dolby, William. *A History of Chinese Drama*. London: Paul Elek, 1976.

[10]Douglas, Robert K. *Chinese Stories*. Edinburgh & London: William Blackwood & Sons, 1893.

[11]Fisk, Craig. "Literary Criticism." Nienhauser, ed. *The Indiana Companion to Traditional Chinese Literature*. Bloomington: Indiana University Press, 1986.

[12]Genette, Gérard. *Paratexts: Thresholds of Interpretation*. J. E.

Lewin, trans. New York & Melbourne: Cambridge University Press, 1997.

[13]van Gulik, Robert H., *Sexual Life in Ancient China: A Preliminary Survey of Chinese Sex and Society from ca. 1500 B. C. till 1644 A. D. 1961.* Leiden & Boston: Brill, 2003.

[14]Hanan, Patrick. *The Chinese Vernacular Story.* Cambridge, MA. : Harvard University Press, 1981.

[15]Hanan, Patrick. *The Invention of Li Yu.* Cambridge, MA. : Harvard University Press, 1988.

[16]Hanan, Patrick, trans. *The Carnal Prayer Mat (Rou Putuan).* By Li Yu. New York: Ballantine Books, 1990a.

[17]Hanan, Patrick, trans. *Silent Operas (Wusheng xi).* Hong Kong: The Chinese University of Hong Kong Press, 1990b.

[18]Hanan, Patrick, trans. *A Tower for the Summer Heat.* By Li Yu. 1992. New York: Columbia University Press, 1998.

[19]Hauf, Kandice. "Review of *The Carnal Prayer Mat*, by Li Yu, translated with an introduction and notes by Patrick Hanan." *Harvard Book Review*, 17/18 (Summer-Fall, 1990): 7-8.

[20]Hegel, Robert E. *The Novel in Seventeenth-Century China.* New York: Columbia University Press, 1981.

[21]Henry, Eric P. *Chinese Amusement: The Lively Plays of Li Yü.* Hamden, CT. : Archon Books, 1980.

[22]Hermans, Theo. *The Manipulation of Literature: Studies in Literary Translation.* London & Sydney: Croom Helm, 1985.

[23]Hightower, James R. "Franz Kuhn and His Translation of *Jou P'u-t'uan.*" *Oriens Extremus* 8, 2 (1961): 252-257.

[24]Hsia, C. T. "Review of *Jou Pu Tuan (The Prayer Mat of Flesh)*, by Li Yü, translated by Richard Martin from the German version by Franz Kuhn." *The Journal of Asian Studies* 23, 2 (1964): 298-301.

[25]Hsia, C. T. *The Classic Chinese Novel: A Critical Introduction.* 1968. Hong Kong: The Chinese University of Hong Kong Press, 2015.

[26]Hummel, Arthur W. *Eminent Chinese of the Ch'ing Period* (1644 – 1912). 2 vols. 1943. Kent, UK: Global Oriental, 2010.

[27] Ingalls, Jeremy. "Mr. Ch'ing-yin and the Chinese Erotic Novel." *Yearbook of Comparative and General Literature*, 13 (1964): 60-63.

[28] Jackson, J. H., trans. *Water Margin*. By Shi Naian. 2 vols. Hong Kong: The Commercial Press, 1937.

[29] Lai, T. C. "Choice Morsels-Some Food for Thought from Yuan Mei and Li Yü." *Renditions*, 9 (Spring, 1978): 47-80.

[30] Lefevere, André. *Translation, Rewriting and the Manipulation of Literary Fame*. London & New York: Routledge, 1992.

[31] Lévy, André. "Jou p'u-t'uan." Nienhauser, ed. *The Indiana Companion to Traditional Chinese Literature*. Bloomington: Indiana University Press, 1986.

[32] Li, Man-kuei. "Li Yü." Hummel, *Eminent Chinese of the Ch'ing Period* (1644–1912), Vol. I: 495-497.

[33] Lin, Yutang. *My Country and My People*. New York: Reynal & Hitchcock, Inc., 1935.

[34] Lin, Yutang. *The Importance of Living*. New York: The John Day Company, 1937.

[35] Lin, Yutang. *The Importance of Understanding: Translations from the Chinese*. Cleveland & New York: The World Publishing Company, 1960.

[36] Mackerras, Colin, ed. *Chinese Theater: From Its Origins to the Present Day*. Honolulu: University of Hawaii Press, 1983.

[37] Man, Sai-cheong. "A Study of Li Yü on Drama." Diss. The University of Hong Kong, 1970.

[38] Man, Sai-cheong. "Li Yu on the Performing Arts." *Renditions*, 3 (Autumn, 1974): 62-65.

[39] Mao, Nathan K. "The Tradition of Seduction in Chinese Literature." *Enquiry* 1, 3 (1967): 1-11.

[40] Mao, Nathan K., and Liu Ts'un-yan. *Li Yü*. Boston: Twayne Publishers, 1977.

[41] Mao, Nathan, ret. *Li Yü's TWELVE TOWERS*. Hong Kong: The Chinese University of Hong Kong Press, 1975.

[42] Mao, Nathan, ret. *Twelve Towers: Short Stories by Li Yü*. Rev. 2nd ed. Hong Kong: The Chinese University of Hong Kong, 1979.

［43］Mao，Nathan，trans. "Tower of the Returning Crane." By Li Yu (1611 - 1680?). *Renditions*，1 (Autumn，1973)：25-35.

［44］Martin，Helmut. "Li Yü." Nienhauser，*The Indiana Companion to Traditional Chinese Literature*. Bloomington：Indiana University Press，1986.

［45］Martin，Richard，trans. *Jou Pu Tuan (The Prayer Mat of Flesh)*. By Li Yu. Translated from the German version by Franz Kuhn. New York：Grove Press，1963.

［46］Martin，Richard，trans. *The before midnight scholar [Jou Pu Tuan]*. By Li Yu. Translated from the German version by Franz Kuhn. London：Andre Deutsch Ltd. ，1965.

［47］Matsuda，Shizue. "The Beauty and the Scholar in Li Yü's Short Stories." *Short Fiction* 10，3 (1973)：271-280.

［48］Matsuda，Shizue. "Li Yu：His Life and Moral Philosophy as Reflected in His Fiction." Diss. Columbia U. ，1978.

［49］Morris，Edwin T. *The Gardens of China：History, Art, and Meanings*. New York：Charles Scribner's Sons，1983.

［50］Nienhauser，William H. ，Jr. ，ed. and comp. *The Indiana Companion to Traditional Chinese Literature*. Bloomington，IN. ：Indiana University Press，1986.

［51］Pym，Anthony. *Method in Translation History*. 1998. Beijing：Foreign Language Teaching and Research Press，2007.

［52］Radó，György. "Outline of a Systematic Translatology." *Babel* 25，4 (1979)：187-196.

［53］Said，Edward W. *Orientalism*. New York：Pantheon Books，1978.

［54］Shen，Jing. "Ethics and Theater：The Staging of *Jingchai ji* in *Bimuyu*." *Ming Studies*，57 (Spring，2008)：62-101.

［55］Shen，Jing. "Role Types in *The Paired Fish*, a *Chuanqi* Play." *Asian Theatre Journal* 20，2 (Fall，2003)：226-236.

［56］Shen，Jing. *Playwrights and Literary Games in Seventeenth-Century China：Plays by Tang Xianzu, Mei Dingzuo, Wu Bing, Li Yu, and Kong Shangren*. Lanham，MD. & Plymouth，UK. ：Lexington Books，2010.

［57］Shuttleworth，Mark，and Moira Cowie. *Dictionary of Translation*

Studies. 1997. Shanghai: Shanghai Foreign Language Euducation Press, 2004.

[58]Toury, Gideon. *In Search of a Theory of Translation*. Tel Aviv: The Porter Institute for Poetics and Semiotics, 1980.

[59]Wang, Ying. "Two Authorial Rhetorics of Li Yu's (1611 – 1680) Works: Inversion and Auto-Communication." Diss. The University of Toronto, 1997.

[60]West, Stephen H. "Drama." Nienhauser, ed. *The Indiana Companion to Traditional Chinese Literature*. Bloomington: Indiana University Press, 1986.

[61]Xia, Jianxin, Tang, Yanfang, Li, Jianjun *et al*., trans. *Selections of Li Yu's Stories*. Beijing: Foreign Languages Press, 2011.

[62]Yang, Winston L. Y., Li, Peter and Mao, Nathan K. *Classical Chinese Fiction: A Guide to Its Study and Appreciation-Essays and Bibliographies*. Boston: G. K. Hall & Co., 1978.

[63]Zhang, Jie. "The Game of Marginality: Parody in Li Yu's (1611 – 80) Vernacular Short Stories." Diss. Washington University in St. Louis, 2005.

[64]埃里克·亨利. 李渔:站在中西喜剧的交叉点上. 徐惠风,译. 戏剧艺术,1989(3):115-122.

[65]爱德华·W. 萨义德. 东方学. 王宇根,译. 北京:生活·读书·新知三联书店,1999.

[66]崔子恩. 李渔小说论稿. 北京:中国社会科学出版社,1989.

[67]冯保善. 李渔. 南京:南京大学出版社,2010.

[68]郭盈.《十二楼》英译研究:以德庇时、茅国权、韩南译本为中心. 北京大学硕士论文,2012.

[69]韩南. 创造李渔. 杨光辉,译. 上海:上海教育出版社,2010.

[70]韩南. 中国白话小说史. 尹慧珉,译. 杭州:浙江古籍出版社,1989.

[71]何敏. 李渔小说在英语世界的研究述论. 中华文化论坛,2013(11)94-101.

[72]黄强. 李渔研究. 杭州:浙江古籍出版社,1996.

[73]李彩标. 李渔四百年:首届李渔国际学术研讨会论文集[C]. 北京:中国戏剧出版社,2012.

[74]李时人. 李渔小说创作论. 文学评论,1997(3):96-108.

[75]李渔.李笠翁曲话.第二版.北京:中国戏剧出版社,1962.

[76]李渔.李渔全集.杭州:浙江古籍出版社,1991.

[77]申丹.叙述学与小说文体学研究.北京:北京大学出版社,1998.

[78]沈新林.李渔新论.苏州:苏州大学出版社,1997.

[79]宋柏年.中国古典文学在国外.北京:北京语言学院出版社,1994.

[80]宋丽娟."中学西传"与中国古典小说的早期翻译(1735—1911)——以英语世界为中心.上海:上海古籍出版社,2017.

[81]孙福轩,孙敏强.李渔三论//李彩标,李渔四百年:首届李渔国际学术研讨会论文集.北京:中国戏剧出版社,2012:163-182.

[82]唐艳芳.李渔《十二楼》英译注释历时对比研究.燕山大学学报,2018(5):34-42.

[83]唐艳芳.建构李渔:论英语世界对李渔形象的操控.北方工业大学学报,2019(6):121-129.

[84]王丽娜.中国古典小说戏曲名著在国外.上海:学林出版社,1988.

[85]吴笛.菲茨杰拉德《鲁拜集》翻译策略探究.安徽师范大学学报(人文社会科学版),2017(6):758-763.

[86]夏洁.德庇时与中国经典早期英译.北京大学硕士论文,2009.

[87]夏志清.中国古典小说导论.胡益民,等译.合肥:安徽文艺出版社,1988.

[88]萧欣桥.点校说明//李渔,李渔全集.卷八.杭州:浙江古籍出版社,1991:1-2.

[89]俞为民.李渔评传.南京:南京大学出版社,2011.

[90]羽离子.李渔作品在海外的传播及海外的有关研究.四川大学学报(哲学社会科学版),2001(3):69-78.

[91]羽离子.评析李渔的长篇小说在欧美的风行.四川外语学院学报,2002(1):25-28.

[92]张春树,骆雪伦.明清时代之社会经济巨变与新文化——李渔时代的社会与文化及其"现代性".王湘云,译.上海:上海古籍出版社,2008.

[93]周领顺,强卉."厚译"究竟有多厚?——西方翻译理论批评与反思之一.外语与外语教学,2016(6):103-112.

[94]赵长江.十九世纪中国文化典籍英译史.上海:上海外语教育出版社,2017.

[95]卓振英.李渔诗赋楹联赏析.北京:外语教学与研究出版社,2011.

# 附录 1

## 林语堂英文著述引用/摘译《闲情偶寄》情况一览<sup>①</sup>

### 1.《生活的艺术》(*The Importance of Living*,1937)

| 原文 | 译文/引文 |
|---|---|
| 　　予于饮食之美,无一物不能言之,且无一物不穷其想象,竭其幽渺而言之;独于蟹螯一物,心能嗜之,口能甘之,无论终身一日皆不能忘之,至其可嗜、可甘与不可忘之故,则绝口不能形容之。此一事一物也者,在我则为饮食中之痴情,在彼则为天地间之怪物矣。予嗜此一生,每岁于蟹之未出时,即储钱以待;因家人笑予以蟹为命,即自呼其钱为"买命钱"。自初出之日始,至告竣之日止,未尝虚负一夕,缺陷一时。同人知予癖蟹,招者饷者,皆于此日,予因呼九月十月为"蟹秋"。虑其易尽而难继,又命家人涤瓮酿酒,以备糟之醉之之用。糟名"蟹糟",酒名"蟹酿",瓮名"蟹瓮",向有一婢勤于事蟹,即易其名为"蟹奴",今亡之矣。蟹乎!蟹乎!汝于吾之一生,殆相终始者乎?所不能为汝生色者,未尝有螃蟹无监州处作郡,出俸钱以供大嚼,仅以悭囊易汝。即使日购百筐,除供客外,与五十口家人分食,则入予腹者有几何哉?蟹乎!蟹乎!吾终有愧于汝矣。<br>　　(《闲情偶寄·饮馔部》肉食第三"蟹",李渔,1991/3:255-256) | 　　There is nothing in food and drink whose flavor I cannot describe with the utmost understanding and imagination. But as for crabs, my heart likes them, my mouth relishes them, and I can never forget them for a year and a day, but find it impossible to describe in words why I like them, relish them, and can never forget them. Ah, this thing has indeed become for me a weakness in food, and is in itself a strange phenomenon of the universe. All my days I have been extremely fond of it. Every year before the crab season comes, I set aside some money for the purpose and because my family say that "crab is my life," I call this money "my life ransom." From the day it appears on the market to the end of the season, I have never missed it for a night. My friends who know this weakness of mine always invite me to dinner at this season, and I therefore call October and November " crab autumn. "... I used to have a maid quite devoted to attending to the care and preparation of crabs and I called her " my crab maid. " Now she is gone! O crab! my life shall begin and end with thee! (Lin, 1937:255) |

---

| 原文 | 译文/引文 |
|---|---|
| 吾观人之一身,眼耳鼻舌,手足躯骸,件件都不可少。其尽可不设而必欲赋之,遂为万古生人之累者,独是口腹二物。口腹具,而生计繁矣;生计繁,而诈伪奸险之事出矣;诈伪奸险之事出,而五刑不得不设。君不能施其爱育,亲不能遂其恩私,造物好生,而亦不能不逆行其志者,皆当日赋形不善,多此二物之累也。草木无口腹,未尝不生;山石土壤无饮食,未闻不长养。何事独异其形,而赋以口腹?即生口腹,亦当使如鱼虾之饮水,蜩螗之吸露,尽可滋生气力,而为潜跃飞鸣。若是则可与世无求,而生人之患熄矣。乃既生以口腹,又复多其嗜欲,使如溪壑之不可厌。多其嗜欲,又复洞其底里,使如江海之不可填。以致人之一生,竭五官百骸之力,供一物之所耗而不足哉!吾反复推详,不能不于造物是咎。亦知造物于此,未尝不自悔其非,但以制定难移,只得终遂其过。甚矣!作法慎初,不可草草定制。吾辑是编而谬及饮馔,亦是可已不已之事。其止崇俭啬,不导奢靡者,因不得已而为造物饰非,亦当虑始计终,而为庶物弭患。如逞一己之聪明,导千万人之嗜欲,则匪特禽兽昆虫无噍类,吾虑风气所开,日甚一日,焉知不有易牙复出,烹子求荣,杀婴儿以媚权奸,如亡隋故事者哉!一误岂堪再误,吾不敢不以赋形造物视作覆车。<br><br>(《闲情偶寄·饮馔部》蔬食第一,李渔,1991/3:234-235) | I see that the organs of the human body, the ear, the eye, the nose, the tongue, the hands, the feet and the body, have all a necessary function, but the two organs which are totally unnecessary but with which we are nevertheless endowed are the mouth and the stomach, which cause all the worry and trouble of mankind throughout the ages. With this mouth and this stomach, the matter of getting a living becomes complicated, and when the matter of getting a living becomes complicated, we have cunning and falsehood and dishonesty in human affairs. With the coming of cunning and falsehood and dishonesty in human affairs, comes the criminal law, so that the king is not able to protect with his mercy, the parents are not able to gratify their love, and even the kind Creator is forced to go against His will. All this comes of a little lack of forethought in His design for the human body at the time of the creation, and is the consequence of our having these two organs. The plants can live without a mouth and a stomach, and the rocks and the soil have their being without any nourishment. Why, then, must we be given a mouth and a stomach and endowed with these two extra organs? And even if we were to be endowed with these organs, He could have made it possible for us to derive our nourishment as the fish and shell fish derive theirs from water, or the cricket and the cicada from the dew, who all are able to obtain their growth and energy this way and swim or fly or jump or sing. Had it been like this, we should not have to struggle in this life and the sorrows of mankind would have disappeared. On the other hand, He has given us not only these two organs, but has also endowed us with manifold appetites or desires, besides making the pit bottomless, so that it is like a valley or a sea that can never be filled. The consequence is that we labor in our life with all the energy of the other organs, in order to supply inadequately the needs of these two. I have thought over this matter over and over again, and cannot help blaming the Creator for it. I know, of course, that He must have repented of His mistake also, but simply feels that nothing can be done about it now, since the design or pattern is already fixed. How important it is for a man to be very careful at the time of the conception of a law or an institution!<br>(Lin, 1937: 42-43) |

**续表**

| 原文 | 译文/引文 |
|---|---|
| 人之不能无屋，犹体之不能无衣。衣贵夏凉冬燠，房舍亦然。堂高数仞，榱题数尺，壮则壮矣，然宜于夏而不宜于冬。登贵人之堂，令人不寒而栗，虽势使之然，亦廖廓有以致之；我有重裘，而彼难挟纩故也。及肩之墙，容膝之屋，俭则俭矣，然适于主而不适于宾。造寒士之庐，使人无忧而叹，虽气感之乎，亦境地有以迫之；此耐萧疏，而彼憎岑寂故也。吾愿显者之居，勿太高广。夫房舍与人，欲其相称。画山水者有诀云："丈山尺树，寸马豆人。"使一丈之山，缀以二尺三尺之树；一寸之马，跨以似米似粟之人，称乎？不称乎？使显者之躯，能如汤文之九尺十尺，则高数仞为宜，不则堂愈高而人愈觉其矮，地愈宽而体愈形其瘠，何如略小其堂，而宽大其身之为得乎？<u>处士之庐，难免卑隘。然卑者不能耸之使高，隘者不能扩之使广，而污秽者、充塞者则能去之使净，净则卑者高而隘者广矣。吾贫贱一生，播迁流离，不一其处，虽债而食，赁而居，总未觉稍污其座。性嗜花竹，而购之无资，则必令妻孥忍饥数日，或耐寒一冬，省口体之奉，以娱耳目，人则笑之，而我怡然自得也。性又不喜雷同，好为矫异，常谓人之葺居治宅，与读书作文同一致也。譬如治举业者，高则自出手眼，创为新异之篇；其极卑者，亦将读熟之文移头换尾，损益字句而后出之，从未有抄写全篇，而自名善作者也。乃至兴造一事，则必肖人之堂以为堂，窥人之户以立户，稍有不合，不以为得，而反以为耻。</u>常见通侯贵戚，掷盈千累万之资以治园圃，必先谕大匠曰：亭则法某人之制，榭则遵谁氏之规，勿使稍异。而操运斤之权者，至大厦告成，必骄语居功，谓其立户开窗，安廊置阁，事事皆仿名园，纤毫不谬。噫！陋矣。<u>以构造园亭之胜事，上之不能自出手眼，</u> | A man cannot live without a house as his body cannot go about without clothing. And as it is true of clothing that it should be cool in summer and warm in winter, the same thing is true of a house. It is all very imposing to live in a hall twenty or thirty feet high with beams several feet across, but such a house is suitable for summer and not for winter. The reason why one shivers when he enters an official's mansion is because of its space. It is like wearing a fur coat too broad for girdling around the waist. On the other hand, a poor man's house with low walls and barely enough space to put one's knees in, while having the virtue of frugality, is suitable for the owner, but not suitable for entertaining guests. That is why we feel cramped and depressed without any reason when we enter a poor scholar's hut.... I hope that the dwellings of officials will not be too high and big. For a house and the people living in it must harmonize as in a picture. Painters of landscape have a (p. 268) formula saying, "ten-feet mountains and one-foot trees; one-inch horses and bean-sized human beings." It would be inappropriate to draw trees of two or three feet on a hill of ten feet, or to draw a human being the size of a grain of nee or millet riding on a horse an inch tall. It would be all right for officials to live in halls twenty or thirty feet high, if their bodies were nine or ten feet. Otherwise the taller the building, the shorter the man appears, and the wider the space, the thinner the man seems. Would it not be much better to make his house a little smaller and his body a little stouter?... I have seen high officials or relatives of officials who throw away thousands and ten thousands of dollars to build a garden and who begin by telling the architect, "For the pavilion, you copy the design of So-and-So, and for the covered terrace overlooking a pond, you follow the model of So-and-So, down to its last detail." When the mansion is completed, its |

| 原文 | 译文/引文 |
|---|---|
| 如标新创异之文人；下之至不能换尾移头，学套腐为新之庸笔，尚嚣嚣以鸣得意，何其目处之卑哉！予尝谓人曰：生平有两绝技，自不能用，而人亦不能用之，殊可惜也。人问：绝技维何？予曰：一则辨审音乐，一则置造园亭。性嗜填词，每多撰著，海内共见之矣。设处得为之地，自选优伶，使歌自撰之词曲，口授而躬试之，无论新裁之曲，可使迥异时腔，即旧日传奇，一概删其腐习而益以新格，为往时作者别开生面，此一技也。一则创造园亭，因地制宜，不拘成见，一榱一桷，必令出自己裁，使经其地、入其室者，如读湖上笠翁之书，虽乏高才，颇饶别致，岂非圣明之世，文物之邦，一点缀太平之具哉？噫，吾老矣，不足用也。请以崖略付之简篇，供嗜痂者要择。收其一得，如对笠翁，则斯编实为神交之助尔。<br>（《闲情偶寄·居室部》房舍第一，李渔，1991/3：155-157） | owner will proudly tell people that every detail of the house, from its doors and windows to its corridors and towers, has been copied from some famous garden without the slightest deviation. Ah, what vulgarity! … (Lin，1937：268-269) |
| 土木之事，最忌奢靡。匪特庶民之家当崇俭朴，即王公大人亦当以此为尚。盖居室之制，贵精不贵丽，贵新奇大雅，不贵纤巧烂漫。凡人止好富丽者，非好富丽，因其不能创异标新，舍富丽无所见长，只得以此塞责。譬如人有新衣二件，试令两人服之，一则雅素而新奇，一则辉煌而平易，观者之目，注在平易乎？在新奇乎？锦绣绮罗，谁不知贵，亦谁不见之？缟衣互裳，其制略新，则为众目所射，以其未尝睹也。凡予所言，皆属价廉工省之事，即有所费，亦不及雕镂粉藻之百一。且古语云："耕当问奴，织当访婢。"予贫士也，仅识寒酸之事。欲示富贵，而以绮丽胜人，则有从前之旧制在。<br>（《闲情偶寄·居室部》房舍第一，李渔，1991/3：157） | Luxury and expensiveness are the things most to be avoided in architecture. This is so because not only the common people, but also the princes and high officials, should cherish the virtue of simplicity. For the important thing in a living house is not splendor, but refinement, not elaborate decorativeness, but novelty and elegance. People like to show off their rich splendor not because they love it, but because they are lacking in originality, and besides trying to show off, they are at a total loss to invent something else. That is why they have to put up with mere splendor. Ask two persons to put on two new dresses, one simple and elegant and original, and the other rich and decorative, but common. Will not the eye of spectators be directed to the original dress rather than to the common dress? Who doesn't know the value of silk and brocade and gauze, and who has not seen them? But a simple, plain dress with a novel design will attract the eyes of spectators because they have never seen it before. (Lin，1937：269) |

**续表**

| 原文 | 译文/引文 |
|---|---|
| 　　开窗莫妙于借景,而借景之法,予能得其三昧。向犹私之,乃今嗜痂者众,将来必多依样葫芦,不若公之海内,使物物尽效其灵,人人均有其乐。但期于得意酣歌之顷,高叫笠翁数声,使梦魂得以相傍,是人乐而我亦与焉,为愿足矣。向居西子湖滨,欲购湖舫一只,事事犹人,不求稍异,止以窗格异之。人询其法,予曰:四面皆实,犹虚其中,而为"便面"之形。实者用板,蒙以灰布,勿露一隙之光;虚者用木作匡,上下皆曲而直其两旁,所谓便面是也。纯露空明,勿使有纤毫障翳。是船之左右,止有二便面,便面之外,无他物矣。坐于其中,则两岸之湖光山色,寺观浮屠,云烟竹树,以及往来之樵人牧竖,醉翁游女,连人带马,尽入便面之中,作我天然图画。且又时时变幻,不为一定之形。非特舟行之际,摇一橹变一象,撑一篙换一景,即系缆时,风摇水动,亦刻刻异形。是一日之内,现出百千万幅佳山佳水,总以便面收之。而便面之制,又绝无多费,不过曲木两条,直木两条而已。世有掷尽金钱,求为新异者,其能新异若此乎? 此窗不但娱己,兼可娱人;不特以舟外无穷之景色摄入舟中,兼可以舟中所有之人物,并一切几席杯盘射出窗外,以备来往游人之玩赏。何也? 以内视外,固是一幅便面山水;而以外视内,亦是一幅扇头人物。譬如拉妓邀僧,呼朋聚友,与之弹棋观画,分韵拈毫,或饮或歌,任眠任起,自外观之,无一不同绘事。同一物也,同一事也,此窗未设以前,仅作事物观;一有此窗,则不烦指点,人人俱作画图观矣。夫扇面非异物也,肖扇面为窗,又非难事也。世人取象乎物,而为门为窗者,不知凡几,独留此眼前共见之物,弃而弗取,以待笠翁,讵非咄咄怪事乎? 所恨有心无力,不能办此一舟,竟成欠事。兹且移居白门,为西子湖之薄幸人矣。此愿茫茫,其何能遂? 不得已而小用其机,置此窗于楼头,以窥钟山气色,然非创始之心,仅存其制而已。予又尝作观山虚 | 　　When a man is sitting in the boat, the light of the lake and the color of the hills, the temples, clouds, haze, bamboos, trees on the banks, as well as the woodcutters, shepherd boys, drunken old men and promenading ladies, will all be gathered within the framework of the fan and form a piece of natural painting. Moreover, it is a living and moving picture, changing all the time, not only when the boat is moving, giving us a new sight with every movement of the oar and a new view with every punting of the pole, but even when the boat is lying at anchor, when the wind moves and the water ripples, changing its form at every moment. Thus we are able to enjoy hundreds and thousands of beautiful paintings of hills and water in a day by means of this fan-shaped window....<br><br>　　I have also made a window for looking out on |

续表

| 原文 | 译文/引文 |
|---|---|
| 牖，名"尺幅窗"，又名"无心画"，姑妄言之。浮白轩中，后有小山一座，高不逾丈，宽止及寻，而其中则有丹崖碧水，茂林修竹，鸣禽响瀑，茅屋板桥，凡山居所有之物，无一不备。盖因善塑者肖予一像，神气宛然，又因予号笠翁，顾名思义，而为把钓之形；予思既执纶竿，必当坐之矶上，有石不可无水，有水不可无山，有山有水，不可无笠翁息钓归休之地，遂营此窟以居之。是此山原为像设，初无意于为窗也。后见其物小而蕴大，有"须弥芥子"之义，尽日坐观，不忍阖牖。乃瞿然曰：是山也，而可以作画；是画也，而可以为窗；不过损予一日杖头钱，为装潢之具耳。"遂命童子裁纸数幅，以为画之头尾，乃左右镶边。头尾贴于窗之上下，镶边贴于两旁，俨然堂画一幅，而但虚其中。非虚其中，欲以屋后之山代之也。坐而观之，则窗非窗也，画也；山非屋后之山，即画上之山也。不觉狂笑失声，妻孥群至，又复笑予所笑，而"无心画"、"尺幅窗"之制，从此始矣。予又尝取枯木数茎，置作天然之牖，名曰"梅窗"。生平制作之佳，当以此为第一。己酉之夏，骤涨滔天，久而不涸，斋头淹死榴、橙各一株，伐而为薪，因其坚也，刀斧难入，卧于阶除者累日。予见其枝柯盘曲，有似古梅，而老干又具盘错之势，似可取而为器也，因筹所以用之。是时栖云谷中幽而不明，正思辟牖，乃幡然曰：道在是矣！遂语工师，取老干之近直者，顺其本来，不加斧凿，为窗之上下两旁，是窗之外廓具矣。再取枝柯之一面盘曲、一面稍平者，分作梅树两株，一从上生而倒垂，一从下生而仰接，其稍平之一面则略施斧斤，去其皮节而向外，以便糊纸；其盘曲之一面，则匪特尽全其天，不稍戕斫，并疏枝细梗而留之。既成之后，剪彩作花，分红梅、绿萼二种，缀于疏枝细梗之上，俨然活梅之初着花者。同人见之，无不叫绝。予之心思，讫于此矣。后有所作，当亦不过是矣。<br>（《闲情偶寄·居室部》窗栏第二"取景在借"，李渔，1991/3：170-172） | hills, called landscape window, otherwise known also as "unintentional painting." I will tell how I came to make one. Behind my studio, the Studio of Frothy White (signifying "drinking"), there is a hill about ten feet high and seven feet wide only, decorated with a miniature scenery of red cliffs and blue water, thick forests and tall bamboos, singing birds and falling cataracts, thatched huts and wooden bridges, complete in all the things that we see in a mountain village. For at first a modeller of clay made a clay figure of myself with a wonderful expression, and furthermore, because my name Liweng meant "an old man with a bamboo hat," also made me into a fisherman, holding a fishing pole and sitting on top of a rock. Then we thought since there was a rock, there must be also water, and since there was water, there must be also a hill, and since there were both hill and water, there must be a mountain retreat for the old man with a bamboo hat to retire and fish in his old age. That was how we gradually built up the entire scenery. It is clear therefore that the artificial hill grew out of a clay statue without any idea of making it serve the purpose of a window view. Later I saw that although the things were in miniature, their suggested universe was great, and it seemed to recall the Buddhist idea that a mustard seed and the Himalayas are equal in size, and therefore I sat there the whole day looking at it, and could not bear to close the window. And one day inspired I said to myself, "This hill can be made into a painting, and this painting can be made into a window. All it will cost me will be just one day's drink money to provide the 'mounting' for this painting." I therefore asked a boy servant to cut out several pieces of paper, and paste them above and below the window and at the sides, to serve as the mounting for a real picture. Thus the mounting was complete, and only the space usually occupied |

**续表**

| 原文 | 译文/引文 |
| --- | --- |
| | by the painting itself was left vacant, with the hill behind my house to take its place. Thus when one sits and looks at it, the window is no more a window but a piece of painting, and the hill is no longer the hill behind my house, but a hill in the painting. I could not help laughing out loud, and my wife and children, hearing my laughter, came to see it and joined in laughing at what I had been laughing at. This is the origin of the "unintentional painting," and the "landscape window." (Lin, 1937: 271-273) |
| 鸟声之最可爱者,不在人之坐时,而偏在睡时。<br>(《闲情偶寄·种植部》竹木第五"柳",李渔,1991/3:304) | Li Liweng said in his essay on "Willows" that one should learn to listen to the birds at dawn when lying in bed. (Lin, 1937: 205) |
| (原文待考) | ... for as Li Liweng has pointed out, those who are wise seldom know how to talk, and those who talk are seldom wise. (Lin, 1937:211) |
| 果者酒之仇,茶者酒之敌,嗜酒之人必不嗜茶与果,此定数也。<br>(《闲情偶寄·饮馔部》不载果食茶酒说,李渔,1991/3:258) | Anyway, Li Liweng has put down on record his sworn opinion that great drinkers of tea are not fond of wine, and vice versa. (Lin, 1937: 240) |
| 如一座园亭,所有者皆时花弱卉,无十数本老成树木主宰其间,是终日与儿女习处,无从师会友时矣。<br>(《闲情偶寄·种植部》竹木第五"松柏",李渔,1991/3:303) | For this reason Li Liweng says that to sit in an orchard full of peach trees and flowers and willows without a pine nearby is like sitting in the company of young children and women without the presence of an austere master or old man, whom we can look up to. (Lin, 1937: 298) |
| 故有兰之室不应久坐,另设无兰者一间以作退步,时退时进,进多退少,则刻刻有香,虽坐无兰之室,若依情女之魂。是法也,而情在其中矣。如止有此室,则以门外作退步,或往行他事,事毕而入,以无意得之者,其香更甚。<br>(《闲情偶寄·种植部》草本第三"兰",李渔,1991/3:284) | Li Liweng advised that the best way to enjoy orchids was not to place them in all rooms, but only in one room and then to enjoy the fragrance when passing out and in. (Lin, 1937: 304305) |

## 2.《古文小品译英》(*The Importance of Understanding*, 1960)

| 原文 | 译文 |
|---|---|
| 　　劝贵人行乐易，劝富人行乐难。何也？财为行乐之资，然势不宜多，多则反为累人之具。华封人祝帝尧富寿多男，尧曰："富则多事。"华封人曰："富而使人分之，何事之有？"由是观之，财多不分，即以唐尧之圣，帝王之尊，犹不能免多事之累，况德非圣人而位非帝王者乎？陶朱公屡致千金，屡散千金，其致而必散，散而复致者，亦学帝尧之防多事也。兹欲劝富人行乐，必先劝之分财；劝富人分财，其势同于拔山超海，此必不得之数也。财多则思运，不运则生息不繁。然不运则已，一运则经营惨淡，坐起不宁，其累有不可胜言者。财多必善防，不防则为盗贼所有，而且以身殉之。然不防则已，一防则惊魂四绕，风鹤皆兵，其恐惧觳觫之状，有不堪目睹者。且财多必招忌。语云："温饱之家，众怨所归。"以一身而为众射之的，方且忧伤虑死之不暇，尚可与言行乐乎哉？甚矣！财不可多，多之为累亦至此也。然则富人行乐，其终不可冀乎？曰：不然。多分则难，少敛则易。处比户可封之世，难于售恩；当民穷财尽之秋，易于见德。少课锱铢之利，穷民即起颂扬；略蠲升斗之租，贫佃即生歌舞。本偿而于息未偿，因其贫也而贳之，一券才焚，即噪冯驩之令誉；赋足而国用不足，因其匮也而助之，急公偶试，即来卜式之美名。果如是，则大异于今日之富民，而又无损于本来之故我。觊觎者息而仇怨者稀，是则可言行乐矣。其为乐也，亦同贵人，可不必于持筹握算之外别寻乐境，即此宽租减息，仗义急公之日，听贫民之欢欣赞颂，即当两部鼓吹；受官司之奖励称扬，便是百年华衮。荣莫荣于此，乐亦莫乐于此矣。至于悦色娱声，眠花藉柳，构堂建厦，啸 | 40. How To Be Happy Though Rich<br>　　From *The Arts of Living* (*Shienching Ouchi*)<br>　　Li Liweng (1611 – 1679)<br><br>　　Money is the means for providing pleasures, yet too much money also entails its disadvantages, and that is why it is difficult to be happy though rich. When the people of Huafeng wished lots of money and children and years〔long life〕for Emperor Yao ( traditional reign, 2357 – 2257 B. C. ), it is recorded that he replied, "Too much money means too many things to attend to." And the people of Huafeng said, "You can give some away." Tao Chukung〔alias Fan Li, c. 473 B. C.〕several times made a thousand dollars and several times gave them away. That was because, like Emperor Yao, he was afraid of the disadvantages of having too much money. To teach rich men to enjoy life would mean to ask them to give money away, which is difficult, to say the least. Having money, one thinks of managing it to let it grow and have more. Once one starts to manage money, there are endless worries and all peace of mind is gone. Also one begins to worry about theft or robbery, or even about being stabbed in the bargain. The worries arising from such fears of theft and robbery are equally demeaning. Furthermore, wealth makes one a target for envy, and one feels no one really cares for him. What chance is there for enjoying life? Such indeed are the penalties of great wealth. Should one therefore conclude that it is impossible to be happy though wealthy? I think not. One cannot be expected to give a great deal of money away, but one can at least refrain from being grasping. This is especially appreciated in times of general poverty. Taking less interest for a loan or cutting one's shares from farmer tenants will immediately be appreciated by the poor, who will be very grateful. One gains a good reputation |

**续表**

| 原文 | 译文 |
|------|------|
| 月嘲风诸乐事,他人欲得,所患无资,业有其资,何求不遂?是同一富也,昔为最难行乐之人,今为最易行乐之人。<u>即使帝尧不死,陶朱现在,彼丈夫也,我丈夫也,吾何畏彼哉?去其一念之刻而已矣。</u><br><br>(《闲情偶寄·颐养部》行乐第一"富人行乐之法",李渔,1991/3:311-312) | when one burns up an I. O. U. even though the debtor has been able only to pay the interest, or when one contributes money to the government or a public cause. This would be quite a contrast to what the rich people of today are doing. It would not hurt one's soul to do so, and would put an end to all envy and enmity. When one hears the tributes of the poor people, it is as good as having two orchestras, and when one receives honors or awards from the government, one's name goes down to posterity. Thus one obtains both honor and happiness. As to amusements, music, women, nice villas, pleasure parties, these things are easily available to the wealthy people as they are not to the poor. So what seemed to be difficult to attain can now be readily achieved. (Lin, 1960:214-215) |
|     穷人行乐之方,无他秘巧,亦止有退一步法。我以为贫,更有贫于我者;我以为贱,更有贱于我者;我以妻子为累,尚有鳏寡孤独之民,求为妻子之累而不能者;我以胼胝为劳,尚有身系狱廷,荒芜田地,求安耕凿之生而不可得者。以此居心,则苦海尽成乐地。如或向前一算,以胜己者相衡,则片刻难安,种种桎梏幽囚之境出矣。一显者旅宿邮亭,时方溽暑,帐内多蚊,驱之不出,因忆家居时堂宽似宇,簟冷如冰,又有群姬握扇而挥,不复知其为夏,何遽困厄至此!因怀至乐,愈觉心烦,遂致终夕不寐。一亭长露宿阶下,<u>为众蚊所啮,几至露筋,不得已而奔走庭中,俾四体动而弗停,则啮人者无由厕足;乃形则往来仆仆,口则赞叹嚣嚣,一似苦中有乐者。</u>显者不解,呼而讯之,谓:"汝之受困,什佰于我,我以为苦,而汝以为乐,其故维何?"亭长曰:"偶忆某年,为仇家所陷,身系狱中。维时亦当暑月,狱卒防予私逸,每夜拘挛手足,使不得动摇,时蚊蚋之繁,倍于今夕,听其自啮,欲稍稍规避而不能,以视今夕之奔 | **41. How To Be Happy Though Poor**<br>From *The Arts of Living* (*Shienching Ouchi*)<br>Li Liweng (1611 – 1679)<br>    The art of being happy though poor consists in one phrase, to think "it could be worse." I am poor and humble, but there are people poorer and more humble than myself. I have a big family to support, but there are people living alone and without children, and widows and orphans. I have to work hard on a farm, but there are people without a farm, or who would rather work hard on their farm like me but cannot because they are sitting in jail. It is a way of thinking, or of looking at it. The same situation may look like hell to one and like paradise to another. On the other hand, always to want to compare oneself with one's betters will breed a state of mind conducive only to one's own misery.<br>    I remember the story of a high official who was traveling abroad. It was summer and his bed was full of mosquitoes inside the net. He thought of his own spacious hall at home, where the summer mat was cooling to the body and many maids would attend to his comforts. The more he |

| 原文 | 译文 |
|---|---|
| 走不息,四体得以自如者,奚啻仙凡人鬼之别乎!以昔较今,是以但见其乐,不知其苦。"显者听之,不觉爽然自失。此即穷人行乐之秘诀也。不独居心为然,即铸体炼形亦当如是。譬如夏月苦炎,明知为室庐卑小所致,偏向骄阳之下来往片时,然后步入室中,则觉暑气渐消,不似从前酷烈;若畏其湫隘而投宽处纳凉,及至归来,炎蒸又加十倍矣。冬月苦冷,明知为墙垣单薄所致,故向风雪之中行走一次,然后归庐返舍,则觉寒威顿减,不复凛冽如初;若避此荒凉而向深居就燠,及其再入,战栗又作何状矣。由此类推,则所谓退步者,无地不有,无人不有。想至退步,乐境自生。予为两间第一困人,其能免死于忧,不枯槁于迤逦踸踔者,皆用此法。又得管城一物,相伴终身,以扫千军则不足,以除万虑则有余。然非善作退步,即楮墨亦能困人。想虞卿著书,亦用此法,我能公世,彼特秘而未传耳。<br><br>(《闲情偶寄·颐养部》行乐第一"贫贱行乐之法",李渔,1991/3:312-314) | thought, the more miserable he felt. He was not able to sleep a wink. Then he saw a man walking about in the court of the inn, seemingly quite happy with himself. He was puzzled and inquired how he seemed to be so happy with the mosquitoes around and was not bothered at all. The man replied, "I once had an enemy and was put in jail. It was summer and the jail was full of vermin. But my hands and feet were tied to prevent me from escape. It was terrible to be bitten by insects and mosquitoes and not be able to do anything about it. There are mosquitoes now. But I move about and they can't touch me. In fact, it makes me happy to feel just the freedom of the limbs alone." The man saw one side of it and the other man saw the other side. The rich man felt quite lost when he heard the story. (Lin, 1960:216-217) |
| 古云:"尤物足以移人。"尤物维何?媚态是已。世人不知,以为美色,乌知颜色虽美,是一物也,乌足移人?加之以态,则物而尤矣。如云美色即是尤物,即可移人,则今时绢做之美女,画上之娇娥,其颜色较之生人岂止十倍,何以不见移人,而使之害相思成郁病耶?是知"媚态"二字,必不可少。媚态之在人身,犹火之有焰,灯之有光,珠贝金银之有宝色,是无形之物,非有形之物也。惟其是物而非物,无形似有形,是以名为尤物。尤物者,怪物也,不可解说之事也。凡女子,一见即令人思之而不能自已,遂至舍命以图,与生为难者,皆怪物也,皆不可解说之事也。吾于"态"之一字,服天地生人之巧,鬼神体物之工。使以我作天地鬼神,形体吾能赋之,知 | 45. On Charm in Women<br>From *The Arts of Living* (*Shienching Ouchi*)<br>Li Liweng (1611 – 1679)<br><br>There is an ancient saying that "the power of exotic beauty fascinates." Exotic beauty means charm, although it has been commonly misunderstood as referring to "good looks" merely. Good looks, it should be understood, can never move us unless it has charm, and only then does the beauty become fascinating and exotic. People who think that all beauties can fascinate people need only stop to think why all the silk dolls and pictures of women can never move one, although probably their faces are ten times more beautiful than living women. Charm in a person is like the flame in a fire, the light in a lamp, and the luster in jewels. It is something invisible and yet seemingly palpable, something which |

**续表**

| 原文 | 译文 |
| --- | --- |
| 识我能予之，至于是物而非物，无形似有形之态度，我实不能变之化之，使其自无而有，复自有而无也。态之为物，不特能使美者愈美，艳者愈艳，且能使老者少而嫁者妍，无情之事变为有情，使人暗受笼络而不觉者。女子一有媚态，三四分姿色，便可抵过六七分。试以六七分姿色而无媚态之妇人，与三四分姿色而有媚态之妇人同立一处，则人止爱三四分而不爱六七分，<u>是态度之于颜色，犹不止一倍当两倍也</u>。试以二三分姿色而无媚态之妇人，与全无姿色而止有媚态之妇人同立一处，或与人各交数言，则人止为媚态所惑，而不为美色所惑，是态度之于颜色，犹不止于以少敌多，且能以无而敌有也。今之女子，每有状貌姿容一无可取，而能令人思之不倦，甚至舍命相从者，"态"之一字之为祟也。<u>是知选貌选姿，总不如选态一着之为要</u>。态自天生，非可强造。强造之态，不能饰美，止能愈增其陋。同一颦也，出于西施则可爱，出于东施则可憎者，天生、强造之别也。相面、相肌、相眉、相眼之法，皆可言传，独相态一事，则予心能知之，口实不能言之。口之所能言者物也，非尤物也。<u>噫！能使人知，而能使人欲言不得，其为物也何如！其为事也何知！岂非天地之间一大怪物，而从古及今，一件解说不来之事乎？</u> | can be seen and yet has no definite shape or body. That is why charm is always mysterious—why a woman with charm is regarded as being exotic, for to be exotic is to be exciting and mystifying, to be that which people cannot quite understand. There are women who make people fall in love with them at first sight, who once seen are never forgotten, and who make men risk all they have, glory, wealth, and even their own lives, in order to possess them. Such is the strange power of women's fascination, something which is elusive and defies all explanation.<br><br>Of all the things that I admire the creator of the universe for, and of all the mysteries of the universe, the charm of personality ranks the greatest. If I were God, I could give my creatures bodily shape and wisdom and knowledge, but I could not give them this something which is invisible and yet seemingly palpable, which exists and yet has no bodily shape, is seen for a moment and disappears again—namely, charm. For charm not only enhances beauty and attraction in women; it can make the old appear young, the ugly beautiful, and the dull become exciting. For silently and secretly it fascinates a man without his being aware of it. A girl who has only a third-grade facial beauty is as fascinating as another one who has better looks, if she has only charm. Take two girls, one who has only ordinary third-grade "looks" but has charm, and the other who has no charm but has better "looks," and put them side by side. People will like the third-grade and not the second-grade beauty. Or again, take a moderately good-looking woman without charm and another who has charm but is totally deficient in good looks and put them together and let people exchange a few words with each of them. People will fall in love with the one who has charm and not with the one who has merely good looks, which goes to prove that charm can substitute for a total absence of good looks. There are today girls who are otherwise common-looking, yet who |

| 原文 | 译文 |
|---|---|
| | can fascinate men even to the point of making them risk their lives for them. The secret lies solely in this one word "charm."<br><br>Charm is something which comes naturally to a person and directly grows out of her personality. It is not something which can be copied from other, for charm imitated is beauty spoiled. To knit her eyebrows was beautiful in Shishih, because it was natural to her, but would be actually disgusting if Tungshih were to assume the same pose, because she was born differently. It is possible to lay down rules for judging a person's face and skin and eyebrows and eyes by certain standards, but as for this thing called "charm," it is something that is immediately felt, but cannot be analyzed or put into words; for in its elusiveness lies its exciting power and fascination.... |
| 诘予者曰：既为态度立言，又不指人以法，终觉首鼠，盍亦舍精言粗，略示相女者以意乎？予曰：不得已而为言，止有直书所见，聊为榜样而已。向在维扬，代一贵人相妾。靓妆而至者不一其人，始皆俯首面立，及命之抬头，一人不作羞容而竟抬；一人娇羞腼腆，强之数四而后抬；一人初不即抬，及强而后可，先以眼光一瞬，似于看人，而实非看人，瞬毕复定而后抬，俟人看毕，复以眼光一瞬而后俯，此即"态"也。记曩时春游遇雨，避一亭中，见无数女子，妍媸不一，皆踉跄而至。中一缟衣贫妇，年三十许，人皆趋入亭中，彼独徘徊檐下，以中无隙地故也；人皆抖擞衣衫，虑其太湿，彼独听其自然，以檐下雨侵，抖之无益，徒现丑态故也。及雨将止而告行，彼独迟疑稍后，去不数武而雨复作，乃趋入亭。彼则先立亭中，以逆料必转，先踞胜地故也。然臆虽偶中，绝无骄人之色。见后入者反立檐下，衣衫之湿，数倍于前，而此妇代为振衣，姿态百出，竟若天集众丑，以形一人之媚者。自观者视之，其初之不动，似以郑重而养态；其后之故动，似以徜徉而生态。然彼岂 | I shall give a few examples of what I saw to show my meaning. I was once in Yangchow, trying to pick a concubine for a certain official. There were rows of women in beautiful dresses and of different types. At first they stood all with their heads bent, but when they were ordered to hold their heads up, one of them just raised her head and stared blandly at me, and another was terribly shy and would not hold her head up until she had been bidden to do so several times. There was one, however, who would not look up at first but did so after some persuasion, and then she first cast a quick glance as if she was looking and yet not looking at me before she held her head up, and again she cast another glance before she bent her head again. This is what I call charm.<br><br>I also remember that on a certain spring day, a number of people including myself were taking shelter in a pavilion to avoid a spring shower. Many girls and women, both ugly and beautiful ones, made a dash for the place. There was one woman in a white dress, however, about thirty years old, who stood by under the eaves outside the pavilion, seeing that there was no more room inside. The other women were all shaking their dresses, but |

**续表**

| 原文 | 译文 |
| --- | --- |
| 能必天复雨,先储其才以俟用乎?其养也出之无心,其生也亦非有意,皆天机之自起自伏耳。当其养态之时,先有一种娇羞无那之致现于身外,令人生爱生怜,不俟娉娉大露而后觉也。斯二者,皆妇人媚态之一斑,举之以见大较。噫!以年三十许之贫妇,止为姿态稍异,遂使二八佳人,与曳珠顶翠者皆出其下,然则态之为用岂浅鲜哉! | there she stood, calm and poised under the eaves, without bothering to do so, because she knew that, exposed as she was, to shake her dress would only make her look ridiculous. Then the shower stopped and people rushed out only to rush back again when the shower came again. They found her quietly standing inside the pavilion, for she had anticipated it. She did not show an air of self-satisfaction; on the other hand, when she saw the other women standing outside with their dresses all wet, she did her best to wipe the water off their shoulders and sleeves, revealing then her infinite charm of movement as if God had ordained this crowd of ugly women to come there with their fussiness in order to show off her beauty to greater advantage. As an observer, I saw it was perfect; in the beginning she showed her charm by her poise when she was standing outside, and then she showed her charm in movement when she was helping the others. But the whole thing came naturally, for she could not have planned it. Her former poise and charm were just as natural as her subsequent activity. She had revealed this inner charm already when she was standing outside the pavilion, quiet and reserved and just her natural self, a charm which was just as effective and suitable to the circumstances of the time as her later movements and activity.... |
| 人问:圣贤神化之事,皆可造诣而成,岂妇人媚态独不可学而至乎?予曰:学则可学,教则不能。人又问:既不能教,胡云可学?予曰:使无态之人与有态者同居,朝夕薰陶,或能为其所化;如蓬生麻中,不扶自直,鹰变成鸠,形为气感,是则可矣。若欲耳提而面命之,则一部廿一史,当从何处说起?还怕愈说愈增其木强,奈何!<br><br>(《闲情偶寄·声容部》选姿第一"态度",李渔,1991/3:115-117) | Some readers may ask, Is it true that charm can never be taught, for we say that one can even learn to be a saint or a sage? I can only say in reply that charm can be learned, but cannot be taught. If it again be asked, Why can't it be taught if it can be learned? my reply is that people without charm can learn it by living together with people who have it. They will acquire it by daily example and contagion, like reeds learning to grow straight in a field of hemp. It comes gradually and naturally by a kind of invisible influence. To lay down so many rules for acquiring charm would be futile and indeed only make confusion worse confounded. (Lin, 1960: 232-235) |

| 原文 | 译文 |
|---|---|
| 　　行乐之事多端，未可执一而论。如睡有睡之乐，坐有坐之乐，行有行之乐，立有立之乐，饮食有饮食之乐，盥栉有盥栉之乐；即袒裼裸裎、如厕便溺，种种秽亵之事，处之得宜，亦各有其乐。苟能见景生情，逢场作戏，即可悲可涕之事，亦变欢娱。如其应事寡才，养生无术，即征歌选舞之场，亦生悲戚。兹以家常受用、起居安乐之事，因便制宜，各存其说于左。<br>　　（《闲情偶寄·颐养部》行乐第一"随时即景就事行乐之法"，李渔，1991/3：321-322） | 52. The Arts of Sleeping, Walking, Sitting, and Standing<br>From *The Arts of Living* (*Shienching Ouchi*)<br>Li Liweng (1611 – 1679)<br>　　There are many ways of enjoying life that are hard to hold down to any one theory. There are the joys of sleeping, of sitting, of walking, and of standing up. There is the pleasure in eating, washing up, hairdressing, and even in such lowly activities as going about naked and barefooted, or going to the toilet. In its proper place, each can be enjoyable. If one can enter into the spirit of fun and take things in his stride anywhere any time, one can enjoy some things over which others may weep. On the other hand, if one is a crude person and awkward in meeting life or taking care of one's health, he can be the saddest person amidst song and dance. I speak here only of the joys of daily living and of the ways in which advantage may be taken of the commonest occupations. (Lin, 1960：258) |
| 　　○睡<br>　　有专言法术之人，遍授养生之诀，欲予北面事之。予讯益寿之功，何物称最？颐生之地，谁处居多？如其不谋而合，则奉为师，不则友之可耳。其人曰："益寿之方，全凭导引；安生之计，惟赖坐功。"予曰："若是则汝法最苦，惟修苦行者能。予懒而好动，且事事求乐，未可以语此也。"其人曰："然则汝意云何？试言之，不妨互为印政。"予曰："天地生人以时，动之者半，息之者半。动则旦，而息则暮也。苟劳之以日，而不息之以夜，则旦旦而伐之，其死也，可立而待矣。吾人养生亦以时，扰之以半，静之以半，扰则行起坐立，而静则睡也。如其劳我以经营，而不逸我以寝处，则岌岌乎殆哉！其年也，不堪指屈矣。若是则养生之诀，当以善睡居先。睡能还精，睡能养气，睡能健脾益胃，睡能坚骨 | 1. The Art of Sleeping<br>　　There was a yogi who traveled about, teaching the secrets of conservation of life force and of prolonging life, and he wanted to teach me. I asked him what he could do to attain longevity and where such blessings were to be found. I thought it would be fine if his methods agreed with my way of thinking, and if not, I could at least befriend him.<br>　　This man told me that the secret of longevity lay in controlled breathing, and peace of mind was to be sought through séance. I said to him, "Your ways are hard and forced, and only people like you can practice it. I am lazy and like motion. I seek joy in everything. I am afraid it is not for me."<br>　　"What is your way then?" he asked. "I should like to hear it and we can compare notes."<br>　　And this is what I said to him:<br>　　In the natural scheme of things, it is meant for |

**续表**

| 原文 | 译文 |
| --- | --- |
| 壮筋。如其不信,试以无疾之人,与有疾之人合而验之。人本无疾而劳之以夜,使累夕不得安眠,则眼眶渐落而精气日颓,虽未即病,而病之情形出矣。患疾之人,久而不寐,则病势日增;偶一沉酣,则其醒也必有油然勃然之势。是睡非睡也,药也。非疗一疾之药,及治百病,救万民,无试不验之神药也。兹欲从事导引,并力坐功,势必先遭睡魔,使无倦态而后可。予忍弃生平最效之药,而试未必果验之方哉?"其人艴然而去,以予不足教也。予诚不足教哉!但自陈所得,实为有见而然,与强辩饰非者稍别。前人睡诗云:"花竹幽窗午梦长,此中与世暂相忘。华山处士如容见,不觅仙方觅睡方。"近人睡诀云:"先睡心,后睡眼。"此皆书本唾余,请置弗道,道其未经发明者而已。睡有睡之时,睡有睡之地,睡又有可睡可不睡之人。请条晰言之。由戌及卯,睡之时也。未戌而睡,谓之先时,先时者不详,谓与疾作思卧者无异也。过卯而睡,谓之后时,后时者犯忌,谓与长夜不醒者无异也。且人生百年,夜居其半,穷日行乐,犹苦不多,况以睡梦之有余,而损宴游之不足乎?有一名士善睡,起必过午,先时而访,未有能晤之者。予每过其居,必俟良久而后见。一日闷坐无聊,笔墨具在,乃取旧诗一首,更易数字而嘲之曰:"吾在此静睡,起来常过午;便活七十年,止当三十五。"同人见之,无不绝倒。此虽谑浪,颇关至理。是当睡之时,止有黑夜,舍此皆非其候矣。然而午睡之乐,倍于黄昏,三时皆所不宜,而独宜于长夏。非私之也,长夏之一日,可抵残冬之二日,长夏之一夜,不敌残冬之半夜,使止息于夜,而不息于昼,是以一分之逸,敌四分之劳,精力几何,其能堪此?况暑气铄金,当之未有不倦者。倦极而眠,犹饥之得食,渴之得饮,养生之计,未有善于此者。午餐 | man to spend half his time in activity and half at rest. In the day, he sits, moves, or stands, and at night he rests. If a man labors by day and does not rest by night and continues this day after day, you can get ready and wait for his funeral to pass by. I try to keep my health by dividing half my time in rest and half my time in activity. If something troubles me and prevents me from sleep, there's the danger signal! I should count my remaining years on my fingers!<br><br>In other words, the secret of good health lies in a good and restful sleep. One who sleeps well restores his energy, revitalizes his inner system, and tones up his muscles. Compare a sick man with a healthy person. A man who is not permitted to rest will get sick; his eyes become sunken, and all kinds of symptoms appear. A sick man becomes worse without sleep. But after a good sleep, he wakes up full of eagerness for life again. Is not sleep the infallible miracle drug, not just a cure for one illness but for a hundred, a cure that saves a thousand lives? To seek health by controlled breathing and the hard exercises of yoga would only involve great concentration and effort to keep awake instead! Would I throw away the best medicine in the world for an untested formula?<br><br>The man left in anger and I did not argue with him.<br><br>An ancient poem goes, "After a long, sound sleep in bamboo-shaded quiet, I feel so far removed from the day's turmoil. If the hermit of Huashan comes to visit me, I shall not ask for the secret of becoming an immortal, but of sleeping well." A modern saying goes, "First rest your mind, then rest your eyes."<br><br>There is a proper time and a proper place for sleep, and there are certain sleeping habits which should be avoided. To be specific, one should rest between 9 p. m. and 8 a. m. To go to bed before nine is too early; it is a bad sign to be craving for sleep like a sick person. To sleep after eight in the |

| 原文 | 译文 |
|---|---|
| 之后，略逾寸晷，俟所食既消，而后徘徊近榻。又勿有心觅睡，觅睡得睡，其为睡也不甜。必先处于有事，事未毕而忽倦，睡乡之民自来招我。桃源、天台诸妙境，原非有意造之，皆莫知其然而然者。予最爱旧诗中，有"手倦抛书午梦长"一句。手书而眠，意不在睡；抛书而寝，则又意不在书，所谓莫知其然而然也。睡中三昧，惟此得之。<u>此论睡之时也。</u>睡又必先择地。地之善者有二：曰静，曰凉。<u>不静之地，止能睡目不能睡耳，耳目两岐，岂安身之善策乎？</u>不凉之地，止能睡魂不能睡身，身魂不附，乃养生之至忌也。至于可睡可不睡之人，则分别于忙闲二字。就常理而论之，则忙人宜睡，闲人可以不必睡。然使忙人假寐，止能睡眼不能睡心，心不睡而眼睡，犹之未尝睡也。其最不受用者，在将觉未觉之一时，忽然想起某事未行，某人未见，皆万万不可已者，睡此一觉，未免失事妨时，想到此处，便觉魂趋梦绕，胆怯心惊，较之未睡之前，更加烦躁，此忙人之不宜睡也。闲则眼未阖而心先阖，心已开而眼未开；已睡较未睡为乐，已醒较未醒更乐，此闲人之宜睡也。然天地之间，能有几个闲人？必欲闲而始睡，是无可睡之时矣。有暂逸其心以妥梦魂之法：凡一日之中，急切当行之事，俱当于上半日告竣，有未竣者，则分遣家人代之，使事事皆有着落，然后寻床觅枕以赴黑甜，则与闲人无别矣。<u>此言可睡之人也。</u>而尤有吃紧一关未经道破者，则在莫行歹事。"半夜敲门不吃惊"，始可于日间睡觉，不则一闻剥啄，即是逻倅到门矣。<br><br>（《闲情偶寄·颐养部》行乐第一"随时即景就事行乐之法"，李渔，1991/3：322-324） | morning is bad for health, like all oversleeping. Where would be the time left for other pleasures? I know a friend who never gets up before noon, and anyone visiting him before noon is kept waiting. One day I sat miserably in his parlor waiting, and with ink and brush ready, I playfully parodied an ancient poem and wrote as follows：<br><br>I am busy sleeping,<br>Throughout the whole morn.<br>If I live to seventy,<br>Five and thirty are gone.<br><br>Although it was done in fun, it is close to the truth. One should only sleep at night as a rule. The pleasure of an afternoon nap is understandable, but is should be reserved only for summer when the day is long and the night is short. It is natural that one tires easily in the heat, and it is as good for a man to sleep when tired as to drink when thirsty. This is common sense. The best time is after lunch. One should wait a while until the food is partly digested and then leisurely stroll toward the couch. Do not tell yourself that you are determined to get a nap. In that way, the mind is tense and the sleep will not be sound. Occupy yourself with something first and before it is finished, you are overcome with a sense of fatigue and the sandman calls. The never-never land cannot be chased down. I love that line in a poem which says, "Dozing off, the book slips out of my hand." Thus sleep comes without his artifice or knowledge. This is the secret of the art of sleeping.<br><br>Next, one must consider the place, which should be cool and quiet. If it is not quiet, the eyes rest but not the ears. If it is too hot, the soul rests but not the body, and body and soul are at loggerheads. This goes against the principle of good health.<br><br>Lastly, we will consider the sleeper himself. Some people are busy, and others have plenty of time. Logically, the man of leisure needs little sleep; it is the busy man who needs it most of all. |

**续表**

| 原文 | 译文 |
|---|---|
|  | But often the busy man cannot sleep well. He rests his eyes in sleep but not his mind. In fact, he gets no rest from sleep at all. The worst of it is to think of something during the half-awake hours of the morning and suddenly remember something he hasn't done or someone he hasn't seen. It is very, very important! He must not sleep another wink or something will be spoiled! That very thought drives away all sleep. He becomes tense and gets up more keyed up than before. The man of leisure rests his mind before his eyes are shut, and his mind wakes up refreshed before his eyes are open, happy to slumber and happier to wake up. Such is the sleep of the man of leisure.<br><br>Yet in this world how many such men are there? All men cannot lead a life with nothing to do. Therefore a method must be found. It is best to dispose of the urgent business of the day in the morning, and delegate to others those things that are not finished. Then one knows that everything is in order and under control. He can afford to seek the pillow and go for that slumber which is described as the "dark, sweet village." He will then sleep as well as the man of leisure.<br><br>Another thing: to enjoy a perfect sleep requires a peaceful conscience. Such a man will not be "frightened when there is a knock on the door at midnight," as the saying goes. He will not mistake the peckings of chickens in the barnyard for policemen's footsteps! (Lin, 1960: 258-261) |

| 原文 | 译文 |
|---|---|
| ○行<br><br>贵人之出,必乘车马。逸则逸矣,然于造物赋形之义,略欠周全。有足而不用,与无足等耳,反不若安步当车之人,五官四体皆能适用。此贫士骄人语。乘车策马,曳履牵裳,一般同是行人,止有动静之别。使乘车策马之人,能以步趋为乐,或经山水之胜,或逢花柳之妍,或遇戴笠之贫交,或见负薪之高士,欣然止驭,徒步为欢,有时安车而待步,有时安步以当车,其能用足也,又胜贫士一筹矣。至于贫士骄人,不在有足能行,而在缓急出门之可恃。事属可缓,则以安步当车;如其急也,则以疾行当马。有人亦出,无人亦出;结伴可行,无伴亦可行。不似富贵者假足于人,人或不来,则我不能即出,此则有足若无,大悖谬于造物赋形之义耳。兴言及此,行殊可乐!<br><br>（《闲情偶寄·颐养部》行乐第一"随时即景就事行乐之法",李渔,1991/3:325-326） | The Art of Walking<br><br>The rich man will go out only in a horse and carriage. It may be called a comfort and a luxury, but it can hardly be said that it fulfills the intention of God in giving man a pair of legs. He who does not use his legs is *ipso facto* deprived of the use of his legs. On the other hand, a man who uses his legs is giving exercise (p. 261) to his entire body. That is why an ancient poor scholar boasted that "a leisurely stroll is as good as a drive." Now to drive or to go on foot are both methods of transportation or locomotion. A man who is used to driving or riding on horseback can learn to enjoy the pleasures of a walk. Perhaps he comes upon a beautiful view or beautiful flowers on the way, or stops to talk with a peasant in his palm hat or meets a recluse philosopher turned woodcutter in the deep mountains. Sometimes one might enjoy a drive, and sometimes a walk. Surely this is better than the obstinacy of that proud scholar of ancient days!<br><br>What the poor man can be truly proud of is not the fact that he uses his legs, but that he does not depend on others for going anywhere. If he is not in a hurry, he can go slowly, and if he is, he breaks into a run. He does not have to wait for someone else, and he is not dependent on the carriage, unlike the rich man who is helpless when the driver is not there. The poor man has fulfilled the intentions of God in giving him legs to walk with. It makes me happy just to think of this. (Lin, 1960: 261-262) |

续表

| 原文 | 译文 |
| --- | --- |
| ○坐<br><br>从来善养生者，莫过于孔子。何以知之？知之于"寝不尸，居不容"二语。使其好饰观瞻，务修边幅，时时求肖君子，处处欲为圣人，则其寝也，居也，不求尸而自尸，不求容而自容；则五官四体，不复有舒展之刻。岂有泥塑木雕其形，而能久长于世者哉？"不尸"、"不容"四字，绘出一幅时哉圣人，宜乎崇祀千秋，而为风雅斯文之鼻祖也。吾人燕居坐法，当以孔子为师，勿务端庄而必正襟危坐，勿同于束缚而为胶柱难移。抱膝长吟，虽坐也，而不妨同于箕踞；支颐丧我，行乐也，而何必名为坐忘？但见面与身齐，久而不动者，其人必死。此图画真容之先兆也。<br><br>（《闲情偶寄·颐养部》行乐第一"随时即景就事行乐之法"，李渔，1991/3:325） | The Art of Sitting<br><br>No one knows the art of living better than Confucius. I know this from the statement that he "did not sleep like a corpse [with straight legs] and did not sit like a statue." If the Master had been completely absorbed in keeping decorum, intent on appearing like a gentleman at all hours and being seen as a sage at all times, then he would have had to lie down like a corpse and sit like a statue. His four limbs and his internal system would never have been able to relax. How could such a stiff wooden statue expect to live a long life? Because Confucius did not do this, the statement describes the ease of the Master in his private life, which makes him worthy of worship as the father of all cultured gentlemen. We should follow Confucius's example when at home. Do not sit erect and look severe as if you were chained or glued to the chair. Hug your knee and sing, or sit chin in hand, without honoring it with the phrase of "losing oneself in thought" [as Chuangtse said]. On the other hand, if a person sits stiffly for a long time, head high and chest out, this is a premonition that he is heading for the grave. He is sitting for his memorial portrait! (Lin, 1960: 262-263) |
| ○立<br><br>立分久暂，暂可无依，久当思傍。亭亭独立之事，但可偶一为之，旦旦如是，则筋骨皆悬，而脚跟如砥，有血脉胶凝之患矣。或倚长松，或凭怪石，或靠危栏作轼，或扶瘦竹为筇；既作羲皇上人，又作画图中物，何乐如之！但不可以美人作柱，虑其础石太纤，而致栋梁皆仆也。<br><br>（《闲情偶寄·颐养部》行乐第一"随时即景就事行乐之法"，李渔，1991/3:326） | The Art of Standing<br><br>Stand straight, but do not do it for long. Otherwise, all leg muscles will become stiff and circulation will be blocked up. Lean on something! — on an old pine or a quaint rock, or on a balcony or on a bamboo cane. It makes one look like one is in a painting. But do *not* lean on a lady! The foundation is not solid and the roof may come down! (Lin, 1960: 263) |

# 附录 2

## 《无声戏》韩南译本篇目一览

| 原文篇名 | 译文篇名 | 译者 |
|---|---|---|
| 丑郎君怕娇偏得艳 | An Ugly Husband Fears A Pretty Wife But Marries A Beautiful One | Chu Chiyu & Patrick Hanan |
| 美男子避惑反生疑 | A Handsome Youth Tries to Avoid Suspicion But Arouses It Instead | Eva Hung & Patrick Hanan |
| 女陈平计生七出 | The Female Chen Ping Saves Her Life With Seven Ruses | Patrick Hanan |
| 男孟母教合三迁 | A Male Mencius's Mother Raises Her Son Properly By Moving House Three Times | Gopal Sukhu & Patrick Hanan |
| 变女为儿菩萨巧 | A Daughter Is Transformed Into A Son Through The Bodhisattva's Ingenuity | Janice Wickeri & Patrick Hanan |
| 谭楚玉戏里传情 刘藐姑曲终死节 | An Actress Scorns Wealth And Honour To Preserve Her Chastity | Patrick Hanan |

# 附录 3

## 《李渔小说选》篇目一览

| 原文篇名 | 译文篇名 | 译者 |
|---|---|---|
| 老星家戏改八字<br>穷皂隶陡发万金<br>（无声戏之《改八字苦尽甘来》） | A Yamen Runner's Horoscope：<br>On a Whim the Old Fortune Teller Revises Horoscope<br>All at Once the Poor Yamen Runner Amasses a Fortune | 滕婷婷 |
| 待诏喜风流趱钱赎妓<br>运弁持公道舍米追赃<br>（无声戏之《人宿妓穷鬼诉嫖冤》） | A Barber's Romance：<br>A Romantic Barber Courts a Courtesan with Hard-Earned Cash<br>A Just Captain Tricks a Swindler with State-Owned Rice | 夏建新 |
| 受人欺无心落局<br>连鬼骗有故倾家<br>（无声戏之《鬼输钱活人还赌债》） | A Confidence Man's Karma：<br>A Naïve Youth Wastes His Inheritance in a Gambling Snare<br>The Swindler Is Ruined by a Revengeful Ghost | 唐艳芳 |
| 吃新醋正室蒙冤<br>续旧欢家堂和事<br>（无声戏之《移妻换妾鬼神奇》） | A Jealous and Scheming Concubine：<br>The Wronged Wife Falls Victim to the Jealous Concubine<br>The Enlightened Husband Restores Peace to the Household | 陈凤姣 |
| 妻妾败纲常<br>梅香完节操<br>（无声戏之《妻妾抱琵琶梅香守节》） | Fickle Ladies and Duteous Maid：<br>Two Ladies Violate Their Duty<br>A Maid Retains Her Moral Integrity | 夏建新<br>李建军 |

续表

| 原文篇名 | 译文篇名 | 译者 |
|---|---|---|
| 寡妇设计赘新郎<br>众美齐心夺才子 | A Handsome Scholar and His Five Fair Ladies：<br>A Jealous Widow Plots to Take in Her Groom<br>Four Fair ladies Conspire to Seize the Handsome Scholar | 夏建新 |
| 贞女守贞来异谤<br>朋侪相谑致奇冤 | A Chaste Wife Wronged by a Frivolity：<br>A Chaste Lady Proves Her Chastity to Refute Slander<br>A Close Friend Teases His Friend to Cause Injustice | 周心红 |
| 说鬼话计赚生人<br>显神通智恢旧业 | A Resourceful Housewife：<br>To Hoodwink the Living with Ghost<br>To Recover the Lost Fortune with Wisdom | 夏建新 |